Love & Dr Devon

Love & Dr Devon

Alan Titchmarsh

SIMON &
SCHUSTER

London · New York · Sydney · Toronto

A CBS COMPANY

First published in Great Britain by Simon & Schuster UK Ltd, 2006
A CBS COMPANY

'Dream Song 14' quoted by permission of Faber & Faber,
from *77 Dream Songs* by John Berryman

1 3 5 7 9 10 8 6 4 2

Simon & Schuster UK Ltd
Africa House
64–78 Kingsway
London WC2B 6AH

www.simonsays.co.uk

Simon & Schuster Australia
Sydney

A CIP catalogue for this book is available
from the British Library.

Hardback ISBN: 0-7432-0771-8
EAN: 9780743207713
Trade Paperback ISBN: 0-7432-0772-6
EAN: 9780743207720

Typeset in Goudy by M Rules
Printed and bound in Great Britain by
The Bath Press, Bath

For
Caroline and Neil

Acknowledgements

I'm enormously grateful to Dr Mike Hayward who advised on matters medical, often at inconvenient times of the day and night, though being a GP he is probably used to this. Any misinterpretations of his advice are my own fault. Thanks also to Wing Commander Neil Mitchell MBE and the staff at RAF Benson who showed me how to fly a helicopter and survive. To my editors Suzanne Baboneau and Rochelle Venables I am, as ever, hugely indebted, and a large helping of gratitude goes to my long-suffering family, my PA Caroline Mitchell and my literary agent Luigi Bonomi. They are, to a man – and woman – unfailingly patient and encouraging in equal measure; two commodities without which any writer is lost.

The best doctors are Dr Diet,
Dr Quiet, and Dr Merryman.

16th-century proverb

Chapter 1

Years ago we discovered the exact point, the dead
centre of middle age. It comes when you are too young
to take up golf and too old to rush up to the net.

Nods and Becks, Franklin P. Adams, 1881–1960

There were just the three of them to start with – Tiger
Wilson, Dr Christopher Devon and Gary Flynn – and they
met on Friday nights in the Hare and Hounds. Well, not
every Friday night, because sometimes Tiger's wife wanted
to be taken out to dinner, and sometimes Christopher
Devon was on call, and sometimes Gary Flynn had a better
offer. But not very often. Which is why, at least three weeks
out of four, they played dominoes in the Hare and Hounds
on a Friday night.

They would like to have played squash. It would have
been better for their self-esteem. But Tiger's right knee had
gone, Christopher's balance was sometimes a bit suspect
and Gary maintained he was averse to anything physical
unless it involved being horizontal.

They never really meant to play dominoes. Dominoes was a game for old men. And they were not old. They were in their fifties. The prime of life. At their peak. Established in their professions. Until recently at any rate.

They met . . . well, they dispute this. Tiger thinks it was at a drinks party, Christopher says they were his patients long before that and Gary claims to have no recollection at all, which most likely pins it down to the drinks party.

The fact that these disparate souls get on with one another at all is pretty remarkable, but they do have one thing in common. Their age. And like most men in their fifties they are at a crossroads. It's not that they have under-achieved. Far from it. They have accomplished what they set out to do. Reached the top of the tree. Well, the higher branches anyway.

Sorted eh? At fifty. In their prime. With just one niggling little question. Is that it?

Not that in the early days of the domino club this had ever been alluded to in so many words. It was more of an undercurrent. A frustration that occasionally erupted thanks to a newspaper article that highlighted the folly of government, or some local injustice that should have been sorted out. The kind of thing that causes most of the population to say, 'They should do something about it.'

Then one day Dr Christopher Devon said, '*We* should do something about it.'

'What sort of something?' asked Gary.

And Tiger said, 'We should form a sort of secret society.'

Chapter 2

And moreover my mother taught me as a boy (repeatingly), 'Ever to confess you're bored means you have no Inner Resources.'

77 Dream Songs, John Berryman, 1914–72

He had been called 'Tiger' from the very beginning. 'Andrew', bestowed at the font, had never been used by anyone except his mother in moments of impatience. She had died when he was fifteen and from then on to his father he was always 'Tiger'. He had gone off the rails a bit after her death. Nothing disastrous, but one or two run-ins with the law for drinking more than he should on a Saturday night, and the occasional AWOL to which his father had turned a blind eye.

But when he left school and refused any form of higher education the paternal foot had been put down. Old man Wilson knew that if he didn't enforce discipline now then heaven knows what would befall his son.

He pushed Tiger in the direction of the only career he

had ever known himself – the RAF. At first Tiger had rebelled. The services with their structured lifestyle were the last thing he wanted. He sought freedom; an escape from the routine of most men's daily lives. But then he discovered flying. The feeling of liberation, at that moment when he penetrated the cloud layer for the first time in an aircraft under his own control, would never leave him. It was the ultimate independence.

He came home with a light in his eyes and told his father of the moment when he knew that a life in the air was for him.

His father smiled knowingly and reached down a book from the shelf beside his chair. Purposefully he thumbed through the pages until he found what he wanted, then handed the book to his son, pointing at the verse on the left-hand page.

Tiger read it slowly:

'Oh, I have slipped the surly bonds of earth
And danced the skies on laughter-silvered wings;
Sunward I've climbed and joined the tumbling
    mirth
Of sun-split clouds – and done a hundred things
You have not dreamed of; wheeled and soared and
    swung
High in the sunlit silence. Hovering there
I've chased the shouting wind along, and flung
My eager craft through footless halls of air;
Up, up the long, delirious, burning blue
I've topped the wind-swept heights with easy grace,
Where never lark nor even eagle flew;
And while, with silent lifting mind I've trod

The high untrespassed sanctity of space,
Put out my hand, and touched the face of God.'

Tiger closed the book, looked up and met his father's eye. 'Thank you.'

His father shrugged. 'I'm glad you found it. Found yourself.'

Tiger never received the acclaim his father enjoyed – high ranking and decorated for his wartime exploits – but he was a respected helicopter pilot and left the service with the rank of Squadron Leader.

Not that he wanted to leave. But the RAF ground their pilots at fifty, and rather than take up a desk job, Tiger had settled for a pension and the chance of staying in the pilot's seat. He now flew for a civilian helicopter company – executives to and from Battersea Heliport, well-to-do passengers to Ascot and Goodwood, bits of filming for TV companies, that sort of thing. It wasn't combat flying, but then the combat part of the job had not been the attraction. He was up in the air, in his own craft; he 'danced the skies on laughter-silvered wings', and that was what mattered.

Wing-Commander Wilson died the year after his son married, so he never saw his grandchildren. While Tiger's nickname had been bestowed as a mark of his father's fondness for the Tiger Moth, Tiger's own children's names – Aisling and Kirsty – were the product of his wife Erica's Scottish and Irish parentage.

So here he was. Sitting pretty with two pretty daughters away at uni. Still married, still flying helicopters and quite comfortably off. And yet he knew that his best days were behind him. The days of high achievement. The days of excitement and hunger. A time when everything seemed to be in front of him; his children young, his wife laughing and carefree. Now that they were all older a different mood prevailed. Not unhappiness, not even discontent. Just some general all-enveloping cloud of acceptance.

Maybe this was how it was supposed to be. Maybe you just had to get used to a gradual winding down. It was a thought that left him sometimes frightened and more often dispirited.

And that's why he had mentioned the secret society. Though, if he were honest, the moment he had done so he felt a bit of a fool.

'So what exactly do you mean by a secret society?' Christopher Devon laid down a three and a two against Tiger's double three.

'Sounds like the Masons to me,' Gary Flynn muttered into his pint.

'Don't be daft,' said Tiger, opening a packet of peanuts.

'Well what then?'

'I don't really know. It's just that it might be a bit of fun to try and make a difference, have a bit of excitement, instead of just whinging about things the whole time and feeling powerless to do anything about them.'

Christopher looked at him sideways. 'You sound like Robin Hood.'

Gary leaned back in his chair and shrugged. 'Why don't you join the Rotary Club?'

'Because I'm happy to play doms with you two but I'm buggered if I want to be surrounded by any more old men.' He picked up a handful of peanuts and tipped them into his mouth.

'Well thank you very much,' said Christopher. 'Are you knocking?'

Gary said, 'Not just yet, thank you,' and put down the five and two.

'Oh, you know what I mean,' said Tiger, through a mouthful of peanuts.

'I thought you'd get enough excitement flying helicopters,' Christopher said.

'But that's just what I do. I mean . . . I want . . . something more out of life.'

Gary folded his arms. 'All right then. We form a secret society. To do what exactly?'

Tiger frowned. 'I haven't quite worked that out yet.'

'I see,' said Christopher. 'We meet in secret and do secret things that we haven't quite worked out yet.'

'At least the Masons know what they're doing,' added Gary. 'Are you going or what?'

'Look,' said Tiger impatiently, 'is it just me or is this a funny time of life?'

Christopher took a deep breath. 'I can tell you that medically it's not funny at all. It's very critical. When a man hits his fifties all kinds of things start to happen. His sperm count goes down . . .'

'Oh, shit!' muttered Gary.

'His libido slackens . . .'

'Double shit!'

'And all kinds of things start to malfunction or drop off.'

'Not much to look forward to then?' said Tiger.

'Depends how you look at it,' replied Christopher. 'Nature can be quite kind really. You see all those chemical processes that happen in the body have side effects. They release other chemicals to the brain that cause us not to

7

mind. We no longer feel a *need* to bonk ourselves senseless every night . . .'

'Speak for yourself,' said Gary.

'Most of us, at any rate.'

Tiger asked, 'But surely we're in our prime now. All those years of experience; there must be some advantage to that?' There was a genuine note of concern in his voice. 'Other bits of us might be falling off but our minds are sharp as a razor, aren't they?' He tipped the rest of the peanuts into his hand and popped them into his mouth a few at a time.

'In some ways, yes. Our reactions are slower and our reflexes not quite what they were but our powers of reasoning are, in many cases, more well developed.'

'There you are then.'

'There I am what?' asked Christopher.

'Three men at the peak of their mental powers and all sidelined by society in favour of younger models.'

'Hey, watch who you're calling sidelined,' said Gary. 'You two might consider yourselves past it but as far as I'm concerned I haven't got there yet.'

'I hate to disabuse you of that conceit,' said Christopher, 'but clinically you are every bit as over the hill as we are.'

Gary raised his voice. 'Is it something in the beer or are you two on a right downer tonight?'

Christopher shrugged. 'Just offering you the benefit of my medical advice, that's all.'

'Well, if it's all the same to you I'd like a second opinion,' said Gary.

'And I would never stand in your way,' beamed Christopher before draining his glass.

Tiger laid down the double five and crumpled up the empty packet of nuts.

'Chips.'

'Jammy devil,' said Gary.

'Another one, gentlemen?' asked Christopher.

'Nah,' said Gary. 'I think I'll be off. All this talk about age has worn me out. And I've someone to meet tomorrow. Someone younger than I am. Considerably younger, who thinks that I'm pretty hot actually.'

'Lucky you,' said Tiger.

'Yes, I am really, aren't I?' Gary grinned. 'Dinner at that little restaurant down by the river, then, with any luck, back to my place. Or hers. I'm not fussy.'

'We know that,' said Christopher under his breath.

'Beats being married,' said Gary.

'How would you know?' asked Tiger.

'Yes, how would you know?' repeated Christopher, getting up from his seat and avoiding Gary's eye.

'Oh, sorry. You know what I mean. Sorry . . .'

Tucked away down the end of a lane in a sleepy and not particularly fashionable Hampshire village is a small but pleasantly proportioned Queen Anne manor house. The River Itchen runs past the end of its walled garden which is peppered with ancient fruit trees that have romantic-sounding names like 'Devonshire Quarrenden' and 'Beauty of Bath', and in early summer the air is filled with the fragrance of old-fashioned roses, clove pinks and lavender. Idyllic. Blissful almost.

Christopher Devon was left the house by a wealthy aunt twenty years ago. She knew he was the only one in her family who would appreciate the garden and the fact that it needed new life breathed into it, rather than being allowed to stagnate. He was a doctor. He understood about life.

About renewal. And he was a gardener. He enjoyed the respite that tending plants gave him in between tending patients.

Daunted at first, Christopher had soon begun to relish the challenge that the garden presented. At weekends he would battle with brambles and briars and barrow in loads of manure from a nearby farm.

For twenty-six years Kate, his wife, was happy to do her bit of battling, too – with patients who made excessive demands, and with two children who had their own needs and necessities. They grew up all too fast, slipping through their father's fingers like dry sand. At almost twenty-four the girl went to Africa to do voluntary work, and the boy, a year younger, to the States where he landed a job in publishing – quite a good one.

Ellie was her dad's girl. The one with the social conscience. Money meant nothing to her; as long as she had something to eat and something clean to wear she was happy. Not for her designer labels and cupboards full of shoes and handbags. A simple soul with a skinny body and long blonde hair, she turned heads in a baggy T-shirt and combats, much to her father's amusement. Walking down the street with her on his arm he felt a million dollars. Always.

She would argue with him about the rights and wrongs of private health care and worry about the state of the rainforest. She would ask why people needed so many cars. She could have been a real pain, but her saving grace was a sense of humour that allowed her to take a joke against herself, and also to take the mickey out of her dad when he got too 'doctory' or when he made pronouncements that she thought were unjust, or plain pompous. She pricked his bubble like nobody else.

Matt was a different kettle of fish. Shy and diffident as a child, he had grown into a confident youth; confident, that is, in everything except his sexuality. Discovering your son is gay is never an easy thing for a father. Christopher suspected before Matt did himself. He could see the outer signs of inner turmoil and did his best to handle them. He tried to hide his disappointment and asked himself why he should be disappointed. Matt was creative, energetic, thoughtful and sensitive. Would being heterosexual have made him a better person?

Kate had been good about it and seemed to find it easier to cope. Christopher had fought to keep the dialogue going, but there was always a slight unease between father and son and he felt it was his fault. Perhaps he should have offered more help – not that Matt ever asked for it. But they rubbed along and kept talking. Eventually it became an accepted part of their lives – Christopher was Christopher and Matt was Matt, and their respect for one another survived.

He missed both his children when they left. He missed the teasing he endured at their hands, and he missed their nearness. Always the first to rise in the mornings, he would walk into their rooms and open the curtains, then turn and see the empty beds, always with a stab of wistfulness.

The marriage to Kate had outlasted those of most of his friends – except Tiger. It had its quiet moments after twenty-odd years, and there were days when it seemed routine, but the fact that underneath it all they actually liked one another made up for the dissipation of that first flush of magical attraction. Didn't it?

With her children off her hands and a husband who seemed to be married in turns to his surgery and his garden, Kate walked out.

It came like a bolt from the blue. Christopher had no inkling at all of her unhappiness, and for that he blamed himself. She was sorry, she said. She was still fond of him, still cared, but wanted more out of life than he seemed able or willing to give. And she wanted it while there was still time.

He did his best to persuade her to stay. Offered to change. To spend more time with her. Asked what he could do to make amends. But to no avail. He even suggested she stay for the sake of the children. But he was too late on that count. They had flown and now so had Kate. It never occurred to him that she might have found someone else.

There was no denying that her leaving affected his work. It was not that he became unreliable, just more irritable. Less tolerant of those underneath him when they mislaid a prescription or muddled up an appointment. From being courteous and unflappable he had become irascible and tetchy; quick to snap and dismissive of patients he considered were wasting his time.

Those around him tried to make allowances, convinced themselves that it was a temporary blip and that soon he would be back to normal. But Randall Cummings, the senior partner in the practice, felt obliged to have a word with him. Things seemed to be improving, until one day, out of nowhere, Cummings said that it would probably be best for everybody if Christopher left the practice. Made a new start. Turned over a new leaf.

Others in the practice were surprised not only at the senior partner's precipitate action, but also at Christopher's tacit acceptance of the decision. The irritability had gone now, to be replaced with a distancing, almost a withdrawal.

There was no farewell party. He just slipped quietly away. Preoccupied. Troubled.

Having devoted himself to medicine for the better part of his life he began to wonder if it had all been worthwhile. What difference had he made? Where was that missionary zeal now? That raw energy that drove him on in his early days as a GP; the days when he felt on top of the job despite the tiredness, the travelling and the endless ministering to the sick. Now he just seemed to be drowning in a sea of forms and regulations. That and loneliness. Not the sort of thing you want to admit to anybody. Loneliness – the unmentionable disease. He tried not to wallow in it. But it had grown ever more enveloping since Kate's departure.

He could feel no bitterness towards her. Just profound sadness at his own myopic self-absorption which had forced her to leave – the long hours, the putting of patients' interests first, the weekends on call, the Christmas dinners interrupted. It had been all his fault. It must have been. What other reason could she have had? Kate seemed apologetic when she left. Apologetic but determined. And she had not kept in touch; that surprised him, and then he began to wonder if she had someone else to care about. Someone of whom her children would not approve.

He had stayed on in the house – it was his only anchor – and decided to set about finding another position. But he was in his fifties. Not the best bet for any practice looking for long-term commitment. He had been scanning the *British Medical Journal* for six months and doing a bit of locum work, but nothing permanent had come along.

It was Ellie who had suggested that he should try to get out more. Told him that he was still a good catch. Said that he should try to find female company.

The idea appalled him. He had been a one-woman man. Never imagined that he would ever be 'on the market' again. And, anyway, where did you look if you wanted to find someone? He didn't want to join a club – they'd all want to talk to the doctor about their ailments – and felt too embarrassed to join a dating agency.

And so the blanket of loneliness enfolded him still further until one night, seated in front of his laptop and surfing the net, he typed in the word 'soulmate' to see what would come up.

The results surprised him. And so did his actions. He had had three assignations now. The first was with a voluptuous widow from Winchester who looked upon him as a personal physician who could solve her bowel problems. He recommended Senokot and waved her off in her chauffeur-driven Mercedes.

The second was with a timid librarian whose interest in gardening, which he thought might prove common ground, turned out to be nothing more than a passion for her local landscape contractor.

The third, and most unsettling, was with a nymphomaniac from Southampton who said that she thought GSH meant Gas Central Heating. Having discovered the relative warmth of his house she had begun to divest herself of more than her opinion on the state of the nation, and Christopher had felt obliged to bid her a fond farewell. Next time he would heed the warning that suggested first meetings should be on neutral ground.

Friday nights in the Hare and Hounds were not the sort of high spot that he had had in mind for his social life. But at least they were undemanding and pleasant. Tiger had enough enthusiasm to lift him out of the mire when he was feeling low and self-absorbed, and Gary was always good for a laugh. Did he really have all those women at his fingertips, or was it wishful thinking?

As for himself, he was content for the moment to look after the orchids in his conservatory, and to try to put the worries of the past behind him. The cymbidiums and miltonias were coming to the end of their flowering season. Spring was approaching, and a new year would, he hoped, bring along a new lease of life. Maybe even someone to share it with. Someone normal, pleasant, loving. That above all. At fifty-five he could really do with a bit of love.

Few people really knew Gary Flynn. He made sure of that. He was friendly, but guarded. He let people speculate on the nature of his employment without ever putting them straight. But that makes sense when you're in the intelligence service. Unless you want everyone to think you're James Bond.

It would not have taken a first-rate sleuth to discover what this civil servant really did, not if they had put their minds to it. Some days he went to the MI5 building on Millbank, and some days he did not. When he did go there he varied his route, just to be on the safe side.

Today he went by train from his home in Winchester to Waterloo and then by bus to Millbank. It was not the shortest route but it made for variety. His open-plan office was shared with other people in the same game. He was not an 'M' or a 'Q', or even a '007', but the fact that he worked where he worked, and that he saw what he saw, made him naturally cautious when it came to making friends.

And that included women. He had never had a lasting

relationship. Never really wanted one. Much. It wouldn't be fair on either of them. He was frequently away, and often on business that while not in itself risky, had risky consequences, and you couldn't expect a woman to settle for that, could you? Better to be a free agent. And yet there were times when he wondered what it was all about. Where was he going? And would he know when he got there?

His current operation involved monitoring the activities of a Chinese diplomat suspected of smuggling illegally acquired currency out of the country. At the moment any definite proof of such activity was lacking and the source of the illicit funding was uncertain. Right now the diplomat was back home in Shanghai, but he would be returning to the UK in the next few days, intelligence suggested, and Gary would be back on the case. The next time Tan Lao Sok tried to leave the country, Gary would be standing in his way. Not that Mr Tan would know anything about it. Until the moment of truth.

In the gym, in the basement of the building, Gary mused on the likely events of the next few days. Sweat poured off his brow as he pulled at the steel oars on the rowing machine. There were people watching Mr Tan in Shanghai and others watching him in Beijing. Being a diplomat he shuttled between the two cities.

The prospect of catching his quarry with the currency did give Gary a frisson of excitement. It was all a bit *Boys Own Paper* for the twenty-first century. Most smuggling operations today involved internet fraud, numbers on screens being shifted between accounts, and it was the Serious Fraud Office and Customs and Excise who took charge. But the diplomatic post held by Mr Tan meant MI5 involvement, which was why Gary was on the case.

He showered and changed, then went back upstairs to his desk, flipping through the *Independent* and the *Guardian* while working his way through a wholemeal BLT sandwich and a cappuccino.

His mind drifted back to the Friday night dominoes and Tiger's suggestion that they form a secret society. He could not help but smile. If only they knew.

Then, in the business section of the *Independent,* his eye lighted on an article about the performance of an ever-expanding chain of Chinese restaurants. It seemed that while everyone else's profits were dwindling, they were celebrating the opening of yet another of their successful eateries under the banner of the 'Red Dragon'.

Gary looked at the caption below the photo and felt a dart of tension run through his body. The new restaurant was in Winchester, and standing next to the owner of this particular franchise, smiling broadly at the camera, was Mr Tan. The devil on his doorstep.

Chapter 3

My wife, who, poor wretch, is troubled with her lonely life.

Diary, 19 December 1662, Samuel Pepys, 1633–1703

The roar of the engines intensified as Tiger raised the collective to increase power. The helicopter rose gently into the hover. His feet on the pedals held the aircraft level, and at fifteen feet he eased the stick forward and powered away into the blue. A moment to savour; always.

His passenger grabbed at the handle above his head as the helicopter surged forward with its nose tipping downwards.

Tiger grinned. 'It's no use hanging on to that, it's coming with us.'

The passenger – a dyspeptic-looking businessman en route for the City Airport – gave a wan smile and let go of the handle as the craft levelled out, checking nervously to see that the briefcase he had put on the rear seat was also still with them.

At two hundred feet the Hampshire countryside opened out beneath them. On this clear, still day there was a crispness and clarity about its features that lifted the spirits. He'd lived here for twenty-five years now, and having flown over the landscape countless times he'd come to know each field and copse, each river and hedgerow almost as though it were his own garden.

The tributaries of the River Test glittered in the early morning sunlight like silver ribbons. Fresh green fields of youthful wheat were spread like emerald velvet between the hedgerows that were about to burst into leaf, and everywhere there were great sprawling cushions of purple-grey woodland.

He could tell at a glance which county was beneath him. Hampshire was predominantly wooded, Wiltshire a tapestry of prairie farming, and Surrey a more heavily populated county where houses spattered the landscape in an untidy rash.

It was Surrey they were flying over now. The businessman had settled down to enjoy the view and, apart from keeping in contact with air traffic control, Tiger said little, happy to start the day quietly. Sometimes, in his imagination, the aircraft slipped away from him and he was flying, dreamlike, under his own bodily power. He could go where he wanted, into any world he chose. Sometimes.

It took just forty minutes to get to City Airport, and having put down neatly on the Tarmac, Tiger escorted his passenger to the small departure lounge and said good-bye. Today was a rarity. A neat dovetailing. Instead of flying back empty he was to return with another passenger. A woman.

Glancing around the sparsely populated lounge he spotted only three likely candidates. A city type with a large attaché case, a power-dressed businesswoman with dark hair tied back in a pony tail, and Kate Devon.

'Hello, Tiger.' She looked at him apologetically.

'Kate! What are you doing here?'

'Waiting for you, I suppose. Waiting for a helicopter anyway, so I suppose that *must* be you.'

'Yes. But where are you expecting to go?'

'Southampton Airport. There's a car there waiting to take me on.'

'Well, I'm your man then.' Tiger picked up her smart Mulberry holdall and gestured towards the door. 'How are you?'

'Oh, you know. Battling on.'

Her lack of enthusiasm surprised him. Her customary fizz was absent. She seemed weary. There were assorted mumbled pleasantries as they walked across the Tarmac, a nod in the direction of the weather, and eventually Tiger asked, 'How long has it been now?'

'Eighteen months.'

'As long as that?'

Kate nodded.

'And how are . . . things?'

'OK. Good days and bad days. Up and down. It's never easy is it? After such a long time. But I made my bed and now . . .' She shrugged.

'Oh dear.'

'No. Not really oh dear.'

'No regrets then?'

'Of course I have regrets. Regrets that my children now have split loyalties. Regrets that I couldn't be content with what I had. Regrets that I needed more.' Then, softly, 'Perhaps I should have been more patient.'

Tiger stowed her bag in the locker at the side of the aircraft, then opened the door and helped her into the
passenger seat. She was smartly dressed in a dark brown
trouser suit, her blonde hair cut into a neat bob.

She and Christopher had always been an attractive
couple: Kate with her ravishing blonde hair and designer
clothes, and Christopher, tall and fair with a smile that
made women go weak at the knees. He had that total lack
of self-awareness that women found irresistible, damn him.
And now . . .

Tiger closed the door and went round to the other side to
climb into his own seat. As he did so he noticed her hands.
They were as neatly manicured as ever, but there was more
jewellery about her now. He glanced at the large diamond
ring on Kate's third finger.

'It's on my right hand,' she said.

Tiger was momentarily embarrassed.

'You can ask, you know,' said Kate.

'I didn't like to.'

'He's a businessman. Quite well off. Very sweet. Very attentive. We travel a lot.'

'Between City Airport and Southampton?'

'No. All over the place – LA, New York, Frankfurt.'

'Goodness.'

Kate smiled ruefully. 'Yes. Look at me; from GP's wife to
jet-setter in two easy stages.'

Tiger concentrated for a moment as he checked his
instruments and started up the engine. He handed Kate a
pair of earphones and then asked for clearance to take off.

While they waited he asked, 'So what does he do?'

'Howie? He's in real estate.'

'An estate agent?'

'He's American. A realtor.' A sardonic note crept into her voice. 'Buys and sells commercial properties.'

'Not very glamorous then?'

'No. But profitable.'

'Where did you meet?'

'I went to a party in the city. With a girlfriend. Howie was there.' She looked across at Tiger. 'It wasn't planned. It just gradually sort of grew.'

'Windjammer three cleared for take off,' came the message over the radio, and Tiger turned his attention to the controls in front of him.

As the helicopter rose from the Tarmac, Tiger manoeuvred it into a neat pirouette. They lifted higher still and then cut a graceful arc out towards the west.

His flight adjustments completed, he asked, 'Where are you living now?'

'Rome, mostly.'

'How nice.'

'Yes. It is. It's a wonderful city.'

'Romantic,' said Tiger.

Kate did not reply, but gazed out across the grey London skyline.

'So where are you off to now?' He asked it more as a way of filling the uneasy silence than anything else.

'Back to Rome.'

'Couldn't you fly from Heathrow?' he asked.

'Howie's meeting me at Southampton. He prefers to fly from there. Quieter.'

'I know what he means.'

Kate's mood was not what he would have expected. There was a hint of melancholy about her now. When she was married to Christopher she was vibrant and lively, often

22

combative in conversation, always exuding an air of bright capability.

He and Erica had seen it coming. The break up. But what could you do? You couldn't say to your friend that unless he pulled his finger out his wife would probably leave him. Especially not when he was a doctor, and the trouble with his relationship was probably that he cared too much about other people to keep his eye on the ball at home. It would be easy to say that Christopher had been selfish about his career, but when that career was concerned with the welfare of the rest of the human race it made a mockery of the usual 'self-centred' accusations levelled at workaholics.

Kate Devon and Erica Wilson had been good friends. Played tennis at the same club. Opened a small bookshop together in Winchester, specializing in topography and travel – Kate had a geography degree, Erica just liked books. Now Erica ran the shop alone, with a bit of part-time help. They had scraped together enough to buy out Kate's share; from being passionate about the shop and its stock Kate seemed to lose interest the moment her marriage ended. Tiger thought she might have thrown herself into it more, but it was understandable, Erica said. Too many memories tied up with the shop; easier to make a clean break.

At least she'll be interested in wherever she's going, thought Tiger. And she's bound to have a book on it. Silly thought.

It was as though she read his mind. 'Funny, isn't it?' she asked through the microphone linked to Tiger's headset. 'All those books packed full of dreams and now I'm realizing them.' Kate turned away to look out of the window and he saw her brush at her cheek with the back of her hand.

They spoke little for the next half hour. Occasionally

Kate would ask the name of a landmark or a house, and Tiger could usually provide the information she wanted. Then they began to circle the airport until finally he lowered the craft gently onto the apron reserved for helicopters.

They sat for a couple of minutes while the engines cooled, then Tiger shut them down and went round to help her out.

'It's been good to see you again,' Kate said, as they walked across to the terminal building. He held open the door and ushered her into the departure lounge.

'Give my love to Erica,' she said. 'Tell her I miss her.' Then she kissed him lightly on the cheek, smiled apologetically, and was gone.

'Doctor Devon, your lunch is ready!'

He could hear the call from the kitchen at the very top of the house. It was like being back at boarding school.

'Coming! I won't be a minute.'

He addressed the envelope, peeled a stamp from the book and stuck it on the letter ready for posting.

'It's going cold, Doctor Devon!' The tone was more insistent.

'I'm on my way.' He tramped down the stairs with the letter, wishing that he could be allowed to get his own lunch, rather than let Luisa make it for him. She was sixty-odd, Italian and irritable, and he really only wanted her to do a bit of cleaning, but she insisted on preparing him a plate of food every day when he was at home. Pasta. Always pasta, with something in it. He was never quite sure what. Today the bits were dark brown. They could be sun dried tomato. They could be sausage. Tasting them would give no greater clue; Luisa's pasta always tasted the same. Glutinous and uninspiring. Food with a flavour bypass.

With any luck she would go before he had finished it and he could consign it to the bin and get a mini pork pie from the fridge and an apple from the bowl. That would do nicely. But Luisa was of the opinion that nourishment should be cooked and arranged into a mountain. How else could a man survive?

He sat down at the table and managed a weak smile. 'Thank you, Mrs Bassani. Pasta. How nice.'

'Your favourite!' she beamed, handing him a spoon and fork.

'Now, Doctor Devon,' – she pronounced his name with a rolling 'r' at the end of the doctor bit – 'I have some bad news for you.'

He looked up. 'Oh dear.'

'I am going away.'

He tried his best to look crestfallen. 'Oh?'

'Yes. I am going away for two weeks.'

'Oh dear.'

'But I make, how you say . . . provision?'

'Provision, yes . . .'

'To make sure you stay clean and well fed.'

'Now, Mrs Bassani, there really is no need . . . I'm sure I can manage without any . . . provision.'

'Oh yes? And who will wash and who will iron and who will make sure you eat?'

She stood with her hands on her broad hips, a white apron over her black cardigan and skirt, her tightly curled hair framing her stern-featured face. She was a caricature of the archetypal Italian momma, straight from central casting.

'Mrs Bassani, if I can't manage for two weeks . . .'

'It may be more. I not sure.'

Christopher knew that this was his last hope of freedom. 'You really mustn't worry yourself, Mrs Bassani. I've been thinking about things and I think it's probably for the best if we . . .'

But he was an amateur. As a doctor in his surgery he might be godlike to his patients and his nurses, but as a mere man in the kitchen of his own home he was putty in the hands of an Italian matriarch in full flood.

'Is all sorted.' Mrs Bassani made it clear that there was no room for further negotiation.

'Sorry?'

'My daughter Maria. She start on Monday.'

'But Mrs Bassani, that really won't be necessary. I'm working for the next few days, so I won't be needing lunch and . . .'

'You no want my daughter?'

'Well, it's not that I don't want her . . .'

'Good. That's all sorted then. Maria start on Monday. She clean and wash and she make you lunch when you are in.'

'Oh, but really, Mrs Bassani, I think just the cleaning . . .' It was a last ditch attempt to salvage some kind of result. It failed.

'No, no no! Her cooking is . . . how you say? . . . no great shakes . . . but she very willing and happy to learn.'

Christopher felt himself drowning in the futility of it all. He thought the mother's cooking was bad enough, but if the daughter's was worse . . .

Mrs Bassani was taking off her apron. If he ate slowly he would be able to leave most of the pasta. He made one more stab at discouragement but it was the briefest of all.

'Mrs . . .'

'Don't worry about my wages. You just give to Maria. She use them for food. And as she not such good cook, she only charge five pound an hour instead of eight. OK?'

With a mouth full of pasta Christopher Devon could only nod and move his eyes in mute agreement.

'Good. That sorted then. I have changed bedding and ironed shirts. Milk in fridge and food for weekend. I see you some time Doctor Devon. Be good!'

And with that she pulled on her thick black coat and walked out of the kitchen towards her car. As the little Fiat with the round lady at the helm pulled out of the drive, the good doctor put down the fork and spoon and got up from the table in search of the pork pie and the apple.

Chapter 4

For secrets are edged tools,
And must be kept from children and from fools.
Sir Martin Mar-all, John Dryden, 1631–1700

'But I thought he wasn't due back until next week?'

'Unfortunately he doesn't always tell us when he has a change of plan.' Gary was looking out of the window and across the river.

His boss was sitting behind a large desk, his heavy head resting on his hands. 'So what now?'

Gary turned round. 'Steady nerves. I don't want to rush it.'

'But you'll keep tabs?'

'Oh, yes, but at a safe distance. We know from experience that he doesn't rush things himself. He won't be going back to China for at least a month if previous trips are anything to go by.'

'Well, he doesn't normally come back to the UK as quickly as this, so supposing he's changed his system?'

Gary considered the question and tapped lightly on the window ledge with his fingertips. 'Unlikely. He can offload quickly at the other end, but he still needs the time to gather funds at this end. I can't see him leaving us again for a while. The important thing is that we don't put the wind up him. He mustn't get even a whiff of the fact that we're on to him. We've made that mistake before, and the moment it happens he'll go to ground. Disappear. Someone else will take over and then it will take us an age to find out who before we can get stuck in again.'

'So why didn't we get him before he made the last trip?'

'We weren't confident he was in possession and we're still not sure where the funds come from. I want to be certain of both. We only get one chance to nab him properly and if we mess it up we're back to square one.'

His boss straightened up in his chair then asked, 'You do think it's worth all this trouble?'

Gary nodded. 'Oh yes.'

'I mean for the amount of money he's smuggling out.'

'Iceberg.'

'Sorry?'

'The money is something concrete that we can get him on. But I'm pretty sure there's more to it than currency smuggling.'

'Well, he's not going to admit to any more than that is he?'

'No. That's why we need him to lead us to others before we jump on him.'

'They're not all Triads, you know,' his boss said wearily.

'No, sometimes it's not that straightforward. There are all kinds of strange things going on now, with the Chinese economy ballooning like it is. More opportunities.'

'Do you need more help?'

'Not for now. I'll carry on with Sarah for a bit. I've got Ben Atkinson doing the foot slogging. We can get him in closer if we need to. I might need some more muscle later on, but for now we can manage.'

'I've heard you say that before. Just make sure that as soon as you think you're getting out of your depth you call for reinforcements. No heroics.'

'OK.' Gary walked towards the door.

'And keep me informed.'

'I will.' He closed the door behind him and murmured, 'Most of the time.'

'So?' Sarah Perry sat on the edge of her desk, dangling her legs.

'I've made sure he knows we can't rush it,' said Gary. 'I think I've bought us a bit more time.'

'And more help?'

'No. I've said we we're fine for now. If Ben can keep providing us with intelligence I thought you and I could manage.'

Sarah frowned. 'Was that wise?'

'Well, look. Who would we get?' He nodded in the direction of two or three other bodies at the far end of the office. 'Wouldn't you rather carry on as we are for now?'

'As long as you think we can cope.'

Gary grinned at her and looked at the long legs, encased in their black-patterned tights, the short skirt, the tight black sweater and the shiny dark brown hair. 'Oh, I think I can cope.'

Sarah grinned back. 'Oh, you wish Mr Flynn! You wish!'

Gary sighed. 'Yes, well, it's not for want of trying.

Anyway, as long as you keep fending me off at least our working relationship isn't compromised. Though why that should be an advantage I can't think.'

Sarah slipped down off the desk and moved across to the water machine. He watched her sinuous walk with a stab of pleasure.

'So what's next?'

'Mmm?' He was miles away. On some beach. Lying next to her.

'I said, what's next?'

'Right. Yes. Strategy. That's what's next. Strategy. We need to find out where the money's coming from and when and how it's leaving the country. And to do that we need some sort of strategy.'

'Meaning?'

Gary drained his cup. 'Meaning we have to see rather a lot of each other over the next few days.'

Sarah screwed up her face. 'Oh, lucky me.'

'Do you want this bath or not?'

Erica Wilson was sitting on the edge of the tub. She was swathed in a white towel, her long brown hair combed back from her face.

'If you like.' Tiger put his head round the bathroom door. 'I remember when we used to share them.'

'Oh don't start that. You can share them with me now if you want except that you're always too busy doing something else.' She wiped a trickle of water from her forehead with the edge of the towel.

Tiger eyed her up proprietorially. She played tennis three times a week in between running the shop, and the regular exercise kept her in good trim.

31

'You look very tantalizing sitting there,' Tiger said as he pulled his shirt over his head.

'Bet you say that to all the girls.'

'Nope. Just the one.' He slipped off the rest of his clothes and slid into the tub.

'Well, you're not in such bad shape yourself, Mr Wilson.' She surveyed him over the rim of the bath. 'You've still got all your hair, not too much grey, and your body's in a tolerable state. Maybe a pound or two more than usual after a long, hard winter, but not bad for a man of advanced years.'

'Do you mind! I'm a bit sensitive about my advancing years at the moment.'

'Why's that? Feeling your age?'

Tiger frowned. 'A bit.'

'Aches and pains?'

'No. Just . . . in other ways.'

A look of concern flickered across her face. 'Is it me?'

He lifted his hand and laid it on her arm. 'No. It's not you.'

'What then?'

'Oh, I was just thinking. You get married because you want to be together, because you just want each other. And then children come along and it all changes. You try your best to make sure that you still care for each other, that you give each other time, and yet it all gets a bit diluted. You're so busy sorting the kids out, worrying about them, ferrying them here and there – they become the entire focus of your life. Then they go and suddenly you're on your own again. You still worry about them – more if anything – but you can't really do anything constructive. So you have to pick up the pieces and start all over again with each other.'

'Is that what it feels like?' she asked. 'Starting all over again?'

'Not completely. It's different. You're sort of starting from a different place. Can you see what I mean?'

'Yes. I suppose it happens to every couple with kids.'

'Those that are still together. By the way, I saw Kate Devon today.'

The introspective mood was broken. Probably, thought Tiger, for the better. 'What?' Erica was surprised. 'Where?'

'I had to fly her from the City Airport to Southampton.'

'Well . . . what did she say . . . what did she look like . . . was she with a man . . . ?'

'Er, answering those one at a time, she said very little, looked stunning – dripping with gold – and was on her way to meet her man who's called Howie and who's clearly not without a bob or two.'

'Oh, poor Christopher.'

'Why poor Christopher?'

'I don't know. It's just that I suppose I'd always hoped they'd get back together.'

'I thought it was me who was meant to stick up for the man and you had to take the woman's part.'

'Not necessarily. I can see why she went. I'm not blaming her. But Christopher's not a bad soul – he's not over keen on the bottle or too physical or anything like that. Just totally wrapped up in his job. Well, he *was* wrapped up in his job. I just wish she'd had more patience, that's all.'

'I suppose she'd argue that she was patient for twenty-odd years.' He paused. 'I wonder if I should tell Christopher. About Howie, I mean.'

'He probably knows.'

33

'He never says anything. Never mentions Kate at all. It's as if she didn't exist.' Tiger handed her the bar of soap. 'Do my back?'

'Go on!' She pushed him forward and began to soap his shoulders.

'I was talking to Christopher and Gary at the pub.'

'Mmm?'

'About . . . well . . . this sort of feeling that you can't make much of a difference any more.'

'Is that how they feel as well?'

'I think so. They won't admit it – Gary in particular – but I'm pretty sure they do.'

'And . . . ?'

'Well, I had this daft idea.'

'How daft?'

'You'll laugh.'

'Try me.'

'I said we should form a secret society.'

'What sort of secret society?'

'I don't know.' Then he brightened. 'To right wrongs and generally make a difference.'

Erica carried on washing his back. 'Like Robin Hood?'

'A bit. But without anybody knowing. I haven't really thought it through. Do you think I'm crackers?'

'Oh, yes. But then I've always thought you were crackers.'

'So it's a daft idea?'

'Yes.'

'And I shouldn't pursue it.'

'I didn't say that.'

'So I *should* pursue it?'

'I didn't say that either. If it makes you happy . . . Provided you don't do anything stupid.' She looked at him;

34

picking up on the earlier part of the conversation. 'You are still happy aren't you? I mean, with us.'

He hesitated for the tiniest split second. 'Of course I am. Like you said, it must be just my time of life, that's all. It makes you take stock. Think about where you're going.'

Chapter 5

I have always depended on the kindness of strangers.
A Streetcar Named Desire, Tennessee Williams, 1911–83

The City of Winchester lies in the valley of the River Itchen. It is handsome and airy, as cities go, and more of a town in terms of its size. Approaching from the east, you can see it lying peacefully in the valley below, snoozing in the summer sun, or hunkered down to avoid the bitter winter winds. The pale buff-grey Norman cathedral dominates not just the green close that surrounds it, but this entire section of the broad valley through which the trout-rich Itchen snakes its way. Once the capital of England, and still home to the lump of wood that purports to be King Arthur's round table, Winchester was, according to the poet John Keats, 'the pleasantest town I ever was in'. Its High Street he found 'quiet as a lamb'. That's all changed now, but he might still consider that some of the side-streets with their 18th-century houses and shop fronts were 'excessively maiden-lady-like'.

'Adventure' was tucked away down an alleyway that ran off the cathedral close – a small double-fronted shop with Georgian windows. Erica rented the ground floor only – there were flats above – and there was just enough room for a tiny kitchenette and loo at the back of the shop, and a small stockroom, though thanks to the bijou nature of the premises most of the stock resided on the floor-to-ceiling shelves.

Today was unlikely to be busy. There were a few new titles to unpack and two boxes of second-hand books to sift through and price up, but Erica was looking forward to a quiet time. Her tennis match was booked in at three and she could be well sorted by then, leaving Brian, the rather wet but willing student, to hold the fort for the rest of the afternoon.

It was at around 11 a.m. that the unexpected visitor arrived. He was an insignificant-looking man in a black anorak, and he carried a black holdall. He wandered up and down the shelves, glanced at Erica's table arrangement of books about the Himalaya – but was clearly preoccupied.

Erica nodded at Brian to keep an eye. The man was obviously shoplifter material. The soft tones of Radio 3 maintained the calm air of tranquility, but for a few minutes Erica and Brian went into surveillance mode.

The only other customer in the shop came to the counter with a copy of James Morris's *Venice*. 'You'll enjoy that,' said Erica, slipping it into a bag but barely taking her eyes off the man in black.

The customer thanked her and left. As if he had been waiting to have the shop to himself, the man came up to the counter. Erica asked pointedly, 'Can I help you?'

'Well, it's more how I can help you,' replied the man.

She didn't like the look of him much. He was quite neat, scrubbed even, but there was something about him that seemed shifty. Slightly seedy. And he smelled too strongly of aftershave.

'Oh?'

'Yes. I represent the local co-operative business venture.'

Erica looked puzzled. 'I don't think I've ever heard of it.' She glanced sideways at Brian who shrugged. Clearly he hadn't heard of it either.

Unabashed, the man continued. 'We are a consortium of local businesses and we run the association as a sort of co-operative. Pooling resources for mutual benefit.'

'What sort of resources?' asked Erica.

'Business expertise, contacts, insurance, that sort of thing.'

'Well, I'm not really sure I need that sort of thing, thanks.'

The man seemed unperturbed. He carried on. 'I think you'll find it really worthwhile to join. We have quite a lot of local businesses on board now and they all know that it makes sense to pull together.'

Erica didn't want to appear obstructive. 'Is it something to do with the local Chamber of Trade?'

'Not exactly. Sort of affiliated but not a part of, if you see what I mean.'

'Well, what does it involve? I'm not sure I have the time for any more commitments, you see.' Erica was hopeful of getting rid of him, but the man refused to budge.

'Oh, it will take none of your time at all. Just a contribution once a month.'

'And what do I get for my contribution?'

'Like I said; the security of belonging to a group of like-minded traders who act together for mutual benefit.'

He seemed to have the phrase off pat. But still Erica was unclear about the benefits of belonging. 'Well, what sort of contribution?'

'That rather depends on the turnover of the business.' He turned and looked around the shop, assessing its likely income. 'In your case I should think we'd be talking in terms of around one hundred pounds a month.'

'A hundred pounds a month!'

'Some traders pay more.'

Erica laughed. 'Well, they might do, but I'm afraid that in my case I don't have the sort of profits that would let me pay a hundred pounds a month.'

'I'm sure we could come to some arrangement,' said the man.

'I really don't think . . .'

'It is negotiable . . .' he offered.

They were interrupted by the pinging of the door bell, and a mother and two small children clattered noisily into the shop. The man stepped back from the counter. 'I'll let you think about it. I'll pop back in a day or two.'

'No. Really, there's no need. I don't think it's for me, I'm afraid.'

The man edged around the mother and children, as if afraid to touch them, and backed out of the door smiling nervously. He pulled up the hood of his anorak and strode briskly off down the alley.

'Well,' said Erica to Brian, 'what do you make of that?'

Brian shrugged. Some days it seemed that all Brian ever did was shrug. In moments of profound irritation Erica longed to ask him for his opinions on the relative merits of Stendhal and Proust – not that she was sure of them herself – but then he was at that difficult age and she didn't want to make him more self-conscious than he already was.

'Brian, can you hold the fort for a minute? I just want to go next door and talk to Isobel.' Brian acquiesced in the only way that Brian knew how, and Erica went out, turned left and pushed open the door of the Belgian chocolate shop.

Isobel, the jolly, spherical lady who presided over the stacked counters of rose and violet creams, bitter chocolate orange peel sticks and bespoke bonbons was busy, as usual, arranging her handmade sweetmeats in small gold boxes to be tied with scarlet ribbon.

She looked up from the lacy frills of her apron straps and said, 'Hello Erica. Can we tempt you?'

'Not today Isobel. Tennis this afternoon. If I ate any of those I'd probably throw up.'

'Oh dear. What a pity.' Isobel looked crushed, disappointed that anyone – even Erica – should use language like that in her little palace of delights. But she got over the unintentional slight almost immediately, and with a bright smile said, 'Just try one of these.' She lifted up a lavender cream with her little steel tongs and handed it over the top of the plate-glass dome of the counter.

Erica gave in. 'Oh, just the one then.' She popped it in her mouth, made appreciative cooing noises that she knew would placate Isobel, and for the next thirty seconds was unable to address the matter she'd come about.

Isobel, always thrilled when a customer expressed admiration of her efforts, went into a little shudder of ecstasy and suppressed giggles, and the amber hair piled upon her head, after the fashion of a walnut whip, quivered in time with her body.

Finally Erica managed to swallow, and to bestow the final acclamation, 'Wonderful, Isobel, I don't know how you do it.'

'Just years of practice you know,' purred Isobel, allowing just a note of self-satisfaction to creep into her voice.

Erica cleared her throat. 'Isobel, have you just had that man in?'

'What man, dear?' She went back to putting her chocolates into their little boxes.

'The one in the black anorak. To do with some co-operative or other.'

'Oh, him. Yes.' Isobel stopped what she was doing. 'Didn't like him at all.' Isobel didn't look serious very often, but she did now. 'Something very odd about him.'

'Did he ask you about joining his co-operative?'

'Yes he did. As if I could afford to.'

'Do you mind me asking what he wanted you to pay?'

'It was quite ridiculous. He wanted a hundred-and-fifty pounds a month. Well, I mean that's just silly isn't it, dear? I couldn't possibly afford that. I know my chocolates are not exactly cheap, but I don't have that sort of profit margin.'

'So what did you say?'

'I sent him packing with a flea in his ear, I'm afraid. I don't like to be rude but he was so persistent, and to be perfectly honest, Erica, I was getting a bit rattled. He didn't seem to take no for an answer. Anyway, fortunately a customer came in and he sloped off. I shouldn't think I'll see him again. I think he got the message.'

'Yes.'

Isobel asked, 'Did you join, then?'

'No,' replied Erica, distractedly. 'No, I didn't. But he

41

said he'd come back, so I don't think he's given up on me.'

'Oh dear! Well, good luck. And if you take my advice you'll do what I did and tell him where to get off next time.'

'Yes. Yes, I will. I'll tell him where to get off.'

Christopher Devon had one last patient to see at the surgery before making his house calls. He was at the start of a locum week in a practice in Romsey and was surprised when a young mother he'd known from his Winchester surgery walked in with her five-year-old daughter. Surprised and thrown a little off balance.

'Mrs Fraser. How lovely to see you. But what are you doing down here?'

The mother looked slightly embarrassed. 'Oh, we moved doctor, shortly after you did.'

'Hello Daisy. How are you?' asked Christopher.

Daisy managed a weak smile before attempting to hide behind her mother's legs.

'Well, how nice to see you both. It must be almost a year since I saw you. Goodness me, Daisy, you have grown, haven't you?'

Daisy, emerging from the other side of her mother with a thumb wedged into her mouth, nodded without looking at him.

'And what can I do for you, Mrs Fraser?'

'Nothing really, Doctor. I spoke to reception and they said I could just pop in after surgery to say thank you.'

'Oh?'

'About Richard.'

'But . . .'

'I know it all went wrong in the end, but I know you did your best. You made his life as comfortable as you could. We just wanted to say thank you for all you did. And we never got a chance to, what with you leaving.'

'No. No, I'm sorry about that.'

Mrs Fraser was in her early thirties. A good-looking woman who had been married to a local farmer. She was always polite and courteous. Deferential to her doctor after the manner of many patients in a country practice. Her husband had been a strapping farmer's lad who had taken on the business himself when his father had retired from their dairy farm near Alresford. Then he had developed kidney trouble. Christopher hoped they would be able to find him a new one. But they had not. Two years later Richard Fraser died, leaving a widow and three children under the age of seven.

Christopher was back there for a moment, back in the bleakness of it all. Remembering the frustration and the anger he felt with himself for not being able to make a difference. For not finding Richard Fraser a kidney and for not taking more of a stand against those who were unable or unwilling to help. If he had done, wouldn't Richard Fraser be alive now? Mrs Fraser cleared her throat, and he came back to the present with a start. 'But are things looking up now that you've moved down here?'

'Yes, thank you, Doctor.'

'So where are you living now?'

'In Wellow. One of the little villages. We're on our own at the moment.'

'I see.' Christopher tried not to appear prying.

'But not for long. Richard's cousin has become a very good friend. Very helpful, you know, kind.'

'Oh. That's good.'

'I don't want them to grow up without a dad. But, well, we'll see.' She looked down at the little girl, now swinging around her legs as a young boy might swing on a lamp post. 'He's very nice your Uncle Tom, isn't he?' she asked.

The child nodded.

'He farms just beyond the town. But it's early days yet. Early days.' She looked reflective for a moment, then gathered her thoughts and spoke more briskly. 'Anyway, Doctor Devon, I don't want to take up any more of your time. But thank you so much. You were very kind. Made it much more bearable.'

'Oh, Mrs Fraser . . .'

'No, really you did. I don't know how we'd have coped without you. Anyway, Daisy's brought you a thank you letter, haven't you Daisy?'

The child nodded.

'Give it to the doctor then,' instructed her mother.

The child reached into her mother's shopping basket and pulled out an envelope that was addressed in a childish scrawl: To Docter Deven.

'Thank you. Thank you Daisy. That's very kind.' He laid the envelope on his desk.

'We'll be going now then. Come on Daisy.' Christopher stood up as Mrs Fraser took Daisy's hand and walked her towards the door. Then she turned. 'I do hope everything turns out all right for you, Doctor. Like it has for me.'

'Thank you Mrs Fraser. That's very kind of you.'

With more murmured encouragement, the mother and daughter left the surgery and closed the door behind them.

Christopher sat down heavily in his chair. However long he might have been a doctor, and however long he carried on being one, he didn't think he would ever get used to the worst injustices of life. To the twists of fate that could deprive a thirty-year-old mother of her husband and three young children of their father.

He picked up the envelope and turned it over in his hand. It had been decorated with brightly coloured flowers, painstakingly drawn out in felt-tipped pens. He used a knife to slit open the flap and pulled out the home-made card inside. It showed a man in brown trousers and a white shirt holding a bucket. He was standing next to a black and white cow in a green meadow dotted with yellow flowers. Above them, in the middle of a blue sky decorated with fluffy white clouds made of stuck on bits of cotton wool was an angel with golden wings.

He opened the card and read the simple legend inside, written out as neatly as a five-year-old hand could manage: Docter Deven – My Hero – Love Daisy xxx.

He laid the card on the desk, leaned forward on his arms and wept.

Chapter 6

Early to rise and early to bed makes a male healthy
and wealthy and dead.
The Shrike and the Chipmunks, James Thurber, 1894–1961

'So have we any idea where they get the money from?'
Sarah Perry was leaning forward on a small sofa in a corner
of the office at MI5.

'Not yet, no,' said Gary. 'I mean, this could just be some
bit of diplomatic PR.' He pointed at the newspaper picture
of Mr Tan. 'You know, doing his bit for Anglo-Chinese rela-
tions. I can't think it's from restaurant tips.'

'What do we know about Red Dragon?' asked Sarah.

'They opened their first restaurant in Canterbury in
2001. The following year it was Bath, then Cheltenham,
then around half a dozen others every year. They now have
twenty-eight of them across the south. I've run a check and
the business seems to be above board – no dodgy accounts
or anything like that.'

She raised her head. 'Have you ever eaten in one?'

'No. But this one's just round the corner from me,' he said, tapping the paper.

'Could we risk it?' she asked.

'What?'

'Going there for a meal. It might be useful to get the feel of the place.'

Gary beamed at her. 'Are you asking me out to dinner?'

'Yes, but not in the way you think. This is purely a business arrangement, and we'll claim it on expenses.'

'Oh, shame. I'd have paid for you if it had been a date.'

'No. I won't put you to that trouble.' She looked at him archly. 'You're old enough to be my . . .'

'Careful!' he warned.

'Brother,' she said.

'Thank you. I'm only just fifty and you're only just still in your thirties.'

Sarah looked indignant. 'Do you mind!'

'Well, you are. Eleven years. Perfect age gap.'

'Says who?'

'Me.'

'Yes, well, that's a matter of opinion.'

'So when's our date then?'

'If you start calling it that there won't be one. Tomorrow night? I can manage that. I can't tonight because Max is taking me to see some art-house movie at the National.'

'His choice or yours?'

'Oh, his. I'm not into all that Japanese stuff. Give me Katherine Hepburn any day.'

She got up and walked to the hat stand to collect her coat.

Gary watched her. When did he not? She really was the perfect girl — long, dark hair that shone like ebony, a personality to keep him on his mettle, a dazzling smile, a figure to die for and legs that just went on and on. The black, tight sweater, the black mini-skirt, the patterned black tights and the long black boots. He shook his head, as if to order his mind, then briefly mused on the fact that he could so easily have been stuck in some macho working relationship with a beer-guzzling, cigarette-smoking guy with halitosis and BO.

He watched as she reached up on tiptoe for her scarf, then cleared his throat. 'Right.'

She turned, putting on her coat. 'So if we go straight from here tomorrow evening then?'

'Yes. Fine. I'll ring up and book. What time shall I say?'

'Well, we don't want to sit there all night, do we? Can we make it lateish?'

'If we said a table for eight thirty? We could take our time then and just see if there are any comings and goings during the evening.'

'Yes. OK then.'

'Take care. See you tomorrow morning.' She lifted her black satchel on to her shoulder and glided out of the office.

How pathetic, he thought. How wonderfully pathetic. He shook his head again, realizing the pointlessness of it all, but still, deep down, wondering if he stood the remotest chance of getting anywhere with her. He caught sight of his reflection in the dark glass of the office next door. It quite surprised him. He looked younger than usual. Thinner. Actually quite fanciable. And he was only just fifty. And she was nearly forty. He laughed out loud; a lone, solitary laugh. Then he slackened his tie, grabbed his leather jacket and turned out the lights.

*

It was only because Tiger had no work that morning that he walked Erica to the bookshop. Otherwise she would have made the discovery on her own.

It was a warm, clear morning. Unseasonably mild. They crossed the cathedral close holding hands, looking up at the grey building as the stealthy rays of sunlight washed over the pale stone. A bell struck the quarter, and Tiger looked at his watch. 'It's a minute fast.'

'If it's all the same to you I'd rather live by cathedral time than Omega time.'

'Yes, well you can't run an airline on cathedral time.'

The conversation stopped when they rounded the corner of the alley and saw Isobel sweeping up broken glass. Erica broke away from Tiger and dashed up to her. 'Isobel, whatever's happened? Have you had an accident?'

'No dear,' Isobel was close to tears, 'not an accident at all. Quite intentional. Look . . .' She nodded in the direction of the left-hand window of her shop. It was shattered. Shards of glass lay on the pavement and among the display boxes of artificial chocolates that were piled up in the once attractive window.

'Vandals. Ruddy vandals.' For Isobel this was the nearest she came to swearing.

Tiger stepped forward to assess the damage. In the middle of the display was a single brick. He turned to Isobel. 'Have you called the police?'

'Oh, they've been and gone dear. I asked them if they wanted to take fingerprints but they didn't seem interested. Said they'd come back later and take down more details. So much of it going on at the moment apparently. Unless they catch the culprits red-handed there's little chance of them ever finding out who did it.'

Tiger shook his head, then turned to take the brush from Isobel. 'Probably just some kids who'd had too much to drink. That's all-day opening for you. You go and have a coffee with Erica, I'll finish clearing this up and then we'd better see about getting your window replaced.'

'But it's curved glass, dear. Special. I don't know if they'll be able to do it.'

'Well, I'll give the glaziers a call and find out.'

'Thank you, Tiger. Thank you so much.' Then she burst into tears.

'Come on,' said Erica gently. 'Come and sit down. We'll help you sort it out.'

The distraught Isobel was taken into the kitchen of Erica's shop while Tiger assessed the damage. It was not too bad. The glass was gone, and the window dressing destroyed, but the carved wooden uprights were intact and there was no sign of disturbance further back in the shop. Poor Isobel. Why did they always have to do it to the nicest people? People whose lives would be turned upside down by one mindless act.

Because it was such a pleasant day, and because he had the day off, Christopher Devon put on old clothes, wolfed down a bowl of porridge and went out into the garden. He would work out there for as long as he could. Until it got dark. Put aside his worries and fill his mind with different problems – rose pruning and snowdrop dividing, revitalizing borders and tidying up flower beds.

He was bent double between 'Madame Pierre Oger' and 'Madame Alfred Carrière' when he heard the voice calling him.

'Dr Devon. Excuse me! Dr Devon!'

He stood up, snagged his arm on a particularly ferocious thorn and said, 'Shit!' Then, recovering himself, 'I'm sorry. I'm off duty today. You'll have to go to the surgery . . .'

The woman laughed.

Christopher unhooked the sleeve of his sweater, picked his way out of the border and walked across the lawn to where she stood.

She was a small, good-looking woman in her forties with short, dark hair. She wore fitted jeans and a baggy sweater; her features were delicate and expressive. She didn't seem to have the manner of most people who came to the door – patients worried about their health, or ladies conducting market research.

'I'm afraid I don't do surveys or anything like that,' said Christopher.

A look of amusement crossed her face. 'I'm glad to hear it. Neither do I.'

She spoke perfect English, but something about her helped him make the connection. 'Oh, goodness! Are you Maria?'

'Yes. I'm sorry. I didn't mean to disturb you. I've come to sort you out.' The words were innocently prophetic.

'No. That's all right. Only you don't . . . I mean . . .'

'I don't look like my mother? No!'

He considered whether it was a good idea to try and ingratiate himself further, but thought better of it. 'Well . . . hello.' He offered his hand, and for the first time in many years experienced a faint feeling of shyness.

She shook his hand firmly and smiled. 'I'll try not to get in your way.'

'Oh, don't worry about that. Do you . . . I mean . . . would you like a coffee?'

She seemed very relaxed, which surprised him. It was not an accusation that could ever be levelled at her mother whose breakneck intensity almost always left him on edge. He reproached himself for wondering how such a plain mother could have given birth to such a beautiful daughter. He had had enough experience of mothers and daughters over the years to know that this was often the case. He put the uncharitable thought out of his head.

'I was saying to Luisa – er . . . your mum – that I didn't really need quite the looking after she seems to think.'

'Oh?'

'She didn't say?'

'No. She just told me to keep the house clean, to do the washing when it was needed and to make sure you had lunch when you were at home.'

'I see.'

He made the coffee and polite conversation. He should have told her he didn't want lunch. Especially as her mother had said she was not a good cook. But somehow he didn't get round to it.

'Shall we start upstairs?' he asked. Then realized the slight *double entendre*. 'I mean . . .'

'Yes, then we can work our way down,' she said, with the merest glimmer of a smile.

He showed her the bedrooms and bathrooms, then his own study on the top floor. 'You won't need to do much in here. Far too messy. I can sort this out myself.'

Maria looked round at the pale oak shelves that lined the wall.

'Sorry. Rather a lot of books. Bit of a vice I'm afraid.'

She walked towards them. 'You like opera?' she asked, pointing at the fat volume of Kobbé.

'Some. Not all. Puccini and Verdi. Some Mozart. One Wagner.'

'Which one?'

'*Meistersingers.*'

Maria nodded. 'The only one I can take, too.'

Christopher was surprised. 'Most folk run a mile from Wagner.'

'I'd run a mile from *Siegfried*,' she said.

Christopher laughed, and a ray of sunlight beamed in at the window. Maria looked out over the garden. 'Wow! Who does that?'

'Er . . . I do actually.'

'I see.' She looked out again, over the green lawns and the beds, but said nothing.

'Shall we go downstairs then?' Christopher gestured towards the door.

They toured the ground floor – sitting room, dining room, hallway and utility room and quite before he knew where he was they were sitting down having lunch together. Not pasta. Not a pork pie and an apple. Instead slices of melon and Parma ham, roasted peppers and boquerones, olives and ciabatta that she had casually pulled out of a raffia basket.

She listened quietly while he explained his modest requirements – a bit of dusting, but not in the study; vacuuming the floors, turfing out the old newspapers, doing a spot of washing and ironing and keeping fresh flowers on the table in the hall. He felt embarrassed about this last request; especially when she smiled gently and looked at him with her head cocked at a slight angle.

'Sorry. Is that a bit much?'

She shook her head. 'Not at all. I think it's rather fine.'

Rather fine. He liked that turn of phrase. Not 'OK', but 'rather fine'.

'And lunch?' she asked.

He hesitated. 'When I'm here, yes. That would be very nice. If it's not too much trouble.'

'Oh, it's no trouble,' said Maria. 'No trouble at all.'

Chapter 7

The appetite grows by eating.

François Rabelais, c.1494–1553

Three meals were enjoyed that night. Christopher Devon ate on his own at the Manor House. Tiger and Erica dined, rather unexpectedly, in the company of Gary and Sarah.

The Wilsons arrived a little before the MI5 contingent, having promised themselves that after their recent excitement they would treat themselves and try the new Chinese restaurant. Erica told Tiger that it would make a pleasant change from the Hare and Hounds. He took the hint and booked. They were shown to a corner table by a solicitous waitress in a gold-edged black silk dress with a generous slit up the side.

Erica noticed the sparkle in Tiger's eye and dug him in the ribs. 'Do you mind not being quite so obvious.'

'Well, I haven't seen anything like that since I flew Singapore Airlines.'

'I didn't know you had flown Singapore Airlines.'

'Only as a passenger. And it was before I met you.'

'Well, you've met me now, so be careful. Anyway, what do you think?'

Tiger looked around him at the interior of the Red Dragon. 'It's smarter than your usual Chinese. Not a bit of flock wall-paper in sight.'

The walls and ceiling were painted black, the picture and dado rails of the old Georgian building were gilded, and black paper lanterns hung from the ceiling, each one emblazoned with a rampant red dragon.

Instead of the usual scrolls of minimalist Chinese art-work, the walls were hung with a mixture of black and white photographs of modern Chinese cities and lengths of plain red silk.

'Very classy,' confirmed Erica. 'I bet we don't have to ask for two number seventeens, a thirty-six and a fifty-four.'

'As long as we don't have to use chopsticks,' muttered Tiger.

'Dr Cummings isn't,' offered Erica, tilting her head in the direction of the fat, grey-haired man sitting in the far corner of the restaurant. A Chinese gentleman sat opposite him, nodding as the doctor spoke softly.

'Adding this lot to his list of patients is he?' asked Tiger with an edge to his voice.

'You don't like him do you?'

'Not much. Not since he gave Christopher the push.'

'It must have been difficult for him.'

'He should have been a bit more understanding. As if Christopher hadn't been through enough. Anyway, he's far too fat for a doctor. And short tempered.'

Their conversation was curtailed by the return of the

waitress bearing a small lacquer tray on which were unidentifiable Chinese canapés. She laid it down on their table with a neat bow, and asked what they would like to drink.

Tiger was about to suggest two halves of lager when Erica cut in and asked for a bottle of chilled Sancerre. The waitress bowed once more, smiled and went off in the direction of the kitchen, returning only moments later with the bottle, pleasingly coated with condensation, and two shapely glasses.

Only four tables were occupied, out of a total of around twenty. 'A bit quiet,' said Tiger, looking around.

'Oh, it's early yet. I expect most folk come at around half past eight.'

Erica was not wrong. Within ten minutes a steady trickle of diners had arrived and the restaurant began to fill up. At eight thirty-five Tiger said, 'Good God!'

'What?'

'Look over there.'

Erica turned in the direction of Tiger's gaze and saw Gary Flynn being shown to a table, along with a slim, dark-haired girl.

Tiger said, with a little too much interest for Erica's liking, 'Who on earth is that?'

'It's Gary,' said Erica flatly.

'I know that. But who's he with?'

'You could always go and ask him,' said Erica, popping one of the hors d'oeuvres into her mouth and giving Tiger a withering look.

'I'd better say hello, or he'll only tell me off later.'

Before Erica could waylay him with a restraining arm, Tiger had risen from the table. He walked across to where

Gary and Sarah were seated and said, 'Are you trying it out as well then?'

He was rather disappointed at Gary's reaction. If he hadn't known better he'd have said that Gary wasn't pleased to see him. In fact he was positively offhand.

'Hi. Yes. Thought we'd give it a try.' He spoke softly and without any apparent enthusiasm.

Tiger turned to Sarah. 'Hi! I'm Tiger, Gary's mate.' He offered his hand.

Sarah shook it and smiled, darting a look across at Gary as she did so.

Tiger read the signals. 'Sorry. Didn't want to muscle in. Just thought I'd better say hello. You know.'

Gary did his best to make amends. 'Yes. Sure. Didn't expect to see you here. Sarah's from . . . Sarah's a friend. We just thought we'd try it out. New place and all that.'

'Yes. Right. Well, enjoy your evening.' Tiger nodded, hesitated, smiled apologetically and then made his way back across the restaurant. He sat down opposite Erica and picked up his napkin. 'That was a bit frosty.'

'I'm not surprised.'

'What do you mean?'

'Here's Gary, come for a romantic night out *à deux*, and one of his beer-drinking dominoes partners lurches over and introduces himself. It's hardly surprising he doesn't welcome you with open arms.'

'I didn't lurch over.'

'You know what I mean.' Erica glanced in Gary's direction. 'Anyway, she does look rather nice. Very classy.'

'Yes,' said Tiger wistfully. 'I was never sure whether he was bullshitting us with all this talk about his sex life. Perhaps it wasn't made up after all.'

58

'A meal in a restaurant with a pretty girl doesn't necessarily mean he's . . . you know . . .'

Tiger grinned at her. 'No?'

'No!'

'Sorry about that.' Gary filled Sarah in on the identity of their visitor and explained that they had known each other for a few years. Did a bit of sport together. He didn't say what. Then he changed the subject. 'Looks a cut above your usual Chinese take-away.'

'Yes. Very smart,' confirmed Sarah.

'And better than a cup of tea down the canteen,' offered Gary. He looked across at her; beautiful and shining in her cream sweater and black trousers. But there was something not quite right. She was preoccupied. Not her usual bouncy self.

'Are you all right?' he asked, as the waitress retreated having brought the wine.

'Yes, fine,' she answered, avoiding his eye.

'No you're not. I know when you're not right. I've worked with you long enough. What's wrong?'

Sarah shook her head and turned away, and he saw her eyes fill with tears. He had never seen her cry before.

'Is it me? Is it something I've said?'

She shook her head again and tried to smile. 'No, it's not you. It's just . . . oh . . . things. That's all.'

He offered her a napkin, and she dabbed at her tears. 'Silly. Not worth it.' She sniffed and brightened quite suddenly, but falsely.

'Is it Max?'

Sarah nodded, and turned away again. Then she said, 'Told me last night. Someone else. Not me any more.'

Gary felt genuinely sorry for a moment or two. He murmured sympathetic platitudes of the 'better off without him' variety, and did his best not to be too hard in his criticism of a man who clearly did not know a goddess when she came up and bit him.

He tried to jolly her out of it, and she seemed to respond. 'Are you hungry?' he asked.

'Not much. But it seems rude not to eat.'

'Anything special, or do you want me to order?' he asked helpfully.

'Oh, anything. I don't really mind.' She began to pull herself together. 'I'm sorry. Didn't mean to bring my private life to work.'

'It's not work exactly, is it?' he asked with just a note of hope in his voice.

She gave him a look that put him in his place. Firm enough but, he hoped, with just a hint of kindness.

He beckoned the waitress to their table, gave the order and then leaned back and looked around. 'They've not stinted themselves have they?'

'No. Boat certainly pushed out. And they have twenty-odd like this?'

'Apparently. Same sort of livery for each one. Not done on a shoestring.'

'And there's nobody here you recognize?' Sarah asked.

'Well, not apart from Tiger and Erica, no.'

'Hardly surprising I suppose. I should think Mr Tan makes a point of not dining in the same place twice.'

'Keep us guessing.'

'But what about the others? The pictures we have of his associates.' Sarah scanned the room as unobtrusively as possible.

'Doesn't look like it. Not yet anyway.'

'No. Maybe it was too obvious a thing to do. Maybe we're wasting our time.'

'Oh, I don't think so,' said Gary. 'Time spent doing things like this is never wasted.' He was pleased she didn't see what he was getting at. He didn't want to rush things after all.

For Tiger and Erica it was still a little strange to be out on their own together after twenty-odd years of being a four-some. Like most parents they did manage to see something of each other alone when the girls were younger, but that was invariably after bedtime. Most intimate conversations during the preceding couple of decades were carried out over the washing-up, or in the bathroom, when there was a chance of not being interrupted. Which was not very often. Erica had, it seemed, only to get into the bath for a steady stream of daughters (if two can be considered a steady stream) to keep coming in and out with this problem over home-work, or that trouble with a boy. They had grown used to it, it had become a part of life. But it did mean that dining out as a twosome had a degree of novelty value. Even if the conversation did, inevitably, turn to Aisling and Kirsty.

The conversation about Aisling's latest boyfriend was interrupted when Erica said, 'Wow! It's him!'

'What?' Tiger was dealing with a particularly crisp spring roll that required all his concentration, and so he did not look up at first.

'That man over there. The one in the corner. He's the one who came to the shop.'

Tiger looked up. 'I'd like to say I understood what you were talking about, but as quite a lot of men come into your shop I can't say that I do.'

'Didn't I tell you? We had a man round the other day, trying to get us to join some sort of shopkeeper's co-operative.'

'What sort of co-operative?'

'He said it was for mutual benefit. Self-help. That kind of thing. Said that lots of shops had already joined and that they found it helpful. I asked if it was something to do with the Chamber of Trade and he said not exactly but that they were affiliated.'

'What exactly did he want you to do?' asked Tiger.

'Well, basically pay a hundred quid a month.'

'For what?'

'For all the benefits it would offer.'

'What sort of benefits?'

Erica shrugged. 'I'm not sure. It wasn't clear really. I went round to ask Isobel if he'd approached her and she said that he'd been in just before he came to see me.'

Tiger looked curious. 'And what did Isobel say?'

'Oh, she sent him away with a flea in his ear. Told him where to get off. He wanted a hundred-and-fifty quid from her. She said she couldn't possibly afford it with her turnover. I mean, how can you agree to pay that sort of money when you've got a tiny shop? It would take a great lump of your profits.'

Tiger put down his fork. 'So this was before Isobel's window was broken?'

'Yes,' confirmed Erica. 'The day before.'

'Are you certain?'

'Of course I'm certain.'

Tiger shrugged and picked up his fork again. 'Probably just a coincidence.'

'What, you mean you think there might be a connection

between that man asking for money and Isobel's shop window being smashed?'

'No. It would have been drunken yobs. There's been a lot of trouble with them lately.'

Now it was Erica's turn to lay down her fork. 'And have any of them been caught?' she asked levelly.

'No,' said Tiger. 'No, they haven't.'

'And has anybody actually seen them smashing shop windows?'

'I don't know.'

'So if it isn't drunken yobs, then who is it?' she asked.

'Well, if it isn't,' said Tiger, 'then I'd say it was some sort of protection racket. But then maybe I've got a vivid imagination.'

'What do you mean?'

'You know what a protection racket is?'

'The sort of thing that happened in America, in the Prohibition.'

'Yes. I've never heard of it happening round here, but you do hear of gangs who go round and ask for money for "insurance purposes". To make sure that your property stays safe. That sort of thing. Veiled threats.'

'But he wasn't threatening,' said Erica. 'He was very calm, very level about it all. It was almost as though he were selling insurance . . .' She heard the words coming out of her mouth.

'Which, of course, he was,' said Tiger. 'Maybe you've hit on it.' Then, softly and quite deliberately he said, 'Bloody hell! Who'd have thought it? I mean, here in Hampshire.'

'But he looks so mild,' said Erica. 'Seedy, but sort of . . . mild . . . I mean, look at him.'

They turned to where the man had sat. But his chair was

no longer occupied. He had left the restaurant, and neither of them had seen him go.

At a quarter to eleven Gary and Sarah decided to call it a day.

'Pity. But I think we had to do it,' said Gary.

'Yes. I suppose it was a long shot,' admitted Sarah. 'Nothing exciting at the kitchen table? You could see it better than me.'

The kitchen table – the one nearest the kitchen door – was the one most frequently occupied by 'management' who could then slip in and out of the restaurant.

'Not really. A few comings and goings. The odd shifty character, but since when has being shifty been a criminal offence?'

'In your case it's borderline,' quipped Sarah.

'You're perking up.'

'Yes. Just a bit. Thanks for tonight.'

'That sounds as though you're bringing the meeting to a close.'

'Yes. Well, I suppose I am.' Sarah reached down for her bag.

'No coffee round at my place then?' Gary asked with a glint in his eye.

'No. Not tonight. Thanks all the same. If I get my skates on I can catch the last train home.'

Gary sighed. 'If you must, but I can always offer you a bed if you want one.'

Sarah looked at him levelly. 'Oh, I'm sure you can, Mr Flynn. It's probably got notches carved on the end of it.'

'Ow!' he said.

Sarah looked apologetic. 'Sorry. Below the belt. I feel a

64

bit sensitive at the moment, a bit bruised. Two years is a long time to be in a relationship and then have it crumble around you.'

'I wouldn't know,' confessed Gary. 'The most I've managed is three weeks.'

'Really? And I thought you had staying power.'

'Not where love is concerned.'

'Love? So we're talking love are we?' asked Sarah looking startled. 'Not just a bit on the side.'

'Slip of the tongue,' said Gary. Then he got up from the table and went to pay the bill.

'You are putting this on your expense account I hope?' Sarah asked.

'Of course,' he said.

But he didn't.

Christopher Devon ate alone that evening, with a tray on his lap. It wasn't as good as his lunch, but that didn't matter. Normally he would have sat in front of the television, but tonight he didn't want the distraction. Instead, he ate his salmon fish cakes in front of a roaring log fire to the strains of Puccini. As Katia Ricciarelli soared through '*Vissi d'arte*' he felt himself transported to another world. A world of calm, a world he had not visited for a long time.

And then it finished. And the room was quiet, except for the occasional crackling of a log. He could not remember feeling quite so emotional since Kate had left. But then he was, he told himself, going through a bit of a phase at the moment. The reappearance of Mrs Fraser and young Daisy had quite thrown him off balance.

Mrs Fraser and Miss Bassani. Except that he didn't know if it was Miss Bassani. Maybe she was married. Bound to be.

She was probably Mrs Whatever. He was surprised that the thought had not struck him before. They had talked about opera and about food but never got round to her private life. He had no idea if she was married. Or had children. Luisa had never said. Never mentioned her family at all until the morning she left. And she wasn't the sort of woman he felt he could ask.

Stupid really. But then Luisa had only cleaned for him for a couple of months, and for half of that time he had been out on call. When he was there, all his time had been spent trying to avoid her, along with her lunches, rather than trying to engage her in conversation. Now he felt guilty. He should have tried harder. Perhaps when she went home she talked about him and said how unappreciative he was of her efforts. And yet Maria had been so friendly.

Anyway, what did it matter? She was just coming in to clean for him. To help him out while he got himself sorted. And she was being paid, after all.

He took the tray into the kitchen and went up to bed.

Chapter 8

In planning for battle I have always found that plans
are useless, but planning is indispensable.
Dwight D. Eisenhower, 1890–1969

The domino club met on Thursday that week. Christopher
rang them to say that he would be unable to make their
usual date thanks to being on call, so Tiger and Gary had
agreed to meet a day earlier rather than postpone.

Settled around their table in the corner of the Hare and
Hounds the conversation turned, as it inevitably did in
Gary's case, to women. Except that on this occasion it was
not Gary who brought the subject up. He seemed a bit
quiet. Which is why Tiger asked mischievously, 'Go well did
it? Your night out?'

Gary didn't look up, but laid down the double six to start.
'Yes thank you.'

Christopher raised an enquiring eyebrow.

'We had a night out at that new Chinese in Winchester,'
confided Tiger.

'What both of you?' asked Christopher.

'Yes. Not intentionally. Just both turned up on the same night.'

Christopher laid down a six and a three. He smiled at Gary. 'That must have cramped your style.'

Tiger laid down a double three. 'Oh, no. He sent me packing very quickly.'

'Well, what did you expect?' asked Gary, rising to the challenge. 'I was hoping for a quiet night out.'

'Sarah,' said Tiger to Christopher, archly. 'Very tall. Very classy. Very young.'

'Do you mind!' Gary put down another domino. 'I wish you'd remember that I'm younger than you two.'

'Not much,' said Christopher and Gary in unison.

'Enough.' And then, 'Can we just finish this game, please?'

'Oh, serious stuff,' said Tiger, and then, obligingly, carried on playing without further reference to Gary's conquest.

It was a couple of games later when the subject returned to the evening at the restaurant. Tiger said, 'Anyway, I've got a project for our secret society.'

Gary spluttered into his beer.

Christopher said, 'I thought that had gone away.'

'No,' said Tiger. 'I was just waiting for the right thing to come along. And I think it has.'

'What sort of thing?' asked Christopher.

'Well, it might not amount to anything, but unless I'm barking up completely the wrong tree I think there's some kind of protection racket going on.'

'That sounds a bit heavy,' said Christopher.

Gary tried to sound offhand. 'What sort of protection racket?'

Tiger filled the two of them in on the events surrounding

the breaking of Isobel's window, and the man in black who had asked both she and Erica to contribute to the funds for 'mutual benefit' and who had been sitting in the Red Dragon that night.

'It does sound a bit of a coincidence,' agreed Christopher. 'But what are you suggesting we do?'

'Make enquiries,' said Tiger. 'Ask other shopkeepers if they've been approached.'

'This guy. The one in the black coat,' asked Gary. 'Have you ever seen him before?'

'No,' said Tiger. 'Never. But I didn't much like the look of him.'

'Not really much to go on, though, is it?' said Gary sarcastically.

'Are you up for this or not?'

Christopher frowned. 'It sounds to me more like something for the police, rather than the Domino Club Secret Society.'

'But they're not interested. Isobel tried to get them involved and they couldn't care less.'

'They've probably got someone on the case already,' said Gary. 'You can't just start sticking your oar in. They'll get narked.'

'There's no reason why they should hear about it.'

Christopher said, 'I didn't really imagine your secret society was going to be doing things quite so ... well ... potentially dangerous.'

'It's not *my* secret society, it's *our* secret society, and anyway there's nothing dangerous about making enquiries,' said Tiger irritably.

'If I were you,' said Gary, with more gravitas than he was usually known for, 'I'd stay well out of it.'

'So you don't want to help?'

'It's not that I don't *want* to help,' said Gary, 'it's just that I don't think I *can* help.'

'How do you know until you try? Honestly. You civil servants, you live such sedentary lives, and then when something comes along that might be a bit interesting you stick your heads in the sand and hope it will go away.'

'Look,' said Christopher, 'I don't really see how, as a local doctor, I can go around asking questions like that. I mean, what does Erica think? Is she happy for you to take the law into your own hands.'

'I haven't necessarily told her yet.'

Christopher looked thoughtful. 'I can imagine what Kate's reaction would have been.'

'Kate would probably have chased them out of the shop with a meat axe!' said Gary, grinning.

'I saw her the other day,' said Tiger. The words came out without his thinking.

'Saw Kate?' asked Christopher. 'Where?'

'At City Airport. Only briefly.' Tiger tried to play it down.

'What was she doing?' Christopher could not hide his curiosity.

'Flying to Southampton.'

'With Howie?'

'So you know about him then?'

'Yes.' His voice was steady. Level. 'American high flier. Everything I'm not.'

'I didn't mean . . .' offered Tiger.

'Oh, don't worry. I'm not feeling sorry for myself. I won't go into terminal decline.'

'I wasn't sure whether to mention it or not. Didn't know whether you knew . . .'

'Yes, I knew. But not from Kate. From someone else. Patients are always happy to keep you up to date on gossip, often in the most lurid detail. She's been with Howie for about six months now. They met salsa dancing. At an executive singles club.'

'Salsa dancing?' asked Gary incredulously.

'They tell me it's huge fun,' said Christopher. Then he looked suddenly sad. 'And full of sexual tension.'

'Well, if it's any consolation she didn't look as if she was having much fun the other day,' Tiger confided.

Christopher drained his glass and sat back in his chair. 'That's a shame. I'd like at least to think that she was happy.'

'Why?' asked Gary. 'She up and left you. Why would you want her to be happy?'

Christopher and Tiger exchanged glances, then Tiger looked down.

'Because after twenty-odd years of marriage,' said Christopher, 'I can't wish her ill.'

'But that's daft. She dumped you.'

'Thank you for reminding me.'

'What you need to do is get yourself someone else pretty sharpish. Someone young. That'll show her.'

Christopher shook his head. 'I don't want revenge, or retribution. I don't even want the satisfaction of knowing that it didn't work out for Kate after she had, as you so eloquently put it, "dumped me". I just want to salvage something out of this mess. Something that will make it worth carrying on. Peace of mind is the nearest I can come to explaining what I want.'

'With another woman?' asked Gary, like a terrier with a bone.

Christopher looked reflective. Then said slowly, 'Maybe. One day. I don't really want to carry on living alone.' Then he turned to Gary. 'Do you?'

Gary shrugged. 'Who knows.'

'That's not an answer.' Now it was Christopher's turn to pursue his quarry.

'I'm not short of a woman, if that's what you mean.'

'Oh we know that. But so far you've not shown much in the way of loyalty, have you?'

'That's a bit unfair.'

'You do seem to enjoy variety,' offered Tiger.

'Yes. Well, maybe I'll change one day. Maybe I just haven't found the right person yet.'

'What about Sarah?' asked Tiger.

Gary felt himself colouring up. He never remembered colouring up before.

'Oh. I think we might have touched a nerve there,' said Christopher mischievously.

'Dream on,' said Gary.

'Us or you?' said Tiger.

'Both. For all you know I might be turning over a new leaf.'

'Can a leopard change its spots?' asked Tiger.

'That's rich, coming from a man with your name,' said Gary, relieved to break the mood. 'Another pint then?'

But none of them seemed to have the appetite for it, and it didn't seem right to Tiger to pursue the matter of the protection racket. Not now. Having been fired with missionary zeal, he went home to Erica more than a little crestfallen. He didn't tell her what he had suggested. He didn't want to be shot down in flames yet again.

*

There could be no denying that Christopher Devon felt a bit of a heel. He hadn't really wanted to let Tiger down, but felt there was simply no way he could involve himself in such a harebrained scheme.

Gary, on the other hand, was now convinced that the Red Dragon figured somewhere in Mr Tan's scheme. He was still not sure how, but he had to find out more about this potential protection racket before Tiger started thrashing around and clouding the water. He hoped he had been sufficiently discouraging over the dominoes without drawing too much attention to himself. What he needed to do was to get Tiger out of the way for a few days. Then he and Sarah could get stuck in. The solution was relatively straightforward.

Tiger sat down at the desk in his office at home and looked out over the cathedral close. Thick grey clouds were looming behind the cathedral, far darker than the pale grey stones of its towers and flying buttresses. For a thousand years the building had nestled there, sheltering the bones of Hampshire's great and good, from St Swithun to Jane Austen. It seemed perverse that he should be looking over something so majestic and musing on something so sordid. The sort of thing you wanted to believe did not happen in peaceful surroundings like these. Petty crime. The manipulation of ordinary people. Maybe it was none of his business, but how could he ignore it as Gary seemed prepared to do? He could understand the reluctance of the local doctor, but he had hoped Gary might have come on board. Gary, who always portrayed himself as Jack the Lad but who now seemed happy to stick his head in the sand. Maybe it was something to do with Sarah. Maybe he really was keen and didn't want to waste his time on anything else.

Tiger gazed beyond the close-cropped grass and the old irregular walls over to the Georgian facades that stared back toward him. Beyond them were the streets of shops where he would have to ask his questions.

Surely it would be fairly simple? He would make a list of all the shops in the half dozen main streets, then ask the manager of each one whether they had been approached by the man in black. Those who admitted they had been visited would most likely be the ones who had refused his offer.

Those who said that they had not seen the man would either have paid the money or had not yet been visited.

Any that had been vandalized would obviously be on the list of those who had declined 'protection'. And if any shops who denied they had been approached said they had been vandalized? Well, that was tricky. They would probably have been the victims of the drunken yobs.

But then he would have to check the timings of the visits from the man with the timings of the vandalism. And what about those who had been approached by the man, agreed to pay, but would tell Tiger they had declined? How would he know who was telling the truth?

He leaned back in his chair. The more he thought about it, the less certain he was of what it would achieve. But he did not have to think for very long. The phone rang. It was the helicopter company. A job had come up. An urgent job. Could he be at Southampton Airport in a couple of hours? With an overnight bag. Well, rather larger than that, actually. He would be away for the best part of a week.

*

'A protection racket?' Sarah was looking out of the window across the Thames towards Lambeth Palace. She turned to face Gary and leaned back on the sill.

'Sounds like it.'

'But could he raise the sort of money we're talking about with a protection racket?'

'Depends on how many clients he has.'

'Well, it explains why the money's in cash.'

Gary drummed his fingers on the desk, it often helped the thought process. 'It just seems a bit clumsy to me, that's all. I mean, I'd expected something a bit more . . .'

'Clever?' suggested Sarah.

Gary nodded.

'You've been reading too many thrillers. Crime is often clumsy. You know that. The obvious motive is usually the genuine one.'

'Yes. But I can't help feeling a bit disappointed.' He got up and walked across to the window to join her, looking out over the skyline. Rain was beginning to fall. The city was disappearing from view. 'Still, I expect you're right. Anyway, we need to get cracking before other parties start interfering.'

'Other parties?' Sarah look quizzical.

'Yes. You're not going to believe this, but Tiger – my mate who came over the other night in the Red Dragon – was the one who woke me up to it. Told me he thought there was something up.'

'How did he know?'

'Oh, his wife runs a bookshop. She had an approach. So did the old biddy who runs the chocolate shop next door. She had a brick through her window the day after she declined to join "the club".'

'And that's why you think there's something in it?'

'Well, it's a lead if nothing else. Worth following up. Not least because the guy who had been asking them both for money was in the Red Dragon the night we were there. Not that we knew who we were looking for. And we've nothing else to go on.'

'No.' Sarah sat down at her desk. 'And we don't know what he looks like, do we?'

'No.'

'But your friend Tiger does.'

'Yes.'

'Couldn't we take him through a few photo fits, or at the very least get a detailed description of the guy so that we've some idea what we're looking for?'

'We could. If he had any idea what I did for a living.'

'Ah. I see. Ask him anything and you blow your cover?'

'Pretty much.'

'So what does he think you do?' asked Sarah.

'He thinks I'm a civil servant.'

'Which, of course, you are.'

'Yes. Just not the sort of civil servant he thinks I am.' Sarah looked thoughtful.

'What is it?' he asked.

'I was just wondering if there was any way we could get the information we need out of Tiger without him knowing what you really do. Get one of our other guys to go and ask him some questions.'

'A bit tricky at the moment', said Gary. 'Right now he's ferrying men from the Ordnance Survey around the Isles of Scilly.'

*

76

Erica didn't really know what made her go and see Christopher Devon. Perhaps it was a combination of factors – Tiger meeting Kate at the airport, the two of them seeing Dr Cummings in the Chinese restaurant. She just felt that she hadn't talked to Christopher for a long time and that it was time to catch up.

When he and Kate had been together the four of them had socialized much more – dined out, even shared the odd weekend away in Bath or Oxford. But since Kate's departure it had been more difficult. Tiger met Christopher regularly on Friday nights, but Erica had hardly encountered him at all, except on the rare occasions when he had dropped Tiger off after their domino sessions.

She had a soft spot for Christopher. He was a gentleman in both senses of the word. Weak, she felt, in some ways, but kind hearted. He deserved better.

She was not at all sure that he would be in when she called on the off chance. She parked in the bumpy lane outside his house and peered over the low flint wall. It was just as she remembered it. And now, as the spring buds were beginning to burst, she saw the tidy garden in the remains of its winter finery. The neatly clipped yew topiary, the low hedges of box, the freshly forked borders running up either side of the flagged stone path that led to the front door of the Queen Anne house. Evenly mown lawns lay to right and left and beyond them, on the far side of the house, the ground sloped gradually away. Here, paths were mown among apple trees that grew in the daffodil-dappled grass that led down to the stream. Such a picture. Such a sadness that it was no longer a happy house.

Erica pushed open the gate and walked up the path to the front door. Before she could ring the bell the door was opened, not by Christopher, but by a petite woman in her forties.

'Maria! What are you doing here?'

'Oh, a bit of this and that. Cleaning mostly. Making sure he's taken care of.'

'I didn't know . . .'

'Mum does it usually. Only she's away and asked me if I'd hold the fort. So here I am. Fort holding.'

Erica heard footsteps coming down the stairs, further back in the hall.

'Who is it?' enquired Christopher's voice. And then he saw her. 'Erica! What a nice surprise.' He came forward and kissed her on both cheeks, then realized that he had interrupted a conversation. 'Do you two know one another?'

Maria laughed. 'Just a little. Our children were at play group together.'

Over coffee the story unfolded. Maria, not wanting to intrude on Erica and Christopher's catching up had gone upstairs to continue her cleaning. They sat at either side of the kitchen table, Christopher toying with a Duchy biscuit and Erica explaining her acquaintanceship with his temporary domestic help.

'My two are a bit older than Maria's but they were good friends for a while when they were little. Then as soon as they went to different schools they drifted apart. I bump into Maria occasionally at the supermarket so we manage to keep up on what they're all doing.

'So she's married?' asked Christopher, doing his best to sound polite rather than curious.

'Divorced.'

'Oh?'

Erica read the question mark. 'Bit of a naughty boy really, Charlie Spicer. A Tarmac sailor.'

'A what?'

'A long-distance lorry driver.'

'Oh, I see. A girl in every port?'

'Well, not *every* port. But certainly a few of them.' She lowered her voice and turned to make sure the door was securely closed. 'I don't know. You know what gossip is. He was just a free spirit I suppose.'

'I bet Luisa had a thing or two to say about that.'

'She did. Then she never mentioned his name again. I never felt Charlie was quite bright enough for Maria, but I may have been unfair. Anyway they were apart enough for it not to work. That must have been four or five years ago now.'

'And is . . .' Christopher got no further with his question.

'No. There's nobody else from what I can gather. Or did I guess the wrong question?'

Christopher looked slightly embarrassed and Erica felt that she had overstepped the mark. 'Sorry.'

'Nothing to be sorry about,' said Christopher, hoping to move the conversation on.

Erica changed tack. 'I just came to see how you were. I haven't seen you for ages and wondered how you were getting on.'

'Oh, I'm managing.' Christopher smiled rather wanly. 'I shall be glad when summer comes, and the better weather. Then I can get outside a bit more. Do a bit more gardening.' He looked out of the window. 'At the moment there's either a bitter east wind or it's chucking it down. This sunny spell's a rarity. I should really be out there now.'

Erica made to get up.

'No. That wasn't an invitation for you to leave. Stay for

a bit of lunch. Maria is a much better cook than her mum. I don't know why it is that we expect all Italian women to be wonderful cooks. It's every bit as ridiculous as expecting every English woman to be able to make a perfect steak and kidney pie. Luisa makes the most dreadful pasta you have ever tasted. It would stick wallpaper to absolutely anything and it tastes just like glue.'

Erica laughed. 'So Maria's offerings are more palatable?'

'She keeps it simple – Parma ham and melon, salami and Italian bread. And that's all I want for lunch – not some sticky goo!'

'You could prepare it yourself, you know.'

'I could. And I was perfectly happy to. It was Luisa who insisted that I be cooked for – helpless single chap and all that.'

'Have you told Maria?'

'Well, no. I tried to. But then she took all this stuff out of her basket and I hadn't the heart to. And anyway . . .'

Erica looked at him with her head on one side.

Christopher met her eye, drew a large breath and said, 'I enjoy her company. That's all.'

Tiger wasn't enjoying anyone's company. He was sitting in his helicopter parked on the island of Tresco. If the weather had been good it would have been great flying. But it wasn't. It was grey, and the cloud base was low. The guys were out surveying whatever they needed to survey, and he was waiting for them to return.

Why this job had suddenly come up he couldn't for the life of him imagine. He thought about Erica working in the bookshop and wondered, just for a moment, if she was thinking about him.

Chapter 9

Anyone watching keenly the stealthy convergence of human lots, sees a slow preparation of effects from one life on another, which tells like a calculated irony on the indifference or the frozen stare with which we look at our unintroduced neighbour.

Middlemarch, George Eliot, 1819–80

'How much do you socialize with him?' Sarah asked.

'About once a week, why?' asked Gary.

Well, if you took me along then I might be able to ask things in all innocence.'

'No. Not possible.'

'Why not? Stag do, is it?'

'Yes.'

Gary was sitting at his desk, tapping away at a laptop. Sarah was doing the same. The exchange took place without either of them looking up, until Sarah said, 'Couldn't you make an exception for me?'

Gary lifted his head. 'Are you teasing me?'

'Why should I do that? I'm just trying to progress this case,' said Sarah. 'Thought I might be able to help.'

She was pushing him. Seeing how long it would be before he gave in. He knew that she wanted to get on with the enquiry but sensed also that she wanted him to feel there might be more. He had been here before. With women who promised much but delivered little. Led you on then dropped you like a hot brick when it suited them. He made to concentrate on the screen, but she refused to let it rest.

'What do you do then, on these nights out?'

'Sport.'

'That's a bit vague. What sort of sport? No. Don't tell me, let me guess. Squash. That's what middle-aged men usually play. Short, sharp and plenty of sweat. Very macho.'

'No.' He didn't rise to the bait. Didn't look up.

Sarah leaned back in her chair and put her hands behind her head, mocking him now as she went through the simple litany: 'Badminton then. All those feathers. Or bowls. Indoor bowls, yes, that's it – nice and gentle. And warm.'

No response.

'Oh, mind you, it could be poker. Lots of interest in poker nowadays. Texas holdall, or whatever it is. Are you part of a poker school?'

Gary stopped and looked her in the eye. 'Dominoes.'

'What?'

'You heard. We play dominoes over a pint. Nothing glamorous, no high stakes, just a bit of fun.'

'But dominoes is . . .'

'If you say it's an old man's game Sarah Perry I shall chase you round this office with a rolled-up newspaper and beat you on the bottom until you can't sit down.'

'Harassment! I could have you for harassment!' she cried.

'Yes, I bet you could.'

She leaned forward on her elbows and stared at him. 'It wouldn't do any harm. Might ginger them up a bit. And if you got Tiger talking about things then I could suggest that we couldn't progress it until we identified the man in black.'

'We?'

'Well, you'd have to let me join in, wouldn't you? Join the domino school.'

'It's not a school it's just a bit of fun, and what do you think the others would say if I took a woman along?'

'Probably be jealous. Anyway, who are "the others"?'

'There's only one. Christopher Devon. Local doctor. Well, he was local, he does locum work now – down Romsey way.'

'Dishy doctor?'

Gary looked up. 'You've perked up, for someone who's just been dumped.'

The cheerful expression on Sarah's face dissolved. 'Thank you for reminding me.'

'Sorry. I mean . . . well . . .' He tried to brighten her up. 'Depends what you call dishy. Tall. Fair-ish. Thinning a bit on top. But he seems to send most women weak at the knees. Thing is, he just can't see it. No confidence.'

'Unlike some I could mention,' retorted Sarah, busying herself with the contents of a file, the spark having died from her eyes. 'So is he married, this doctor?'

'Divorced.'

'Any attachments?'

'Not that I know of. Anyway, why are you so interested?'

'Just curious. If you take me with you I'd like to be a bit prepared, that's all. Only doing my research.'

Why he felt a need to go along with her he could not say,

83

though to any outsider it would have been obvious that he would do anything, well, almost anything, to please her. After half an hour he heard himself say that he would think about it, which was about the nearest he could come to resisting her charms. For now.

The weather was slightly better, otherwise Tiger would have had to wait longer than anticipated at the helicopter terminal on St Mary's. He had dropped the Ordnance Survey team on St Agnes and been instructed by his base to fly to St Mary's and pick up a co-pilot. The firm had been a pilot short for a month now, without any sign of a replacement for old Eric who had finally retired to his cottage in Dorset. The new pilot would be billeted with him for the rest of the week, sitting in the left-hand seat, before doing any independent flying, just so that safety procedures could be confirmed and so that Tiger could make sure the new recruit was up to scratch. There were only two men in the Ordnance Survey team so the new pilot could conveniently be accommodated.

He had a name and a description. Sam Ross. Red hair. About thirty-five. Medium height. He scrutinized the passengers as they came off the Penzance helicopter. He wondered if his expected contact had missed the flight until a voice asked, 'Are you Tiger?'

He turned around to see a redheaded thirty-five-year-old of medium height. 'I'm Sam Ross,' she said.

Tiger covered his embarrassment at making the obvious false assumption and shook her hand. 'Hi! Tiger Wilson. Can I take your bag?'

She shook her head. 'No thanks. I can manage. Where do we go?'

Tiger indicated the small cafe. 'Coffee first?'

'Yeah. Thanks.'

Had Tiger been expecting a woman, this is not the sort of woman he would have been looking for. Sam Ross was bright-eyed with short red hair. Her eyes were light blue and her skin pale except for the lightly flushed cheeks. She seemed almost too slight to be a helicopter pilot. Her fingers were long and delicate – those of an artist – but her slender figure presumably belied her strength.

They sat down at a table. Tiger was surprised at how relaxed she seemed to be. He was expecting a kind of worried intensity – the sort that usually accompanies someone embarking on a new job, in a new place and with new people. Instead, Sam Ross seemed totally at ease.

'So you know the Jet Ranger?' he asked.

'Pretty well. Flown them for two years now, along with Squirrels.'

'And how long have you been flying altogether?'

'Oh, since I was eighteen. Got my private pilot's licence in my twenties. Couldn't keep me out of the sky after that. But I never thought I'd be able to do it for a living.'

'We do have female airline pilots.'

'Yes, but it's bloody hard. And there are lots of men who wish we weren't there.'

'Oh dear.'

'Sorry. Did that sound a bit heavy?'

Tiger shook his head.

'Didn't mean it to be. But you do get looked up and down a bit. I think a lot of guys think you must be . . . you know . . . the other way.'

'And you're not?' teased Tiger.

Sam frowned in mock admonishment. 'Please!' Then she

grinned. 'No. Far too interested in . . . well . . . let's not go there. Just . . . ordinary . . . that's all.'

Given a dictionary and asked to choose a word that would describe Sam Ross, 'ordinary' was not the one that Tiger would have picked.

Whatever else Erica had expected to find when she rounded the corner into the alley it was not Isobel and a pile of glass. She had been there. Done that. But this morning the scene was repeated. Isobel was standing in the middle of the alley with her broom. The only difference was that this morning it was not Isobel's shop window that had been smashed. It was Erica's.

Christopher Devon took the phone call in his temporary surgery in Romsey. It was from one of the partners in his old practice in Winchester.

'I only called to see how you were doing,' said Reggie Silverwood. 'Find out if you were surviving.'

'Oh, I'm surviving, Reggie. What about you?'

Christopher had got on well with Dr Silverwood since he had first arrived at the practice. By then, Randall Cummings had taken the role of senior partner, but Reggie was part of the old guard and determined to remain on a part-time basis for as long as he could. He was a GP of the old school, greatly respected by his patients and with a bedside manner that inspired confidence even in the most nervous and insecure. He might not be the most go-ahead and dynamic of physicians, but his value as a father figure who would be admired and revered by the more senior members of his panel was not lost on Dr Cummings. He was the practice's grand old man, and as long as he just about pulled his weight, Randall Cummings was prepared to let him stay.

Christopher was fond of Reggie. He used to see him regularly at the surgery, and very occasionally for a drink after 'office hours'. He was a small, bird-like man, with wire-framed glasses and a slight stoop, often seemingly preoccupied by some conundrum of life upon which his brain was deeply engaged.

He sounded, today, a little more weary than usual. 'Oh, just about surviving, too, but I don't know for how much longer.'

'That sounds a bit defeatist Reggie. Not like you.'

'Mmm. Well, maybe the time's come for me to pack it in.'

Christopher made his surprise clearly audible. 'Pack it in?'

'I think so.'

'Oh, it'll just be a temporary blip, Reggie. You'll have had a few cases that have got you down. You know how it is. Never two without three and all that.'

'Mmm. I'd like to think so. But it's a bit more than that.'

Christopher paused before replying. 'Is it Cummings?'

There was a silence at the other end of the phone. 'Reggie?'

Dr Silverwood cleared his throat. 'Not at all sure I understand, Christopher. Things going on. Things I can't really believe. Perhaps I'm mistaken. Confused.'

Christopher spoke seriously. 'Reggie, do you want to talk?'

'Not sure I should.'

'I think you can to me. Why don't you come round for a drink? What about tonight?'

'Oh, I'm not sure . . .' murmured Reggie.

'It would be nice to see you.' Christopher played a card that he thought might work on a man who had devoted his life to the well-being of others. 'And anyway, the evenings are rather long for me now, being on my own. It would be good to see you. Cheer me up a bit.'

Reggie took the bait. 'Well, I suppose I could drop in for a quick one. See how you are. What time would suit?'

Christopher looked at his watch. 'Say half past seven? I finish here at six and that will give me time to get home and light a fire. Stay for supper if you want.' He knew the invitation would be declined, but he wanted to make the offer all the same.

'Oh, no. I won't put you to all that trouble. A glass of Scotch will do nicely. Then I'll be off home to Betty.'

'OK Reggie. I'll see you at half past seven.'

Chapter 10

Actions receive their tincture from the times,
And as they change are virtues made or crimes.
'A Hymn to the Pillory', Daniel Defoe, 1660–1731

In the same way that toast always lands butter-side down, and the wine bottle is always empty when you fancy just one more glass, so family disasters invariably happen when one of you is away from home.

'Did you call the police?' Tiger asked.

Erica assured him that the police had been and gone, convinced, once more, that it was drunken yobs who had put a brick through her shop window.

'And you know it was a brick?'

'It was there among the books. Thank God the window has a secure barrier at the back of it otherwise the place would have been open and anyone could have got in.'

'But didn't the alarm go off?' he asked.

Erica spoke softly. 'Brian forgot to set it. I was playing tennis and I left him to lock up.'

'Oh, God! Didn't you drill it into him? Especially after Isobel's window being smashed.'

'Tiger, he is a grown man. And he's not our child. I can't treat him like an imbecile.'

'That's clearly what he is.' Tiger was angry. Not only at Brian's apparent stupidity, but also because of the fact that he was distanced from the action. Unable to help. Unable to take charge.

'There's no need to have a go at me,' Erica said, wounded by his tone.

'I just can't see how he could have been so daft, that's all.'

'Yes, well I think he knows that now and it won't do any good to keep going on about it. The glazier's coming to fit new glass this afternoon and so we should be safe by tonight.'

'Have you made sure it's reinforced glass?'

'Tiger, I'm not completely incapable. I can get a new window fitted.'

'And what about the man in black? Any sign of him?'

'No. None. And if he does come back you can be sure he won't be going anywhere until I've asked him a few questions.'

'No,' said Tiger. 'Don't make him suspicious. We don't want to frighten him off.'

'Tiger, that's exactly what I *do* want to do. If it *is* him who's responsible I don't want him thinking he can intimidate me by lobbing a brick through my window.'

'Erica, you don't know what he'll do next. I don't want you getting involved.'

'I think it's bit late for that. I *am* involved. More than you at the moment. And it'll take us all afternoon to clear the broken glass out of the window.'

90

He felt deflated. Detached from it all. Unable to connect with Erica who was clearly rattled by his attitude.

'Look, I'm sorry I'm not there. I'll be back by the end of the week. But just don't do anything . . . you know . . . hasty.'

'So when *are* you back?'

'Friday afternoon. These guys finish here on Friday lunchtime and I'll fly them back then.'

'Right. It'll be good to see you.'

'The only thing is . . .'

'Yes?'

'Would you mind if I went to play dominoes? Only I want to talk through all this with the guys and see if they have any ideas.'

'No. Fine. If that's what you want to do.'

He could hear the disappointment in her voice. 'I won't be late back. And, anyway, I'll see you for an hour or so before I go.'

'It's up to you.'

He should have been more thoughtful but his mind was focussed and his vision was blinkered. And, anyway, she didn't sound very welcoming right now.

Sam Ross was a natural. She handled the Jet Ranger with practised precision and Tiger commented, at the end of their second flight, 'I don't know why I'm here. You don't need me at all.'

'I should hope not,' she replied with an amused grin. 'Far too independent.'

'Well, next week you'll be on your own. The second helicopter's being serviced now and she'll be ready on Monday.'

Tiger sat back in the left-hand seat as Sam circled the tiny island of Samson. The weather had cleared, and what little cloud there was had gathered in a thin skein on the distant horizon. The early spring sun had turned the sky a soft shade of forget-me-not blue, and the water beneath them was pure turquoise. The sands of Samson were the colour of white ground pepper, and the whole scene could easily have featured in a Caribbean holiday brochure.

'Wonderful isn't it?' asked Sam.

'Blissful.'

'I've always wanted to live here,' she said.

'Idling?' he asked.

'Oh, I'd find enough to keep me occupied. Taking pleasure flights probably.'

Tiger chuckled. 'I think you'd get bored of that.'

'S'pose so. But it's nice to dream.'

The Ordnance Survey men said little, and were put down on St Martin's, the long, bone-shaped island at the north-eastern corner of the group. They asked to be picked up in two hours, so Sam lifted up the aircraft and headed south-wards toward St Mary's.

'Do you dream a lot?' asked Tiger, idly.

'A bit.'

'Not happy with what you're doing then?'

'Perfectly happy.'

'So?'

'Oh, you know. It'd be nice to have somebody to share it with, that's all.'

'I see.'

'Do you?' she asked, he thought rather pointedly.

'Yes,' he replied.

'You share yours then?' She banked the helicopter to the

left of Hugh Town and tilted over towards Agnes, lining up with the white lighthouse.

'Thirty years now.'

'God, that's impressive. One ex of mine said that you only get twenty-one years for killing someone. Not much of an advert for a lasting relationship.'

'That's a bit of an old chestnut.'

'So was he.' She grinned. 'I'm in no rush. I can wait.'

Tiger looked out of the window at the white stump of the lighthouse, it's lantern glinting in the sun as they wheeled around a couple of hundred feet above it. Sam was right, it was blissful out here. A different world. He watched as the foaming water broke over the rocks and sprayed into the air. Out here among the gulls and the seals you could be a million miles from anywhere.

Gary Flynn was deep in thought, poring over papers at his desk and sipping the black coffee at his right hand. With a pen he traced down the sheet of paper line by line, noting times and locations. Before him lay the weekly life of Mr Tan, as collated by the likes of Ben Atkinson whose job it was to tail a suspect and make notes of their every movement. Thanks to the assiduousness of some foot-slogger, Gary even knew what Mr Tan had for lunch at the Savoy Grill and who he ate it with.

There were visits to a Savile Row tailor, to Lobb for handmade shoes, and to Davidoff for cigars.

'Doesn't stint himself, does he?' murmured Gary, noticing that Mr Tan had spent £4,400 on two pairs of handmade loafers.

'So he's not just doing it for his country then?' asked Sarah.

'I should think that's the last thing he's doing it for. I think Mr Tan's main concern is Mr Tan – and family.'

'Large one is it?'

'Three sons and a daughter. The way he's bringing them up I should think they'll have high expectations in later life.'

'Not if he's spending it all on shoes,' remarked Sarah. 'Mind you, I could have got a dozen pairs of Jimmy Choo's for what he's spent on a couple of pairs of loafers.'

Gary looked up. 'You've seen this?'

'Of course.' Sarah looked impassive.

'Notice any patterns? Anything odd.'

'Only one thing.'

She was giving little away. Gary pressed her further. 'And?'

'I'm wondering about Mr Tan's health. Do we know if he's fit and well?'

'I think he is. He's in his forties, smokes like a chimney, but they all seem to out there. I think he's as healthy as your average Chinese male city dweller who has a capacity to overindulge. Why do you ask?'

Sarah came over to Gary's desk and leaned over his shoulder. He could feel her warmth. Smell her scent. Her closeness affected his heart rate. He concentrated hard on the papers.

She pointed to several entries over a period of a few days. 'Look at these. Harley Street. But two different addresses.'

'Odd. Do we know who he was seeing?'

'No. There are several consultancies in each building but Harley Street being Harley Street – and a model of discretion – we couldn't tell who he saw when he was inside the building. Each one houses anything up to half a dozen specialists.'

'Could have been getting a second opinion.'

'Yes,' agreed Sarah. 'I'd thought of that.'

'Otherwise what?'

Sarah shrugged. 'No idea. Unless he's flogging them cheap drugs.'

'It's quite possible,' said Gary. 'But what's his source? We've no record of him visiting anywhere else that could supply them, have we?'

'No. But they could easily be knocked off.'

'Do we have records? Of stolen drugs? Serial numbers and suchlike.'

'We do. I've got the guys checking it out.'

Gary closed the file and got up from his desk. 'There's something there. Something I'm not seeing.'

'If it's any consolation I can't see it either,' admitted Sarah. 'I've thought of everything – drugs, money laundering, protection rackets. I just can't make the connection as yet.'

'We need more time to work this out.'

'Well that much is obvious,' she said.

Gary paused, walked to the window, surveyed the view across the river and then turned to her. 'And how are you doing?'

'Me?'

'Yes. You know. After your . . . local difficulties.'

She was caught unawares by his concern. 'I'm fine. Thank you. Fine.'

He said nothing for a moment.

Sarah frowned. 'Why do you ask?'

'Oh, you know. Just like to make sure that my staff are all right. Don't like to think that they might be suffering in silence.'

'Suffering?' Sarah gave a slight laugh. 'I suppose that might be pushing it. I have my moments. You know . . . on those evenings where there's nothing on the box and I've run out of stuff to read. But I'm getting on with my life.'

'How?'

'Just by . . . getting on . . . blocking it out.'

'Funny,' said Gary. 'I always thought of you as having a mad social life. Out every night.'

Sarah smiled ruefully. 'Me? No. Home bird really. Not a clubber. Can't think of anything worse.' Then she said briskly, 'Anyway . . . what about Mr Tan?'

'I'd rather talk about you, to be honest.'

'Steady on, Mr Flynn, or I might begin to think you really care.' She walked across to her desk and dropped down into the chair.

Gary kept staring out of the window. Would that be such a terrible thing? he thought.

The fire was crackling in the grate at the Manor House. Christopher had broken open a new bottle of Laphroaig and had poured a tot for himself while waiting for Reggie Silverwood to arrive.

Half past seven came and went. Eight o'clock. At eight-fifteen Christopher phoned Reggie's home. Betty answered. 'No. I thought he was coming for a drink with you.'

At eight-thirty he phoned the hospital, and at eight-thirty-two he learned that Reggie Silverwood had been involved in a motor accident. He was lying unconscious in the Hampshire Royal Infirmary.

Christopher looked at the old doctor lying in the bed. Without his glasses and his usual look of thoughtful preoccupation his features seemed more relaxed. But his skin was pale, almost translucent. It was a look Christopher had seen before. He feared the worst.

There were no other cars involved, confirmed the house-man. From the condition of the driver when they had found him it looked as though Dr Silverwood had had a heart attack at the wheel, then plunged down a ditch off the main road just before the turning to Christopher's house. His condition was stable, but the next twenty-four hours would be critical.

Christopher nodded. He had said the same words himself enough times to know their underlying truth.

Reggie's accident was a blow. He had been a kind and generous colleague and a good if reserved friend. But gnaw-ing away inside was the regret that they had not had a chance to talk, for Reggie to share whatever it was that was troubling him. Christopher suspected that he knew the likely cause. But for the moment all he could do was wait.

Chapter 11

An office party is not, as is sometimes supposed, the
Managing Director's chance to kiss the tea-girl. It is
the tea-girl's chance to kiss the Managing Director.
Roundabout, Katharine Whitehorn, 1928–

When the man in black reappeared in the shop, both Erica
and Brian were taken by surprise. Erica had really not
expected to see him again. The fact that he would dare to
come back had never seemed likely, but here he was, large
as life, with the same anorak and the same holdall under his
arm.

There were several customers in the shop this time, brows-
ing the shelves. Erica caught Brian's eye and motioned him
to join her in the stockroom. The man in black, true to form,
was scrutinizing a shelf on Polar exploration, waiting for the
shop to empty.

'It *is* him, isn't it?' asked Erica.

Brian, breaking the habit of a lifetime, decided to forgo
his usual shrug and nodded.

'Right. You hold the fort. I'll call the police on my mobile from the yard and I'll be back in the shop as soon as I can. Keep him talking.'

Erica ignored the look of horror on the youth's face at the prospect of having to make conversation with anybody, let alone a criminal, and sent Brian back into the shop to face the enemy.

A few minutes later she slipped into the shop and locked the back door.

It seemed an age before the three customers departed, one without buying anything, and the other two with small travel guides.

The man approached the counter.

'I was wondering if you had had any further thoughts on my suggestion?' he asked. 'I think I could offer you a special rate.'

Erica had no time to reply. The bell on the door of the shop pinged and she glanced across to see two sturdy police-man blocking out the light.

'So what happened?' There was an edge in Tiger's voice.

Erica could tell he was not happy, and knew that the information she was about to give would not improve things. 'They had to let him go.'

'What?!'

Erica held the telephone away from her ear for a moment, then continued, 'They said they were sorry but that they had no reason to hold him. There was no way they could connect him with the broken windows, and he had nothing else on him that gave them any cause to sus-pect that he had anything to do with it.'

'But what about the demand for money?'

'They said he denied that he had asked for anything. Then they asked me if he had actually threatened me and I had to admit that he hadn't. I think as far as they were concerned he might just as well have been selling *The Big Issue*. They were very sympathetic but said there was nothing else they could do until they had some sort of evidence.'

'Did they take his fingerprints?'

'I don't know. They might have done. They took him down to the police station but then came back and said they'd had to let him go. I think they were hoping that they might have frightened him off. They seem to think he was pretty harmless.'

'But that's ludicrous,' Tiger fumed.

'But we don't know, do we?' asked Erica. 'We're only making assumptions.'

'Yes, but they're based on . . .'

'What? What are they based on? That we don't like the look of him? That it was a bit of a coincidence that two windows were broken within a few days of him asking us if we'd like to join his "Friendly Society".'

'It doesn't sound very friendly to me,' muttered Tiger. 'Oh, bugger. Why did it have to happen while I was away?'

Impatience showed through Erica's voice. 'I'm sorry. If I'd thought, I could have asked him to delay his return until you'd come back.'

'That's not what I meant.'

'Well, I don't like you being away any more than you do. But sometimes things happen and I have to tell you about them, even if you don't want to hear.'

He felt guilty now. Guilty at having a go at her. Guilty at not being there when she needed him. 'I'm sorry. I'll be back soon.'

'And when are you next away? Do you know?'

'No. 'Fraid not. This one came out of the blue and I don't know what I've got on next week.'

Erica became aware that she was sounding like a whinge-ing wife. She tried to make amends. 'Well, whatever. We'll just make sure we have some decent time together this weekend.'

'Yes, please.'

They hung up with one or two bridges mended, but an overall feeling of dissatisfaction. After thirty years, she still did not like him being away.

The kitchen table at the Manor House was laid out with the now customary antipasto – olives and salami, rocket leaves with Parmesan shavings and other Italian delicacies.

'I'm getting rather used to this,' said Christopher.

Maria looked troubled. 'Oh! I'm sorry. Would you rather have something else?'

He grinned. 'That's not what I meant at all. I meant it's very nice.'

She smiled with relief. 'I'm glad I got it right, then.'

'Are you sure you won't join me?' Christopher asked.

'I can't have lunch with you every day. I'm supposed to be cleaning. If mum got to hear about it I'd be in deep trouble.'

'Even if it was by invitation?'

'Even then. Mum would tell me to know my place. To "looka after da doctorr".'

Christopher laughed. 'That was scarily accurate.'

'Yes. It is a worry, isn't it? I might grow into her with age.'

'No. Highly unlikely.' He put on a mock-serious voice.

'As a doctor I can tell you that the measurements of your bones and your general demeanour indicate that it is more than probable that you will retain your slender figure into old age, regardless of your genetic background.'

'Is that so?'

'No. I just made it up, but it sounded very plausible, don't you think?'

She held him with a measured look. 'You know, I thought you'd be such a serious man.'

Christopher sat back in his chair and dabbed a trickle of olive oil from his chin. 'Why?'

'Well, you're a respected doctor.'

'I don't know about the respected. And I'm a bit worried about the serious.'

'So you're not serious then?' she asked.

'Oh I can be. I can be very serious. But I've had rather enough of that. Apart from . . .' His mind wandered for a few moments over the events of the previous evening, and he saw the image of Reggie Silverwood lying in the bed. 'But I really do think I should snap out of it. Get myself out more.'

'Where to?' she asked, breaking off from cleaning the cooker.

'I haven't been to the opera for ages. A bit of Puccini, or Verdi, that's what I need.' He stood up and went to fill the kettle. For a few moments he was unsure of what to say, then he asked brightly, and in what he hoped was a suitably casual tone, 'Do you want to come?'

'What?'

'To the opera. You said you liked Italian rather than German, so come and hear one with me.'

'Oh, I couldn't possibly.'

'Why not?'

'For a start, my mother . . .'

'Your mother's not in charge of my social life.'

'I know she's not but . . .'

'Well, then, there's no reason why you shouldn't come with me.' Then it occurred to him that she might not actually want to go with him. That she might have someone else to share her evenings.

'But, of course, you probably have other things . . . someone else to . . .'

Maria butted in. 'No. It's not that. I just . . . well . . . if you're sure . . . ?'

'Quite sure. I'll get hold of the programme for Covent Garden. See what's on. You can bet your life it'll all be Wagner and Strauss, but we'll have a look and see what we fancy. If that's OK?'

'Fine. Lovely.'

Their conversation came to a gentle end. Christopher made them both a coffee and left Maria to drink hers as she worked in the kitchen, while he took his upstairs to his study. He sat down at his desk and looked out over the garden and the long, narrow grass path that he had cut in a line from his study window to the old yew tree at the far end. There was a white-painted seat beneath the ancient tree with its low-sweeping branches, and it occurred to him that it had been over a year since he had sat there with anybody. It also occurred to him that a few minutes ago, for the first time since he could remember, he had used the word 'we'.

On Thursday night the men from the Ordnance Survey decided that they would go out under their own steam.

Tiger and Sam had dined with them in the hotel every other evening, and the conversation had not exactly flowed, so he was not sorry when they said that on their last night they'd go off on their own.

'Do you want to eat in your room?' he asked Sam.

She looked marginally crestfallen at the thought and so he asked, 'Or shall we go and find somewhere together?'

At this she brightened. 'There's a seafood restaurant down by the harbour. Lobster and crab, that sort of thing,' she suggested.

No matter how long a man has been married, and however loyal he is to his wife, there are moments when he finds himself on his own in the company of an attractive woman, when he can forget for a while that he is spoken for. No harm comes of it, in most cases, and it is extremely good for morale. It shows him that he can still be good company, still court an admiring glance from someone who is not bound by loyalty or family ties.

Tiger looked at Sam sitting across the table from him and saw how the candlelight played in her eyes. Saw the coppery tints of her hair, the delicate curve of her chin and the warm smile, and for a while at least he remembered what it was like to be young and in love. Not that he was in love with her. But he did find her very attractive. She had the knack that some women do of listening as though you are the only person in the room. Of cutting out the rest of the world entirely. At least, that's how it felt to Tiger. For one evening at least, he could be single again. And desirable. Not disloyal, but just happy in his own imaginings. Somewhere else. With someone else. Dreaming a little. Indulging his fantasies.

'I do like it here,' she said.

'Yes. A good find.' He came back from his reverie and topped up her wine glass.

'So do you know what you'll be doing next week?' she asked.

'Not until Saturday morning. The usual flexible life.'

'Some people couldn't cope with that.'

'What about you?'

'Got used to it,' she said, and took a sip of wine. 'Makes for a nomadic life. Maybe that's why I'm still single.'

'Do you mind that?'

'Oh, sometimes. Other times it's OK. Depends where the job takes me. If it's coming to places like this, then I can hack it. But if I'm stuck in some seedy B&B or a motel that has nylon sheets and walls as thick as cardboard, I'd happily swap it.'

They were interrupted by the arrival of their food. Tiger had steak and fries, Sam a grilled lemon sole. The young waitress laid them down and did a little bob before leaving them to eat.

'*Bon appétit*,' said Tiger.

'And you. And thanks for being so welcoming. Some guys wouldn't take quite so kindly to a girl invading their patch.'

'Oh, I don't really see it like that,' said Tiger. 'There's enough to go round.'

They talked easily over the meal. Tiger telling about his father, then about his time in the Air Force – the countries where he had flown and stories of narrow escapes. Of helicopters falling off the sides of ships, of others that crashed into the sea. And then he became aware that he was doing all the talking.

'I'm sorry. All these *Boy's Own* stories. Boring the pants off you.'

Sam shook her head. 'No, you're not. It's good to hear someone who's keen on their job.'

'Yes, but I can talk about other things.'

'Like what?'

'I don't know. English topography.'

'That's a conversation stopper if ever I heard one.'

He noticed that her face lit up when she laughed.

'Well, I can tell you about lighthouses and burial mounds and barrows.'

'OK, then,' she teased, 'so what do you know about the Scilly Isles?'

'For a start I know that if you call them that the inhabitants will shoot you. They're called "Scilly" – a bit like the Scots hating to be called Scotch.'

'Anything else?'

Tiger took a deep breath. 'I know that the island of Samson was inhabited until eighteen fifty-five and that Harold Wilson, who was Labour Prime Minister from nineteen sixty-four to nineteen seventy and nineteen seventy-four to nineteen seventy-six, used to have a holiday home on St Mary's.'

'Is that it?'

'I also know that the gardens on Tresco hardly ever have a frost and that means they have the finest collection of Mediterranean plants in Britain. Will that do for starters?'

'What a mine of information you are.'

'I know. Deadly, isn't it?'

She shook her head. 'Oh, I don't think so. You can make people laugh and that's what's important.'

Tiger looked reflective. 'Yes. Only I don't seem to have done that a lot lately,' he murmured.

He ordered a glass of red wine to accompany what was left of his steak, conscious of the fact that the following morning they would be flying. Finally, at a quarter to midnight, Sam said, 'I think we'd better be going.'

They walked along the harbour wall and looked out across the calm water, where pleasure boats and fishing smacks bobbed on their moorings, and the halyards of yachts chimed gently against their masts in the evening breeze. The moon was almost full, and casting its light in silvery shards across the rippling water.

As they approached the door of the hotel at the far end of the harbour they stopped and gazed at the view.

'Perfect,' murmured Tiger. 'Just perfect.'

'Yes,' she agreed. 'Perfect.' Then she turned and kissed him on the lips.

Chapter 12

Thy wife shall be as the fruitful vine: upon the walls of
thine house.
Thy children like the olive branches: round about thy
table.

Psalm 128.3

As far as Christopher was concerned, Friday should have
been a day off much like any other day off. He had
explained to the Romsey practice that he would be unable
to cover for them that day. He did not feel a need to explain
why. It was his birthday. Nobody else needed to know, but
he wanted to be at home on his own. To potter about. Take
time to reflect. Maybe have a beer with his lunch.

Maria did not work on Fridays, so there would be no
Italian delicacies today. He had not told her of the day's significance. He got up at half past seven to a clear blue sky
and the sound of blackbirds and thrushes singing their
hearts out.

He sipped his morning coffee and looked out over the

frosted grass, sparkling in the early slant of amber sunlight that filtered through the branches of the yew tree. The dew on the cobwebs that stretched across the topiary box bushes glinted like diamonds. A good day to be up early. A good day to have a birthday.

But then his thoughts turned to Reggie Silverwood. He would call later for an update on his progress. And to Maria. He wondered what she would be doing. She had no children at home now, Erica had said, so how would she fill her day? And then he thought about Kate. He tried not to think of her too often. To do so was to be overtaken by a deep sadness born of guilt and errors of omission. He tried not to slip into the 'if only' frame of mind, and as he felt the black mood approaching, he jinked his mind sideways, as a hare jinks in a field when chased. He could usually rely on it to work. Today he wasn't sure.

He showered and changed into his gardening clothes – jeans and an ancient fleece – then wandered outside, down the flagstone path that led to the greenhouse. He turned the key in the lock, opened the door and inhaled. That aroma of leaf and flower, of compost and dampness always gave him a moment of pleasure. The first lungful of growth-laden air was every bit as uplifting as the first mouthful of champagne and, the doctor told himself, less damaging for the liver.

He picked up the long-spouted watering can and moved among the plants, feeling the compost in their pots and dispensing liquid refreshment where it was needed. He pulled off a browning leaf here, a faded flower there, murmuring to his charges as he did so.

For the next hour he sorted through them, making a mental note of which plants needed potting on come the warmer weather, and which were really past their sell-by date and would be better replaced by new stock.

The cymbidiums were all but over now – only the occasional waxy flower remained on their long and arching stems. In June they would be stood outside, to make room for brighter flowers – the geraniums and fuchsias that blazed their way through the summer. He knew that his tastes were simple. It didn't bother him. Rarity had never been an attraction.

The frost had melted from the grass now, leaving a dusky grey dew. He left the greenhouse and walked along the side of the house, past borders where daffodils were bursting their buds, and walls festooned with jasmine and japonica, and as he turned the corner he saw two people walking up the path to the front door.

In that split second before being able to identify them it occurred to him that the Jehovah's Witnesses were getting up earlier nowadays. The feeling that followed was one of relief and delight.

'Ellie? Matt? What on earth?'

They stood before him on the path, smiling broadly.

'But you're in America and you're . . . but you're here!'

Ellie walked up and wrapped her arms around him, laying her head on his chest. 'Happy birthday Dad.'

Matt hung back for a moment, then came forward and kissed his father softly on the cheek. 'Happy birthday Pa.'

Christopher stepped back for a moment and surveyed them both. He shook his head. 'I'm sorry. But why . . . ? I mean, it's not a special birthday or anything . . .'

'Yes it is,' confirmed Ellie. 'It's yours.'

'I tell you what, Dad,' said Matt, 'it's bloody cold out here. Can we go inside?'

With Christopher's arms around each of their shoulders they walked up the path to the front door.

They had come, they said, to cheer him up. Matt was on his way to a meeting in London and Ellie had a week off between changing locations with her charity in Africa. They had not planned ahead much, but when each had realized they would be free during the same week, they had decided on a surprise visit.

He looked at them sitting on either side of the kitchen table – Ellie as ever in clothes that would grace no fashionable shop, but looking as elegant as only she could in a pair of combat trousers and a sweat shirt emblazoned with the words 'Feed Africa', lest anyone should be in any doubt as to her intentions. Her fine fair hair was gathered up behind with a tortoiseshell clip. Her skin pale and clear and dusted with freckles courtesy of the African sun.

Matt wore a charcoal-grey sweater that had been revealed, along with the scarf around his neck, when he took off his thick overcoat. His features, if anything, were more refined nowadays. He had lost all remains of his childhood pudginess and turned into a youth every bit as handsome, in his father's eyes, as Michelangelo's *David*. You could have cracked an egg on his cheekbones. His hair was dark and curly. Nobody was quite certain where that had come from.

Ellie talked avidly about her work – laying on water, teaching people how to grow things, helping them to help themselves. Matt was more reticent. 'Oh, it's fine, you know. Busy. New magazines being launched. Company shake-ups.'

'And have you heard from your mum?' asked Christopher.

They both nodded, but seemed a little reticent. 'Now and again,' said Ellie.

'Mmm,' said Matt.

'Think she's pretty busy,' offered Ellie. 'Travelling a lot.'

Matt asked 'You've not . . . ?'

'No,' cut in Christopher. 'No, I've not seen her for quite a while now.'

'I see.'

He made to brighten the mood. 'So, how long are you staying? Shall we go out to dinner? I can cancel what I was going to do . . .'

'Well, I can stay for a few days,' said Ellie, 'but Matt's got to go in a couple of hours.'

'You've come all this way and you can only stay a couple of hours?' asked Christopher.

'Sorry, Dad. It was that or nothing.'

Christopher was anxious not to appear ungrateful. 'Oh, I'm not nagging or anything. It's just that . . . well . . . I'm glad you thought it was worth it.'

Matt looked quizzical. 'What?' Then he shook his head. 'Just because we're away from home now doesn't mean . . .'

'But you'll stay for lunch?'

'Of course. In fact . . .' He reached down for the holdall that he had carried in with him and put it on the table. 'Everything you need for a birthday lunch.'

Matt unzipped the bag and lifted out cheeses and paté, a bottle of champagne, crackers and pickle and, finally, a hand of bananas.

'Bananas!'

'And . . .' said Ellie, with theatrical finality dipping into the bag and pulling out a plastic tub, 'Marks and Spencer's custard!'

Christopher threw back his head and laughed. Bananas and custard had been their father's favourite since they could remember.

In the time before lunch they caught up on their lives – Ellie giving chapter and verse on her relief work, and Matt listening intently and only occasionally chipping in with an aside until Christopher turned to him and asked, 'So it's all going well with you.'

'Sort of. A bit up and down, but I'm managing.'

'And you're happy?'

Matt smiled. 'You always ask that.'

'I know. But it's only because, well, you know . . .'

Matt nodded. 'I know. Yes. Yes, I'm happy. So far . . .'

'And the job?'

Matt sighed. 'A bit tricky to be honest. But I'm hopeful of resolving things. I just wish we could get on with it, but the money men keep getting in the way. The world seems to be run by accountants now. They call the shots, I guess.'

Christopher chuckled.

'What?' asked Matt.

'*I guess*. Sorry. You suddenly sounded very American.'

'Oh dear. *I suppose*, then. Is that better?'

Christopher shook his head. 'It doesn't really matter. Just glad to have you here.'

'You didn't expect us then?' asked Ellie.

'Not at all.'

'Well, you can blame him.'

'What?'

'It was Matt who said we should come.'

'I was coming anyway,' mumbled Matt, 'I just thought it would be nice if we were both here, and Ellie managed to engineer a break and . . . well . . . here we are.'

113

'Thank you,' said Christopher. 'Thank you very much. You've made my day.'

'So, are you getting out, Dad?' Ellie asked. 'Are you meeting people?'

'Of course I am. I meet people every day.'

'I don't mean patients. I mean . . . special people.'

'I've always maintained that everybody is special . . .' said Christopher, prevaricating.

'When you want to you can be so irritating,' moaned Ellie.

Matt sat quietly, munching on a cracker.

'I play dominoes every Friday . . .'

'Oh, that's great. You'll meet just the right sort of people down the pub!'

'And,' he countered, with increased volume, 'I have just invited someone to the opera.'

'Good!' cried Ellie positively. 'Are we allowed to know who?'

'Her name's Maria.'

'And . . . ? What does she do?'

Christopher smiled weakly. 'She cleans for me.'

'Oh.'

Matt looked doubtful.

'Now there's no need to look like that. She's not your average cleaner. She knows about opera and . . . things. And she's Italian. Well, part Italian. She speaks perfect English. Anyway, there's nothing in it. It's just an evening out. But she's very pleasant and I enjoy her company and . . .'

He became aware that they were both gazing at him and trying not to smirk. He stopped speaking in mid flow. 'Are you teasing me?'

'No, Dad,' said Matt, maintaining a deadpan expression. 'If you want to go out with a cleaner then that's fine. But just make sure she's not after your money.'

Christopher was not sure whether he was serious or not.

'Well I think it's lovely,' offered Ellie. 'At least it's a start.'

'What?' asked Christopher. 'You think I can work my way up through the animal kingdom from a cleaner and probably end up with a real lady?'

Ellie got up from the table and walked behind her father, draping her arms over his shoulders and putting her head next to his. 'I don't care who you go out with as long as it makes you happy.'

Christopher shot a look at Matt, who shrugged. 'Up to you, Dad. Just be careful, that's all. There are gold-diggers everywhere.'

Christopher thought he detected the merest hint of a smile on Matt's lips. At least he hoped he did.

'Oh, shut up, Matt!' cried Ellie. 'Don't listen to him, Dad.'

Christopher had heard enough. 'What about you two?' he asked. 'Any men on the horizon?' He realized, with the merest hint of irony, that he only needed to enquire about the one sex.

Ellie flopped down in her chair again. 'I've got one guy trying it on, but I'm not very keen. He's a doctor.'

Christopher raised an eyebrow.

'Yes, but unfortunately he's not like you. Got an ego the size of a house. Thinks he's God's gift. Trouble is, he is rather. Bloody fit. Sickening really.'

He turned to Matt. 'How about you?'

Matt avoided his eye. 'Yes. There is a guy. We share an apartment.'

Christopher waited and did not fill the silence.

Then Matt looked at him and smiled. 'We've been together for six months.'

'Good. I'm glad,' said Christopher. And then, 'Anyone like coffee?'

Matt wanted to say more, but he felt that the moment had passed, and so he picked up an orange from the fruit bowl and began to peel it.

Matt gave his father a farewell hug and strolled down the garden path with the empty bag under his arm. Christopher returned to the kitchen table. 'Do you think he's all right?'

Ellie nodded. 'Oh, he's all right. Big shake-ups at work. Came to London for a big meeting.'

'And what about – you know – his private life?'

'Still finds it difficult to talk about it, but I think he's happy.'

'What he was saying . . . about gold-diggers. Do you think he's really worried?'

'I think he's just worried that you might be taken advantage of. Doesn't want you to get hurt.'

Christopher sighed. 'I don't want to get hurt myself. Again. The trouble is that if I just sit here and wrap myself in cotton wool I'm not going to meet anybody. And then I just start looking inwards the whole time. It's not a good thing, Ellie. And, anyway, I'm starting off gently. I'm not committing myself to anything. You'll like Maria. She's very nice. And fun . . . and . . . well, you'll meet her on Monday. I hope you like her.'

'And if I don't?' she teased.

'You will. I know you will.'

*

116

Gary looked pleased with himself. He was leafing through a report and making satisfied little grunts as he did so.

'What are you looking at?' asked Sarah.

'A police file on our friend who was trying to sell protection.'

'How have you got that?'

'Well, I tipped the wink to the Hampshire Constabulary and asked them to keep an eye open. Said that if they managed to collar him to be very gentle on him and let him off lightly. But that I wanted chapter and verse on who he was.'

'And you've got it?'

Gary tapped the file. 'I've got it. It seems that he went back to see Erica again and she called the police. Fortunately someone was sharp enough to stop them from being too heavy and our man in black – Kevin Whittier – has been released into the big, wide world again. No clues though. He's got no previous form.'

'But it's unlikely he'll go back to demanding money, isn't it?'

'For a while I should think. But he might lead us to someone bigger. We're keeping tabs on him.'

'Oh,' said Sarah, with a hint of disappointment in her voice. 'Does that mean that I can't come to the domino club tonight?'

'It means you don't *have* to.'

'Shame really. I was quite looking forward to it.'

'Well, come then. I don't mind.' He wondered whether he should have said it. It was nothing more than vanity really. But Tiger and Christopher had given him such stick for not being able to hang on to women that he wanted to show them the sort of woman he could get if he put his mind

117

to it. Not that he had got her just yet. But given time . . . and if she really did want to come.

'Fine. I will.'

So it was done. And there was no way he could back-track.

Tiger wished there was some way *he* could backtrack. It had been nothing more than a kiss, but he would be fooling himself if he tried to believe he had not enjoyed it. And it was definitely more than a peck.

The following morning nothing was mentioned, but Sam seemed to have an extra sparkle in her eye. An extra spring in her step. And Tiger's mind was racing. Should he say anything? Best not. Best let it lie. Try to pretend it was nothing more than some flight of fancy after a glass too many.

But as they flew the helicopter back to Southampton he would glance at her occasionally when she wasn't looking, and enjoy her close proximity. He knew they were foolish thoughts. Knew they might lead him into trouble. But at the same time he felt exhilarated. Alive. Invigorated. Twenty years younger. The warning bells should have been ringing loudly at the catalogue of clichés that were running through his mind. But they were not. Or if they were, he was block-ing them out. He hoped that he and Sam would be able to work together again. He must work out how they could.

Ellie took the phone call at four o'clock in the afternoon. 'Dad? It's for you. The Royal Infirmary.'

He took the handset from her, fearing the worst. 'Dr Devon? This is Mark Armstrong, the houseman at the Royal.'

'Hello. Yes?'

'I'm afraid it's bad news. Dr Silverwood died an hour ago. Quite suddenly. We got him through the night and thought there was some hope he'd pull through, but then I'm afraid he took a turn for the worse and there was, well, nothing we could do. I'm so sorry. His next of kin have been informed, but I thought you'd like to know as well.'

'Right. Thank you.' Christopher put down the phone.

'Is it serious?' asked Ellie.

'Yes, sweetheart. It's very serious.'

Chapter 13

Meaningful relationships between men and women don't last.

There's a chemical in our bodies that makes it so we get on each other's nerves sooner or later.

Woody Allen, 1935–

Gary was not disappointed by the reactions of Tiger and Christopher that evening. Their jaws could scarcely have been lower as Sarah sat down next to him at the table in the Hare and Hounds. Why they chose this particular pub none of them could recall. But it was conveniently situated, and while not being especially grand it had a decent log fire during every month with an 'R' in it, the regulation number of horse brasses and copper warming pans on the wall and a good pint of real ale in the pump. They usually commandeered a table in the far corner to the right of the fireplace where they could see the comings and goings as well as the spots on the dominoes.

Christopher had nearly rung to cancel, but Ellie said

that she wanted an evening to pamper herself, and he knew that would mean at least three hours in the bathroom.

Tiger had managed to placate Erica. She had not minded that he needed a couple of hours with his mates, but she wondered why he was so distracted. Perhaps he was just pre-occupied with the break-in.

Gary went through the introductions, then asked, 'Well, are we playing?'

Tiger and Christopher pulled themselves together. Tiger went for the drinks while Christopher emptied out the dominoes onto the table. It wasn't until they had played a couple of games, both of which Sarah managed to win, that the conversation began to flow.

'So how did you two meet?' Tiger asked, attempting to break the ice. Gary seemed temporarily lost for words so Sarah cut in. 'At a club. The usual sort of place.'

'So you saw him across a crowded room?' asked Christopher.

'Something like that.'

'He has a terrible reputation you know.'

Gary cut in. 'Do you mind not running me down? I brought Sarah here for a pleasant evening out, not for a replay of the Spanish Inquisition or a bit of character assas-sination.'

'Sorry,' said Christopher. 'We'll try to be on our best behaviour.' And then, to Sarah, 'It's just that we've never been allowed to meet any of the others.'

Sarah smiled mischievously. 'Oh, so there have been others have there?'

'Well,' said Tiger, 'he's not a young man. He's very experienced.'

'No. I'm sorry. This conversation has got to stop,' said Gary.

Christopher looked contrite. 'Yes. How very rude.' He turned to Sarah, 'It's just nice to see him suffer for a change. He's so much younger than we are, you see, and he usually reminds us of that.'

'Really?' countered Sarah. 'He doesn't look it.'

Gary shot her a look, then got up and went over to the bar for another round.

Geoff, the barman, grinned at him. 'Wishing you'd not brought her now? Giving you a bit of stick are they?'

'Just a bit,' murmured Gary. 'Just a bit.'

Sarah turned to Tiger, 'I'm sorry to hear about the shop.'

'Yes, bit of a shock,' confirmed Tiger.

'And you think it's some sort of protection racket?'

Tiger looked a little alarmed.

'Oh, it's all right. Gary told me. But he told me not to tell anyone else.'

Tiger relaxed a little. 'Yes. Well, we've no proof as yet. But I want to ask a few questions in the High Street – of the shopkeepers – and see if I can make any sense of it.'

'So you've no idea where he came from? No clue as to who's behind it?'

'None. But I just think that it's too much of a coincidence that our shop window and the one next door were broken just after we'd declined the offer of his help.'

Sarah nodded, then decided to let the subject go. Gary returned with the drinks and handed them round.

Then Sarah turned her attention to Christopher. 'So how long have you been a GP?'

'Oh, nearly thirty years now.'

'Always around here?'

'Not at first. But for the last twenty or so.'

Sarah sipped at her glass of white wine. 'Never thought of going private? Harley Street or anything like that?'

Christopher laughed. 'No. I'm not a specialist. Just a general practitioner. Aches, pains, wounds and rashes, you know.'

Gary watched Sarah warily. He knew where she was leading.

'How does it work then? Harley Street? If you need a specialist how do you find one? I mean, you wouldn't just knock on doors would you?'

'Well, not quite, but almost. It's rather different to the way it used to be. Much more open. Years ago your doctor would probably have recommended you to someone. Or if you had a health-care insurance scheme then they'd do the same.'

'And now?'

'Well, some firms advertise. You can ring them up and make an appointment.'

'So you could shop around. You know, go to several specialists and get different quotes?'

'Certainly. Harley Street has become competitive, just like anywhere else.'

'And there would be nothing to stop you talking to several different people if you wanted a second opinion?'

'Not at all.'

'Is it all specialist medicine there, then? Rather than aches and pains?'

'Oh, it tends to be. Things like cosmetic surgery. Complimentary medicine. Transplants. And simple operations, too, for private patients. People who can afford not to wait.'

'I see.' Sarah paused and considered the facts.

Taking advantage of the lull, Gary butted in, nervous of

the fact that Sarah had slipped into interrogation mode. 'Er, look, if we want to make that restaurant for dinner I think we'll have to be getting along.'

Sarah looked across at him. 'Oh. Are we going out for dinner?'

Gary responded without a flicker. 'Yes. I've booked.'

'Not the Red Dragon?' asked Tiger.

'No. Not tonight.'

'Good.' He sipped his pint then added, 'I'm not sure about that place. Not since we saw our "protection man" there. It's rather put me off it.'

Christopher chipped in, 'I've not been there yet. Was the food any good?'

'Not bad at all,' confirmed Tiger. 'But I'm not sure you'd want to go.'

'Why not?'

'Saw Randall Cummings sitting in a corner. Talking to the owner. At least I take it that he was the owner. He was Chinese. Looked very proprietorial. Thought Dr Cummings must be adding him to his clientele.'

'I've never met him,' said Gary. 'What does he look like?'

And then they noticed Christopher.

'Are you all right?' enquired Tiger.

'Sorry?' replied Christopher absently.

'Only you look a bit pale.'

Gary took Sarah to a gastropub down by the River Itchen. He thought she would protest the moment they left the Hare and Hounds, but she seemed surprisingly amenable.

The Seahorse was as different as could be from the pub where they played dominoes. While the Hare and Hounds offered dark-stained oak and an abundance of horse brasses, the Seahorse maintained the air of a sophisticated bistro. The walls were painted pale yellow and hung with posters of vineyards. Candles provided most of the light, and from behind the bar came a warm glow that spread an air of contented comfort over the scrubbed pine tables and the well-heeled clientele.

'I don't know why I've come,' Sarah protested gently.

'Probably my irresistible charms,' offered Gary.

'Not specifically,' she said matter-of-factly.

'Why then?'

They were seated at a table for two in a corner. With the sort of view that both of them enjoyed. From here they could do for pleasure what they were trained to do for a living. Watch people.

'Because I'm curious.'

'Curious about what?' he asked.

'About you.'

Gary was disconcerted. She'd never admitted anything so remotely personal before. Always treated him as though he were either an obstacle to her progress or a stray dog that had temporarily invaded her patch.

'In what way?' he asked slowly.

'Well,' she said, 'you're either a complete male-chauvinist bastard, or a lifelong commitment-phobe, or an insecure coward where relationships are concerned, and hide behind a protective barrier that's composed of the other two.'

'I think you've lost me,' he said.

Sarah shook her head. 'I don't think so.'

Gary took a sip of his wine and put down the glass, all without looking at her. 'So which of those three – it was three wasn't it? – things do you think I am?'

'Let's take them one at a time. If you were a complete male-chauvinist bastard you'd have taken advantage of me more than you have.'

He looked up at her and murmured, 'Must be losing my touch.'

She continued. 'All right then, *tried* to take advantage of me.'

Gary looked offended. 'I thought I'd made a pretty good stab at it.'

'No. Not by some men's standards. Then there's the commitment phobia.' She mused for a moment. 'You see, I could well believe that. Did you have any pets as a child?'

'A hamster.'

'There you are then.'

'What do you mean, "there you are"?'

'Hamsters. Shortest-lived of any childhood pet. What do you get out of them? Three years – if you're lucky. Puts you off long-term relationships for life.'

'That's absolute bollocks.'

Sarah shook her head. 'Oh, no. Well-known fact. If you'd had a dog you'd have been much more ready to commit.'

'I'm glad you didn't study philosophy at university because with this turn of mind you'd have been a disaster.'

'No, but I did study social anthropology and you fit the bill exactly.'

He opened his mouth to speak, but Sarah cut in, 'And then we come to what I consider to be the most likely cause.'

'Which is?'

'You are a plain and straightforward insecure coward.'

'Don't be ridiculous. How could I be a coward when I've had so many . . .'

'Ah, so it's true what they were saying in the pub? You have had a lot of relationships.'

'I'm fifty!' he cried, rather too loudly. One or two of the other diners looked round.

'Well, that's most of them informed. They'll probably send round a birthday cake in a minute.'

'I'm fifty,' he whispered. 'Of course I've had lots of relationships. Who hasn't?'

'And how long have they lasted? On average.'

Gary looked exasperated. 'I haven't worked it out.'

Sarah stared at him in silence.

'Well, I managed three months once. No. No – six months. Half a year. That's not bad.'

'How long ago?'

'Ooh . . . ten years.'

Sarah pretended to write on an invisible notepad. 'Six months, ten years ago. Patient clinically incapable of sustaining a relationship.'

Gary leaned back in his chair. 'What's this got to do with anything? I mean, why are you so interested?'

Sarah looked him in the eye. 'Because I want to know if I'll be wasting my time.'

That night Sarah did not catch her train from Winchester to London. Instead she became, as she would have put it, another notch on Gary's bedpost. They made love looking up at the stars in Gary's penthouse: which is what he called his top-floor flat with a Velux window. Sarah slept peacefully in his arms as Gary gazed at the outline of Orion through the darkened glass. There was a certain satisfaction in the conquest, but also a slight nervousness that he could not pin down. Normally it would not have troubled him. He wondered why it should do so now.

Erica lay awake for a long time. She rolled over at one point and put her arms around Tiger. He did not respond. He acted as though he were asleep, but she was sure he was still awake. Eventually she drew away from him, turned over and moved to her own side of the bed. She heard the clock of the cathedral strike one. Then two, Then three. Then she fell into a fitful, uncomfortable sleep.

Christopher sat up until midnight talking to Ellie, catching up on her African exploits and asking about Matt. It seemed that most of the information he gleaned about Matt came from Ellie.

'I do worry,' confided Christopher.

'So do we,' said Ellie.

'What do you mean?'

'About you. We worry about you.'

Christopher laughed it off. 'But I'm far too old to be worried about.'

'That's so typical. Just because you're a parent you think that all the worry is one way. We worry about you every bit as much as you worry about us.'

'But why?'

She came over and sat on the arm of the chintz-covered chair. 'Because we love you.'

Christopher looked up at her. 'That's very kind,' he said softly, and stroked her arm. 'And mum?'

'Yes. We love her too,' murmured Ellie. 'In spite of it all.'

'You mustn't blame her, you know.'

'Hard not to.'

'Ellie, if I thought that you did, I'd be very upset.'

'Well . . .'

'You don't, do you?'

'Dad, she went off and left you.'

'Yes. But it was my fault.'

'How could it be your fault?'

'Because I was neglectful. I didn't pay her enough attention.'

'But you have a tough job. You're a doctor, you're bound to be preoccupied and stuff. But at least you were here. It wasn't as if you were away for weeks on end or anything.'

'But even so . . .'

Ellie spoke more softly, 'Dad you did your best, that's what matters. Sometimes things don't work out the way they should. But that's no reason to feel you've failed.'

'Listen to you. You're not supposed to talk like that. I'm the one with all the experience. I should be the one making value judgements.'

She leaned into him. 'I'm sorry. I just hate to see both of you so unhappy.'

'You think your mother is unhappy?' There was a note of surprise in his voice.

'She doesn't say so, but I can tell. I know it's not what she thought it would be.'

'With Howie?'

Ellie nodded.

'In what way?'

'Oh, I don't think the grass is as green as she imagined.'

'Mmm. It seldom is.' He patted her arm and made to rise from the chair. 'So what will you do tomorrow?'

'Oh, go into town. Have a look around. Maybe buy a few new T-shirts.'

'No designer dresses?'

'No need for them yet.'

'Shame. I'd love to see you in a posh frock. Just for once.'

'Oh, you will, one day. I've not gone all butch. Just practical. There's not much call for an LBD out there.'

'LBD?'

'Little black dress, Dad.'

'Oh, yes, of course. LBD,' he murmured absent mindedly.

'Dad, are you sure you're all right?'

Christopher broke out of his reverie and smiled gently. 'Yes. I'm fine.'

'Is it something to do with this afternoon? That phone call.'

'Yes. You remember Dr Silverwood?'

'Old Dr Silverwood? The little man with the beaky nose and the glasses?'

'Yes. Well, he's died.'

'Oh, I'm sorry. You were rather fond of him, weren't you?'

'Yes. I was rather. And . . . well . . .' He paused to think, then said, 'Can I ask you something?'

'Of course.'

'If you knew someone had done something which you thought was wrong, and yet to mention it might cause even greater problems in its own way, would you mention the thing which was wrong, whatever the circumstances, or would you keep quiet thinking that the smaller wrong was preferable to the greater one that would occur as a result?'

Ellie thought for a moment, then said carefully, 'I think it depends on whether you thought that the person might do the wrong thing again.'

Chapter 14

One would be in less danger
From the wiles of a stranger
If one's own kin and kith
Were more fun to be with.

'Family Court', Ogden Nash, 1902–71

At half past nine on Saturday morning, while Ellie was still asleep, Christopher rang Randall Cummings at his home. The phone was answered in the abrupt manner he had become used to.

'Randall, it's Christopher Devon.'

'Yes?'

'I need to see you. Can I come round?'

'It's not very convenient. I've a golf match in an hour.'

'It won't take long. I can be with you in fifteen minutes.'

'You'll have to take your chance. I might be here, I might have gone,' and Cummings put the phone down.

Christopher took a deep breath to calm himself. Cummings'

manner had not improved in the intervening months. He was as terse and peremptory as ever. But then, with Christopher Devon, he probably felt he had need to be.

Cummings' house was in a neighbouring village, within a stone's throw of the Itchen Valley Golf Club. Maybe, Christopher mused as he drove there, if he'd joined the golf club things might not have turned out the way they did. A pity he'd always subscribed to the 'good walk spoiled' school. But no. Cummings would never have been his type, and golf was never his game. He'd rather spend his time outdoors in the garden.

He pulled up alongside the high brick wall that surrounded Cummings' house. It was the sort of house more usually associated with a professional footballer than a family practitioner. It was barely five years old – brick built with a red tile roof and a white-pillared portico. A row of three garages stood beside the sweeping Tarmac drive and to enter the premises any caller had to press a button in the brick pillar by the electronically controlled gates. They were made of black wrought iron, with gilded spears at the top of each upright. It seemed to Christopher an appropriate indication of the owner's character.

He got out of his car and pressed the call button. There was no reply, but after a few seconds a low hum indicated that the gates were opening. He drove up to the front door and parked his mud-caked Volvo estate alongside a gleaming silver Mercedes. The boot was open, and he could see a red leather golf bag filled with clubs lying within it.

As he approached the pillared portico the front door opened, and a large, grey-haired man in plus fours and a lemon-yellow cashmere sweater walked out onto the broad apron of steps.

'Hello, Randall,' offered Christopher.

'You'll have to be quick,' growled Cummings, looking at his watch. 'I have to leave in ten minutes.'

Christopher looked at his own watch, and then turned round to look at the golf course across the road, barely two minutes away on foot. 'Right. Can I come inside?'

'Can't we talk here?'

'I'd rather not.'

Cummings shrugged, turned and walked into the house. Christopher followed him.

Once inside the cream-coloured marble hallway, dominated by a large chandelier which was lit even at this early hour, Cummings rounded on Christopher. 'I don't like being bothered at home. Especially at weekends.'

'Randall, I don't relish having to come and see you whatever day of the week, but I wanted to talk to you. I think you know what it's about.'

'Why should I?'

'Randall, nobody knows why I left the practice. Why I really left. And I don't want to have to tell them.'

'What do you mean?'

'You know perfectly well what I mean.'

'Are you trying to blackmail me?'

'Don't be ridiculous. This isn't some cheap thriller. Of course I'm not trying to blackmail you, though heaven knows I'd have enough grounds.'

'What then?'

'It's got to stop. You've got to start being more even handed.'

'What do you mean by that?'

'You can't reserve your best treatment for the people who can pay most.'

'That's a slanderous allegation.'

'It would be slanderous if it weren't true.'

'So what's brought all this on? Why the pricking of conscience now?'

'You know perfectly well that my conscience was pricked the moment I knew what was going on. And I said so at the time.'

'So?'

'Mrs Fraser came to see me the other day.'

'Which Mrs Fraser?'

'The Mrs Fraser whose husband died because he couldn't get a kidney transplant.'

Cummings pushed his hands deep into the pockets of his plus fours. 'Lots of people die because they can't get a transplant. There are more people who need organs than there are donors.'

'But Mr Fraser could have got one, if you'd not decided that money was more important than ethics.'

Cummings' face began to turn red. 'If you're telling me that I made an error of judgement . . .'

'Of course I am. Of course you did. You gave a kidney to someone who could pay for it.'

'Are you saying . . . ?'

'Yes I am. You bumped them to the top of the list and ignored those who were already there and it's got to stop.'

Cummings glowered, his face now a deep shade of crimson. 'If you're threatening me . . .'

'I'm telling you how I feel, that's all. I'm a doctor, like you, and I didn't become a doctor to make a fortune.'

Cummings threw back his head and laughed. 'Ha! That's rich, coming from you. Left a manor house by your auntie, and a small private income. When have you ever had to struggle, eh? When have you ever wondered where the next meal was coming from?'

'That really isn't the point.'

'Oh, yes it is!' Cummings was getting into his stride. 'It's exactly the point. You've always looked down on me because of my background. You with your Cambridge education and your flower-bedside manner. You never could stomach the fact that I was the senior member of the practice – apart from Reggie Silverwood – and much good he was.'

'That's rubbish and you know it. And Reggie Silverwood was a good doctor who cared for his patients.'

'And are you saying that I don't?'

'I'm saying that you're not even handed. And while we're on the subject of Reggie, what happened on Thursday?'

Cummings was caught off guard. 'What do you mean?'

'Reggie rang me. There was something wrong. He wasn't himself.'

'Probably been at the bottle.'

'You know Reggie never touched the stuff until after hours. Ever.'

'What then?'

'Had he rumbled you, Randall?'

'Don't be ridiculous. Anyway, there's not much point in talking about it now, is there? Not after his accident. It's very sad. But there we are. Had a better innings than most, just bloody bad luck.'

'You're sure it was just bad luck?'

'Of course I am. Had a heart attack and lost control. Not unusual in a man of his age.'

'Well, the post-mortem will confirm whether it really was an accident.'

'Post-mortem? What post-mortem?'

'I'm going to speak to the coroner. To ask for one. Just to make sure.'

Randall Cummings coloured up again, this time it looked as if he might actually burst a blood vessel. 'Just exactly what are you implying?'

'I don't know, Randall. I just want an easy conscience, that's all. I'd like to be able to sleep at night knowing that I'd done all I could.'

'All you could to what?'

'Save lives.'

'You sanctimonious bugger. Get out!'

'I'm sorry, Randall. Sorry that I'm not prepared to put my head in the sand. It might suit your *modus operandi*. It might make for a quieter life for me. But I can't do that.' Christopher turned and walked down the steps without looking back. He got into his car and started the engine, but before he could let off the handbrake, the silver Mercedes shot past him and with a squeal of tyres on Tarmac, Randall Cummings sped out between the iron gates with barely an inch to spare. By the time Christopher had turned into the road the car was out of sight.

Tiger tried to avoid working on Saturdays, especially when he had been away for much of the preceding week. But today he had to call in at the helicopter hangar at Southampton airport to check his workload for the following week and to tell the mechanic about a couple of things that needed attending to.

He was sitting in the office going over paperwork when Sam walked in. She looked worried. Not her usual carefree self.

He looked up and saw it was her. Then he saw her expression. 'Are you OK?'

'Not really, no.'

'Why? What's the matter?'

'My aircraft. There's a problem with the engine.'

'Can't they fix it?'

'Not until the end of the week.'

'But we're supposed to have an express delivery system so that we're not out of the sky for any longer than we have to be.'

'I know. But the particular part they need doesn't exist in this country, can you believe? They have to get it from the States and that's going to take three days, and then they have to fit it.'

'Bugger!'

'Yes, bugger!' Sam flopped down in the chair at the desk that butted on to the front of the one Tiger sat at. 'So I'm sorry. It means you'll have company next week again.'

'Oh?' he tried to sound level. Even in his tone.

'Yes. The boss says he thinks it would be good if I kept you company, then at least I won't be completely wasting my time.' She paused. Then said, 'If it's all right with you?'

'Yes. Yes, of course. No problem at all.'

Sam looked out of the window at the low grey clouds. 'Let's just hope we get some better weather, and some decent locations.'

'Yes,' said Tiger. And his mind began to wander.

Gary propped himself up on his elbow and looked at Sarah lying on the pillow next to him. She looked more beautiful than ever if that were possible. Her long, dark hair lay on the pillow like some raven wave, her face was calm and relaxed. He thought he could even detect the faintest smile.

Carefully he stroked a few stray strands from the side of her face and she murmured something so softly that he could not hear. Then she opened her eyes, looked startled for a moment, then relaxed again.

'I'm glad it didn't last,' said Gary softly.

'Mmm? What?'

'That frightened look. Do you want some coffee?'

Sarah shook her head. 'No. Tea. Please.'

Gary bent down and kissed her on the cheek, then slid out of bed and walked down the few steps that led into the living area. He crossed to the kitchen in the far corner.

Sarah watched him go. 'Nice bum.'

'Thank you.'

'For someone your age.'

He turned and looked at her.

Sarah rolled over in the sheets until she was lying on her stomach looking directly at him. 'Nice other things as well.'

Gary picked up a towel from a pile of washing in the kitchen and wrapped it round himself.

'Well, well . . .' said Sarah.

'What?' asked Gary, filling the kettle at the tap.

'That's not a word I would ever have associated with you.'

'What isn't?'

'Embarrassment.'

He put the kettle on the hob and walked back towards the bed. 'How do you know I'm embarrassed?'

'Because you've gone just a tiny bit pink.'

Gary pushed her so that she rolled onto her back once more, then he pulled the sheet away from her and gazed at her body. 'And you're quite a lot pink,' he said, bending down and feathering her stomach with kisses.

They had their tea and coffee later, when they could no longer stand the insistent whistling of the kettle.

Chapter 15

If you would be happy for a week take a wife; if you would be happy for a month kill a pig; but if you would be happy all your life plant a garden.

Anon, mid-17th century

Christopher was shaking by the time he drank his own cup of coffee in the kitchen at the Manor House. But at least he had done it. Cleared his conscience. Up to a point. Whether it would make any difference only time would tell. And how would he know? Now that he was no longer a part of the scene, how could he tell what went on on a daily basis?

But the alternative – to make a formal complaint about Cummings – would have thrown the local practice into chaos; undermined all confidence in the other doctors whom he knew had nothing to do with Cummings' Machiavellian manoeuvres.

He had thought long and hard about it. Wondered whether he was being cowardly in not taking it to a higher authority immediately. But in the end decided on calmer tactics. The warning he had given was as far as he would go, for now. If he discovered the merest suggestion that Cummings was still on the make then he would have to go further, but hopefully he had made enough of a point with this shot across Cummings' bows.

Ellie came down, bleary and tousled, at around half past ten. 'Mm . . . hello,' she murmured, opening the fridge and hauling out a pint of milk.

'Hello you. Sleep well?'

'Yup.'

'How did I know that?'

Ellie smiled a beatific smile without opening her eyes. 'Do I look relaxed then?'

Christopher grinned. 'Just a little.'

Ellie squinted at him. 'Oh. It's more than you do,' she said. 'What's happened?'

'I just faced up to what we were talking about last night, that's all.'

'And did it work?'

'We'll have to wait and see, my love.' He drained his mug. 'So are you ready for your shopping trip?'

'Do I look ready?'

'Well, if you get your skates on I'll drop you in town.'

Ellie snapped awake. 'Give me twenty minutes and I'm yours.'

True to her word she appeared at the bottom of the stairs at the appointed time. 'Anyway, Dad, what are you doing going into town on a Saturday? I thought you'd be happier in the garden.'

'Er . . . I'm just dropping in on Maria.'

'Maria? Oh, yes, your cleaning lady.'

141

'I do wish you wouldn't call her that.'

'I didn't mean to call her that. I'll try it again.' She cleared her throat. 'Oh, Maria!'

'Better.'

'Why are you calling in on her, or is that too personal?'

'Because she asked if I'd look at her roses. I think they might have a bit of canker.'

'And you being a good doctor she thought you might be able to sort her out?'

'No. Me being a good *gardener* she thought I might be able to sort *them* out.'

They walked together to the car, and Christopher said, 'I don't know why you're grinning like that. There is absolutely nothing funny about canker on roses.'

He had expected a small garden with a few forlorn rose trees within it. What met his eye on that spring Saturday morning was an altogether different sight.

Maria's house was a small Georgian terraced cottage a few streets away from the cathedral close. It would once have been a busy street, but Winchester's one-way system meant that it was now a cul-de-sac. What was formerly a down-at-heel cottage had now, thanks to the freedom from traffic and the associated dust and grime, gone up in the world.

The house fronts were stucco, and painted in different colours – soft yellow, pale blue, warm cream and even blush pink. Not one of the front gardens had been given over to car parking. Instead, they all retained their low-pillared walls and contained either modern minimalist gardens – yuccas, bamboos and pebbles – traditional cottage-garden plants or tiny squares of lawn surrounded by borders brimming with daffodils.

Number 34 was the gem among them. Christopher cast his eye over the mixture of plants that jostled for position in the small tapestry that was Maria's front garden. There were Lenten hellebores and miniature narcissi, euphorbias and hardy cyclamen, dwarf irises and lungworts. Variegated ivy scrambled over the low wall, and one or two small trees – as yet unidentifiable in their leafless state – pushed up among the floral carpet through which ran a sinuous river of gravel to allow its owner to get closer to her charges. It was a plantswoman's garden, put together with skill and good taste, and Christopher was taken aback.

His reverie was broken by the sound of her voice. He looked up to see her standing in the doorway. 'Don't look too close. It's a bit early in the year.'

Christopher raised his hands in amazement. 'It's wonderful. I've never seen so much crammed into such a small area.'

'I wonder if it's a bit busy sometimes.'

'No. It's perfect.' He opened the gate and walked down the path to greet her. 'I thought it would just be a bit of a rose bed with a few tired old bushes in it.'

She smiled. 'It was when I came here.'

'How long ago?'

'Oh, five years now. I've been busy changing it since then.'

Christopher looked round. 'So where's the rose bush?'

'It's in the back garden. Do you want to come and have a look?'

Maria led him through the house. It was tastefully decorated in palest creams and white. A small cottage, it nevertheless had an open, airy feel to it. On the walls were pencil sketches of human figures. At the windows hung

143

swathes of muslin that filtered the morning light. She took him through to the kitchen at the back of the house – a sleek, modern room with pale wooden work tops and a pair of French doors that looked on to the tiny back garden.

It was a simple creation, centred by a rectangular box-edged bed sliced into four triangles. On the wall at the end, a lion's head fountain spurted into a lead cistern. There were cones of box and yew at strategic points, and everywhere, the same skilful mixture of plants that had been evident in the front garden.

Christopher shook his head. 'I had no idea.'

'What?' she asked, innocently.

'That you were such a good gardener. I mean, I saw you looking at mine, when I took you round on that first day, but I thought it was because . . . well . . . you couldn't understand it.'

'Oh no. It was envy. I'd never seen so much garden!'

'Well you've made the most of this patch.' He brought his eyes to focus on his immediate surroundings now. The kitchen was fresh and white with no traditional Welsh dresser. Instead floor-to-ceiling bookshelves ran down one side. He glanced at some of the authors – Elizabeth David and Beth Chatto, Nigel Slater and Christopher Lloyd. Gardening mixed up with cookery and with fiction – Paul Coelho and Kazuo Ishiguro, Jilly Cooper and Rosamunde Pilcher.

'Oh, don't look. I keep meaning to sort them out, but they always seem to get muddled up.'

'Bet you know where they all are though.'

'Yes, I do, funnily enough.'

She made coffee while he sat at the table. 'And the rose? The one with the canker?'

Maria pointed out of the window. 'That one over there in the corner. "Souvenir de la Malmaison". It's lovely and pale pink but it doesn't seem very happy.'

'No,' confirmed Christopher. 'I gave up with mine years ago. Too weedy.'

'Do you think I should do the same?'

'Well, I don't like to condemn any patient out of hand but I think you'd be better off planting something with a stronger constitution.'

'Any suggestions?'

'Try "Jacques Cartier". It never seems to get diseased and it flowers for most of the summer, too. It is a bit bigger though.'

'Thank you, Doctor.'

'That'll be five guineas.'

She laughed. 'Very reasonable.'

'Or I'll settle for a cup of coffee.'

They sat at the kitchen table and for the next half hour they talked easily about gardens and plants, about books and cooking.

There was a moment where he came close to confiding in her. Wanted to tell her where he had been early that morning. Wanted her opinion on what he should do, whether he should take it any further. He would have liked to hear her point of view. She seemed worldly wise without being hard, experienced without being embittered. He opened his mouth to broach the subject but instead found himself saying: 'I've made enquiries about the opera. There's a performance of *Tosca* at Covent Garden next Wednesday. Would that be any good?'

'Perfectly fine.'

'You don't need to look in your diary?'

Maria shook her head. 'It's not exactly packed with social engagements.'

Christopher made to get up. 'Right. Well, I'd better be going. I'll see you on Monday.'

'You're about then? Not on call?'

'No. Not next week. They've given me a week off.'

He tried not to sound too worried, and Maria did not like to pursue the subject. Instead, she said brightly, 'Right, well I'll make sure you have some lunch, then.'

Tiger was not getting on too well. Having finished his paperwork at the airport he had gone into Winchester and begun his inventory of shops, thinking that if nothing else it would take his mind off Sam. He battled with himself over her. Half the time he wallowed in the pleasurable thought of being next to her for another week. Wondering where it might lead. Then his conscience would get the better of him and he would tell himself that nothing else must happen.

The shopkeepers he questioned did not exactly welcome him with open arms on a busy Saturday morning, neither were they forthcoming with much information. What had seemed at the outset to be a fairly straightforward exercise had turned into a maze of confusion. A bit like his mind. One or two shopkeepers said they had been visited by the man in black. Others claimed no knowledge of him. Not one of them admitted to paying anything, and only one other shop had suffered any form of vandalism. They had indeed been visited by the man in black and declined his offer. Tiger saw his first glimmer of hope, until the shop-keeper explained that the vandalism had involved someone being heartily sick on their doorstep the previous

Saturday night. This was not a tactic that Tiger would have suspected would be employed by the man in black.

After an hour of futile questioning he realized he was getting nowhere. He walked around the corner to the bookshop where Erica was working the morning shift, Brian having gone to see his mother in Bournemouth.

'You look a bit down in the mouth,' said Erica. 'No luck?'

Tiger leaned against one of the towering bookshelves. 'Bloody useless.'

'I'm glad.'

'What do you mean?'

'Well, if you'd found something you'd have gone at it like a dog with a bone, and I don't know that I want you getting mixed up in something like this.'

Tiger looked disappointed. 'But you said yourself that the police weren't doing anything about it.'

'I know, but I'd just like to see if that warning they gave him has any effect. Maybe they'll have frightened him off and you won't need to get involved.'

Not get involved. Something about the words echoed around his head.

'Are you all right?'

'Mmm?'

'Only your mind's been somewhere else since you came back. Did you have a bad week?'

Christopher had threatened Randall Cummings with a post-mortem to warn him off more than anything else. To show him that he was not trusted, that he could not take the law into his own hands. If he were going to carry out his threat he could not put off ringing the coroner any longer. He'd known Monty Loveday for many years.

147

Perhaps he could arrange a post-mortem with the minimum of fuss. Not raise too many eyebrows, just in case it proved negative.

Monty was not a golfer. Neither was he keen on shopping with his wife. Old cars were his thing, and Christopher was fairly confident of catching him at home on a Saturday, even if he would not be best pleased to be dragged away from his Wolseley with hands covered in oil.

'Monty, I'm sorry to bother you on a Saturday.'

'Christopher, the car's in bits and I can't get to the bottom of the fuel problem, so to be perfectly honest I'm glad of the break.'

Christopher could picture him in his green overalls with *Castrol* emblazoned on the left breast, like some ageing racing driver making a long-overdue pit stop. Monty was tall and gangling, a fifty-year-old man with the body of an adolescent, all the better for reaching the inner recesses of the 1938 Wolseley, Twenty-Five Super Six Series III, which rejoiced under the name of Veronica.

'Bit of advice, Monty.'

'Oh, that sounds ominous.'

'I've got a death that I'm a bit suspicious about. I was wondering of you could authorize a PM.'

'How suspicious?'

'Well, the cause of death was thought to be accidental, but I'm not certain.'

Monty sounded serious. 'Christopher, you know as well as I do that if you think that death was in suspicious circumstances then you should be talking to to police, not to me.'

'I know.'

'So?'

'I don't want to make ripples if there's no need. But I just

148

want to satisfy myself that the death was due to an accident, nothing else.'

'Christopher, I'd like to help. But I really don't see how I can. Not without involving the police.'

'Of course. No.'

'Is it anybody I know?'

'Reggie Silverwood.'

'Oh, poor Reggie. Very sad. But straightforward surely? You don't really think his death was suspicious do you?'

'I don't know. I just wanted to be certain.'

'Christopher, I know you were very fond of the old boy, but from what I've heard his death was an open and shut case. Had a heart attack, didn't he? Ended up in a ditch. How could his death be suspicious?'

'I'm not sure. Perhaps you're right. Perhaps I'm clutching at straws.'

Monty sounded puzzled. 'I'm getting the feeling you're not telling me everything, Christopher.'

'Oh, it's just a thought. Look, never mind, Monty. I'll get back to you if I need to. I'm sorry to bother you on your day off.'

'I'm not concerned about that. But if you have worries, Christopher, you really should voice them to the police. You don't need me to tell you that.'

Christopher put down the phone and reasoned with himself. Randall Cummings might be greedy. He might be lining his pockets more than he should, but there would be no way he would actually have brought about Reggie's death. He told himself he was overreacting. It was time he stopped.

It occurred to Christopher that he had not spoken to Betty Silverwood since Reggie's death. He called her to offer his condolences. She was, as she had always been, a stoic doctor's wife who faced up to life's vicissitudes with sanguine acceptance. Like Reggie, she preferred their private life to be private, but Christopher had met her on a number of occasions over the years – when the practice had organized a dinner, or occasionally when she came to pick Reggie up from the surgery.

He wondered whether it would be better to write or to call on her, but a phone call seemed to be preferable. Then at least he could be both personal and brief, without the distance of a letter or the imposition of a house call.

'It was a bit of a shock,' she admitted. Reggie's customary capacity for understatement and calmness in the face of all difficulties was clearly a characteristic shared by his wife. But her voice wavered a little, and Christopher hoped she would not mind if he asked a few more questions.

'He'd seemed fine,' she continued. 'A bit more thoughtful than usual. A bit preoccupied. But then you're all like that from time to time, aren't you?'

Christopher voiced his agreement, then asked, 'But he'd not said anything? Said that he was worried about anything in particular?'

'No. Not at all. No more than usual.'

'So have you set a date for the funeral?'

'No. Not yet. Anyway, it'll be a service of thanksgiving rather than a funeral.'

'Oh, I see.'

'Yes. Seems a bit pointless having a funeral when there's no body. Reggie left his body to science, you see. Once his organs had been donated. He was very keen on that.'

Chapter 16

Who shall decide, when doctors disagree?
'Epistles to Several Persons', Alexander Pope, 1688–1744

'I really can get myself on to a train, you know,' said Sarah.

'Yes, but I want to make sure.'

'Why? Can't wait to get me out of your hair?' She looked at the top of his head. 'Not that there is much of it.'

'Are you complaining?'

'No,' she said. 'No, I'm not.'

Gary walked her up to the platform of Winchester station. They were not holding hands. She had hers on the strap of the satchel that hung from her shoulder. His were plunged deep into the pockets of his leather jacket.

'Why me?' he asked, matter-of-factly.

'Why not?'

'Well, you've fended me off for months. Why the sudden change of heart?'

'Who knows?'

'You will come back? I mean, you can tell me if it was just a one-night stand.'

'Is that what you'd prefer? Is that what you're used to?'

'Used to, yes. But not what I'd prefer.'

The distant rumble of the train broke them off. They stood back as it thundered alongside the platform and drew to a halt. The electric doors slid open.

'You could stay if you want,' he said. 'You don't have to go back.'

'No clothes,' she said. 'Can't wear these all weekend.'

'But you could come back when you've got them.'

She stepped up on to the train and turned to face him. 'Maybe next time.' She leaned forward and kissed him on the cheek, then the doors slid closed and the train pulled slowly out of the station. He waved, then watched the train until it was a tiny dot at the end of the track.

Gary was at a loose end. He could go back to his flat and read the papers. He could go for a run. Instead he walked into town and paid a visit to Erica's bookshop.

'We don't see you here very often,' said Erica. 'Going on holiday?'

'I wish,' said Gary. 'Too much on. Just thought I'd come and pick up a bit of reading – something to take my mind off work.'

'Do you need any help?'

'Well, you could point me in the direction of China.'

'You'll find China down the third alleyway somewhere between Borneo and Denmark.'

'And I thought *my* geography was shaky,' murmured Gary.

'Oh, we're a world apart in here,' said Erica. 'Anything in particular?'

'Well, not so much a travel guide as a book on Chinese culture. That sort of thing. As up to date as possible.'

'Hang on.' Erica came out from behind her counter and led the way to the third aisle. 'I think we've something fairly new. Came in a couple of weeks ago. Now then, where are we . . .' She scrutinized the shelves in the section marked China. 'There you are . . . up there. The one with the dreary cover. Can you reach it, or shall I go and get the steps?'

Gary stretched up and pulled down the thick book. '*Modern China: Its Economy and Changing Culture*. I see what you mean about the dreary cover.'

'The title's not especially exciting either, is it? I'm sure we can find you something a bit more inspiring than that. Wouldn't you rather have something with more photographs in it?'

'No, this'll be perfect.'

'If you're sure. I think on the whole I'd be happier with something a bit more exciting myself.'

But Gary was adamant. He paid for the book, took it home, and for the rest of the afternoon immersed himself in the culture of the East. It took his mind off Sarah for a while, and it was not a wasted exercise. He had never met Mr Tan, but now he seemed to be able to see him, if not more clearly, then at least through a glass darkly.

Monday morning dawned cold and damp. It was not the perfect day for gardening and, anyway, Christopher had other things on his mind. He greeted Maria warmly, but she could see that he was preoccupied.

'I'm nipping out for a while,' he told her. 'I should be back about lunchtime.'

'Fine. Lunch at about one?'

He turned towards her and she felt the need to reassure him. 'It's only cold stuff so it doesn't matter what time. But I can do some soup to warm you up.'

Her kindness pricked his conscience. 'Thanks. That will be lovely.' He looked at her for a moment, unsure what to say, then smiled hesitantly and turned to go. He stopped at the door. 'I really am grateful, you know. I do appreciate it.'

She looked down. 'Oh . . . it's nothing.'

There were no more words between them, just a glance. To Christopher, in that split second, it seemed that some-thing had touched him – reached out and reassured him. He hoped that he wasn't convincing himself there was more to it than there was. In spite of his worries about Randall Cummings and Reggie Silverwood the existence of Maria in his life, and the return of Ellie, had cheered him up more than he could have imagined. Ellie. He must make time for her. Tonight he would cook her supper. Talk to her more. They had only spoken in fits and starts since she had come home. On Saturday she had gone out shopping and then off to see a friend in the evening. On Sunday she had gone to see more friends while he pottered in the greenhouse. Tonight he would make up for it. Cook her something special. But first he would go to the hospital.

Dr Armstrong was apologetic. 'I'm sorry you didn't know. It didn't occur to me to say at the time.'

Christopher was standing in front of the young doctor in his office at the end of one of the wards. 'So the organs were removed straight away?'

'Almost immediately, yes. The corneas, kidneys, the other useful bits.'

'And the rest of the body?'

'Off to a teaching hospital. I'm not sure which one.' Then he looked a little apprehensive. 'It was all done quite properly. All the forms were signed.'

'Yes, yes, I'm sure. I should have realized. Reggie was always so keen on his patients carrying donor cards it would have been surprising if he hadn't carried one himself. It was stupid of me not to remember.'

Christopher made to go, then he turned at the door. 'How long have you been working here, Mark?'

'Oh, about eighteen months. Why?'

'Do you have many dealings with Dr Cummings?'

'Not if I can help it. Scares the pants off me. Gruff old bugger.'

'Not popular then?'

'Not much. The patients are terrified of him and most of the nurses are wary. Oh, he's all right, I suppose. But a bit too autocratic for most of us.'

'Is that all? There's nothing else about him that people don't like?'

Mark Armstrong laughed. 'I'd have thought that was enough. He's not very friendly, not very chatty. A bit hard to get to know. But then with a bark like that no one really wants to make the effort. You get him in to see his patients, but he doesn't make a point of fraternizing with anyone. Keeps himself to himself.'

Christopher nodded thoughtfully. 'I gather he signed Dr Silverwood's death certificate?'

'Yes. He happened to be on the ward when he died. Said he'd do it as Dr Silverwood was a colleague.'

'And did he know about Reggie's organ donor card?'

'Yes. Well he must have done. In fact, I think he alerted us to it. Yes, that's right. He said he would put in a call to someone.'

'And did he?'

'No. We have our own procedure for organ donation and so it was taken in hand here.'

Christopher sighed with relief.

'Is something wrong Dr Devon?'

'No. Not this time, thank God.'

Mark Armstrong looked at him quizzically. 'You used to work with Dr Cummings, didn't you?'

'Yes. Yes, I did.'

'Can't have been easy.'

'No.'

'But you moved on?'

'Yes, Mark. I moved on.' He nodded a farewell and left the doctor's room, murmuring to himself as he went, 'But I'm not sure where to.'

This particular Monday morning found Tiger apprehensive. He'd been unable to settle to anything over the weekend, with the events of the previous Thursday evening playing over and over in his mind. He tried to rationalize. It had been a kiss, for God's sake, a simple, single kiss. It might never happen again. But then his mind went into that peculiar self-destruct overdrive: did he want it to be that simple? Had he enjoyed it? Yes. Would he like to do it again? Yes. No! But yes. Would he like it to go further? Yes. No! Definitely not. But if it did, what would it be like? And wasn't it good to feel like this? Like what? At sixes and sevens. But excited. Alive. There was something of the fairground ride about it – the highs, the lows, all mixed together and leaving him confused but somehow elevated from the humdrum of daily life. It was, he knew, a dangerous brew.

He checked in at the helicopter base at Southampton airport and found himself scheduled for a flight to Leeds Bradford Airport with Sam in the left-hand seat.

He hadn't felt so nervous in years, but there were two city executives in the back so the conversation was strictly business. The flight was uneventful and the two gents were dropped off midmorning.

It was a wait and return job. Tiger and Sam had three hours to kill. They refuelled then went to the waiting room. He wondered how they would pass the time. He did not have long to wait.

'Let's hire a taxi,' said Sam.

'What?'

'We could run up to the moors. Take in the view. Have a cup of tea.'

Tiger laughed. 'Nice thought. There's only one problem.'

'What's that?'

'If they finish their meeting early and get back here to find we're up on the moors or off having a cup of tea I can't see they'll be best pleased.'

'No. I suppose not.'

He wondered what she was thinking. Wondered even if she had forgotten that it happened. Maybe he was making too much of it. Then she broke the tension.

'The other night . . .' she said.

So there it was; she had mentioned it. 'Yes.'

'I'm sorry if what I did upset you. I didn't mean to.'

'Didn't mean to do it?'

'No. Didn't mean to upset you.'

'Well you didn't upset me.'

'So you don't mind?'

'No.'

She turned to him and smiled. 'That's all right then.'

When Sarah arrived at work that morning she found Gary sitting behind his desk looking particularly smug.

'Hello. You look pleased with yourself. Something you'd like to share?'

'I thought we'd already done that,' he said.

'Oh, very clever. So is that look the sort of look I'm going to get every morning from now on?'

'Probably not.'

She hung up her coat and turned round. He flattered himself that he detected a look of disappointment. 'Oh?'

'Had a bit of a breakthrough at the weekend. At least I hope it was a breakthrough.'

'Go on.' She came over and perched on the edge of his desk and he made an extra effort to avoid looking at her legs for too long.

'Well, what did we notice about Mr Tan last week? Where did he go?' asked Gary.

'To the Chinese restaurant . . . the . . . whatsitsname . . . the Red Dragon.'

'Where else?'

'Er . . . assorted business meetings . . . and Harley Street.'

'Exactly.'

'So it's Harley Street that's important. I was right,' she said triumphantly.

'It's Harley Street that *could* be important. I'm not saying that I know for sure, but I've been doing some research.'

'Drug running. Is that it? You've found evidence?'

'No. Not yet.'

'What then? Don't tell me. Mr Tan's into dodgy cosmetic surgery. He leaves all his patients looking like the Bride of Wildenstein and then does a runner with the money?'

'He could do, but I think it's unlikely.'

'So what's left?'

'Transplants.'

Sarah looked puzzled. 'He's selling his organs?'

'Not his. Other people's.'

'How could he do that?'

Gary was warming to his subject. 'Well, if you've been reading the newspapers over the past year or so . . .'

'Which I have . . .'

'You might have seen bits about corpses being relieved of their organs before they were released to relatives for burial.'

'Yes.'

'It seems there's a massive market out there, and an illegal one at that.'

'Illegal in what way?'

'Criminal gangs work out deals with undertakers – or even dodgy hospital staff – and arrange for the removal of body parts for sale to transplant companies.'

'Transplant *companies*?'

'Yes. If you have enough money they'll find you a heart or a kidney or whatever you want, and arrange a transplant.'

'You make it sound like buying a car.'

'A very expensive car.'

'So you think Mr Tan is involved with dodgy undertakers?' asked Sarah, sliding off Gary's desk and walking round to her own.

'Not necessarily. Let me set this out for you. The National Health Service is all well and good except that waiting lists are still far too long, regardless of what the government says. Result? More and more people are going private, so they can skip queues. But that still presupposes, where transplants are concerned, that there are enough organs to go round.'

'Which there aren't,' chipped in Sarah.

'Correct. So, another private market develops, where the very rich can go completely independent and book into a Harley Street clinic, for instance, which specializes in transplants.'

'So if you're rolling in dosh, but need a new kidney, you can get one straight away?'

'Exactly. But where do these organs come from?

'Corpses?'

'Not always.'

'No. I remember reading about poor people in some country or other who will sell a kidney to earn money.'

'That's right. In Moldova, for instance – desperately poor country, sandwiched between Romania and the Ukraine – people actually mortgage their bodies. They'll sell one of their kidneys for a few thousand quid. And what does it sell for to a prospective patient? Go on, guess.'

'Ten grand?'

'As much as ninety-five thousand pounds.'

'Bloody hell!' Sarah sat back in her chair. 'But what makes you think Mr Tan is involved? He's never been to Moldova – at least not since we've been tracking him.'

'No. But Moldova's only one of the countries involved. Israeli patients fly to Turkey and get most of the Moldovan kidneys. There are brokers in New York who work with

Russian immigrants; rich Palestinians go to Iraq, and Nigerian doctors can help you out if you live in South Africa.'

Sarah whistled. 'So it's a world-wide trade?'

'You bet. And one involving a hell of a lot of cash. They reckon that the bone theft industry in the States . . .'

'Bone theft?'

'Yes, they use bones for transplants, too – about four hundred thousand of them every year – and for grinding up to make dental filler.'

Sarah grimaced.

'Yes, look after your teeth. Anyway, the bone theft market in the States is worth about five hundred million dollars a year.'

'What about over here?'

'In the UK it's illegal to profit from trading in body parts. That means all such trading is driven underground. It wasn't always the case in other countries. There are new restrictive laws in India now. And that means it's recently been overtaken in the transplant export market by which country?'

'China?'

'Got it in one, Miss Perry.' Gary leaned back in his chair and folded his arms behind his head. 'The organs you can buy in India come mainly from live donors but China's do not.' He paused.

Sarah leaned forward in her chair. 'Go on.'

'Well, it's not very nice. Condemned prisoners in China are shot through the head to avoid damaging their organs which are then sold.'

'That's gross.'

'Well, it's a fact of life. There are figures from Amnesty International.' Gary rifled through the papers on his desk.

'Here we are. In 1996 they reported that ninety per cent of all transplanted organs in China come from executed prisoners.'

Sarah stood up and walked to the window. 'How depressing.'

'Depressing but unbelievably lucrative. If you're stinking rich but your life depends on a new kidney, you'll spend whatever it takes to get one.'

'And Mr Tan can oblige?'

'Probably. Of course, I don't know for certain. It's only a thought. But we can't link him with drugs, and if he's not visiting Harley Street for private medical reasons it seems to me that it would make sense of everything we've seen. Or am I jumping to conclusions?'

Sarah shook her head. 'No. Not necessarily. But it's one heck of an assumption.'

Chapter 17

The sage has the sun and moon by his side. He grasps
the universe under the arm. He blends everything into
a harmonius whole, casts aside whatever is confused or
obscured, and regards the humble as honourable.

Chuang Tzu, c.369–286BC

Christopher couldn't remember when he had last lit a
candle. He thought he'd make an effort. It would be the last
time he would see Ellie for a while. She'd be with him until
the end of the week, she had said, but he reckoned that
most evenings she'd be catching up with her mates and so
he would make the most of tonight.

'Are we dressing for dinner?' she'd asked. With tongue in
cheek he'd replied, 'Of course,' but he was surprised when
she came down in a sparkly top with her long fair hair cas-
cading over her shoulders.

'You know, when you make an effort it's quite amazing
what you can look like,' he teased.

'Yes. Well, it's just a shame you didn't do the same.'

'I'm always smart,' he countered.

'Except when you're gardening.'

'OK. Point taken. Would you like me to go and change?'

'Don't be daft. Only kidding. Anyway, this is probably the last chance I'll get to wear anything decent before I go back to Africa.'

'I thought you'd be out on the town.'

'Not out. In. It's better to see my friends at home, then we can talk properly instead of shouting over all that loud music.'

Christopher smiled. 'I thought I was supposed to think like that, not you.'

'Oh, I don't know, Dad. I can't take the racket like I used to.'

'At twenty-three?'

'And three-quarters.'

Christopher poured her a glass of wine and they sat down at either side of the old oak table in the kitchen. 'I don't remember when I last did this,' he said.

'That's sad,' said Ellie. 'Maybe you'll be doing more of it soon. Have you asked her round to dinner?'

'Who?'

'Who do you think? Maria, of course.'

'No. Not yet. Don't want her to think I'm pushing things. We're going to the opera on Wednesday, though. *Tosca*. At Covent Garden.'

'Safe.'

'What do you mean?'

'Well, not much time to talk. Except in the interval. Not much time to get to know one another.'

'We're getting to know one another quite well, I think. I told you – I've been to look at her rose bush – and she sits down with me for lunch some days.'

Ellie giggled. 'How romantic! You've been to look at her rose bush . . .'

Christopher sounded hurt. 'Well it's all right for you. I mean people of your age are expected to go on dates and go out to dinner. It's the most normal thing in the world. People of my age are already fixed up, and when you're not, and you want to do something about it, it seems much more calculating. You don't seem to be able to do anything without it having . . . great significance.'

'And does this one have great significance?'

'I don't know yet. It might have.'

Ellie took a sip of her wine, then said, 'Would you *like* it to have great significance?'

Christopher thought for a moment. 'Yes. I think I probably would,' And then, 'But it's early days.'

'Are you still worrying about mum?'

'Of course.' He took a gulp of the wine. 'Never stop.'

'Dad, I know I shouldn't really say this . . .'

Christopher looked up from his glass.

'You're going to have to get a life of your own.'

He sighed. 'Fancy you having to tell me that. How very grown-up.'

'No. Not grown-up. Just realistic. I know it might seem disloyal, and I don't want to be disloyal to either of you but . . . well . . . mum's made her own life now. You can't just sit back and let life slip away. Who cares if you have to go out on a date or two? You're not that old. You're still quite dishy.'

'Me? Dishy?'

'Yes! Some of my friends' mums go quite weak at the knees whenever your name is mentioned.'

'Don't be silly.'

'They do! You're a good catch.'

'For a gold-digger?'

'That's just Matt being protective.'

'Of me or your mother?'

'Both. I think really he'd like you back together . . .'

Christopher interrupted, 'I don't think that's being realistic . . .'

'But I know he wants you to be happy, too.'

'But cautious?'

Ellie shook her head. 'I think you're naturally cautious. I mean you haven't exactly made an effort to find a new partner have you?'

Christopher took a deep breath. 'I did go on the internet.'

'What?'

'Well, it seemed an innocuous sort of thing to do. I just typed in "soulmate" to see what would come up.'

Ellie's eyes lit up. She leaned across the table on her elbows. 'What happened?'

'Disastrous. One hypochondriac, one rather dull librarian and one who was . . . how shall I put it? . . . rather keen on the physical side of things.'

'Dad! You didn't . . . ?'

'No I did not. I got her out of here before her feet could touch the ground.'

'You invited her round here?'

'Well, I thought it might be a bit more private. I didn't want to do my . . . courting . . . in public. In front of patients, with them all nudging and winking.'

'I'd never thought of that.'

'No. Most people don't. There's no anonymity when you're the local doctor. They all mutter and give each other knowing glances. Well, they would if given half a chance. So I thought I was safer here. Wrongly as it turns out.'

'But Maria. She seems very nice.'

Ellie noticed that her father's whole demeanour changed at the mention of her name. The hunted look disappeared. His face relaxed.

'Yes. She is. And she likes gardening. And opera. Your mum never . . . well . . .'

'No,' said Ellie softly.

'And we talk. A lot. About all kinds of things.'

'And there's no other man in her life?'

'Not as far as I can make out. I mean, I haven't asked her or anything. But there's no sign of a man round at the house. Her children have left home. Apparently she's divorced, so Erica told me. Has been for some time.'

'Well I think it's lovely.'

'Do you now?' Christopher got up and walked over to the Aga. 'I only hope you think the same about your dinner. What would you say to a little fish?'

'Hello little fish,' she said.

Tiger and Erica were sitting down to a meal of their own when the call came at half past ten that evening.

'Mr Wilson?'

'Yes.'

'Do you think you could come down to the police station please? We've caught someone trying to break into your shop.'

They went down together. Tiger drove.

'Do you think it's him?' asked Erica.

'They didn't say.'

'If they've got him that would be such a result.'

'Yes. I'd like to punch his lights out.'

Erica seemed surprised. 'That's not like you.'

'Well, we've never been done over like this before. I didn't realize how I'd feel about it I suppose.'

'Well, now you know.'

'Yes. I mean, we're not that well off. Comfortable, yes, but not rolling in it. And whatever we've got we've earned. It just pisses me off that somebody else thinks they can have it by lobbing a brick through your window. It's as if they're saying "Why waste your time working for it, mate, when all you need is a bit of muscle?" It makes me angry.'

Erica rested her hand on his arm as he was driving. 'It really doesn't matter you know. Not that much.'

'It does matter. It matters to me.'

She sat quietly for the rest of the journey. The police station was only a few minutes away. They parked outside and walked up the steps.

Tiger spoke to the young policeman behind the desk. 'The name's Wilson. You caught someone trying to break into our shop.'

'Oh, yes sir. Would you like to come this way?'

The young policeman – he could only be in his early twenties, thought Tiger – led them down a corridor and tapped on one of the side doors. 'Come in.'

The policeman showed them in. 'Mr and Mrs Wilson, sir. The shop owners.'

'Ah, yes. Come in.'

The room was small. There was nobody in it but a plain-clothes policeman. An overweight man in his forties with an open-necked shirt and a brown jacket. One wall of the room had a large window in it, and on the other side of the

168

window was another room. A room with a table surrounded by several chairs.'

'Mr Wilson, Mrs Wilson.' He nodded at them and shook their hands. 'Detective Sergeant Evans. We caught someone trying to break into your shop tonight – through the front door. I know you had a bit of bother last week, and just wondered if you've seen any of these before.' He gestured in the direction of the window. 'They can't see you. It's special glass.'

Tiger and Erica looked through the window at the three teenage youths slumped around it. Then they looked at one another. Erica shook her head. Tiger sighed. 'No, Sergeant. No, we've not seen any of them before.'

The sergeant registered their disappointment. 'It would have been neat if it had been the guy you complained about last week, I know. But we just wondered if there was any way you could associate him with these three.'

'No, I'm afraid not.'

'Well, they've had a go at one or two other shops as well. Maybe we've found our men. With any luck, the two things won't be related and hopefully you won't hear any more from your caller.'

Tiger nodded. 'Well, thanks very much. What do we do now?'

'They didn't manage to get in. Our lads caught them in the act of trying. Bashed the lock a bit, but the shop is still secure. We can sort it out from here. Though you'll probably want to claim on your insurance for any damage.'

He saw the worried look cross Erica's face. 'Only a bit of paint work. Nothing serious. We got them before they could really get stuck in.'

'So what will happen to them?' asked Tiger.

'Oh they'll probably go to a detention centre for a bit. It might help. It might not. Only time will tell. But at least we've stopped them for now. I'm sorry to have called you out, but hopefully this will be an end to your troubles.'

If only it were that easy, thought Tiger.

Gary, at home alone in the 'penthouse' flat, found his mind musing on two things. Sarah was the first, and Christopher was the second. Sarah had said she could not see him that night. She did not say she couldn't see him any night, but she did seem to be asserting her independence; stopping him from thinking that the conquest had been made; showing that she was not necessarily his for the asking. It did not surprise him. He knew she wouldn't be that much of a pushover, even if the easy way they had climbed into bed on Saturday night might have given that impression. Life, and love, he knew was seldom that straightforward. He would play it cool. As long as he did not have to play it cool for too long. Having been intimate with her once, he was quite keen to be intimate with her again. He also had another feeling. Had some difficulty in identifying it. It was a kind of unease. He tried to put it out of his mind.

Christopher occupied his mind for professional reasons. He could do with talking to a doctor, and Christopher was the only one he knew. There were sources at work that he could talk to, but that would mean putting his cards on the table, and at the moment all he had was a theory, nothing more. There was no hard evidence. He wondered if Christopher would level with him, confidentially. Tell him what he knew about the transplant trade in Britain. Of course, he might not know anything at all. He was a GP, a family doctor. But then he must have had patients in need of transplants.

He just needed to get a better feel for the lie of the land. The sort of feel you could not get by reading a book or a newspaper. But how to broach the subject without making Christopher suspicious?

Maybe he could give the impression that he was taking Tiger up on his 'secret society' idea. It was a bit risky, and a bit far fetched, but just supposing the domino club secret society took an interest in finding out more about illegal transplants.

'Ha!' He heard himself laughing out loud. It was a fatuous idea. And a dangerous one. Risky professionally, too, for someone in his position. But there was no danger in simply talking about it, was there? Without giving his own position away. He could make sure the subject was dropped before they ever thought about actually *doing* anything. Anyway, he knew Christopher would be reluctant to get involved in anything medical, and Tiger? Surely this would be too much of a big issue for him, too?

Well, he could at least talk to them, as mates, about this thing he had been reading about. Get their take on it – Christopher from a medical point of view and Tiger? Well, he could pretend to talk to Tiger about transport arrangements. How would they get the organs from one place to another? He could stop them from talking to anyone else and, equally important, he could make sure that he wound up their 'involvement' before they appeared to get anywhere. And at least it would give him a chance to talk things over with someone other than Sarah. Both Tiger and

Christopher were bright. They might even add their own bit of knowledge.

Oh it was ludicrous all right, but every now and again, the ludicrous yielded results. Put like that, he had nothing to lose.

Chapter 18

A kiss can be a comma, a question mark or an exclamation point.

That's basic spelling that every woman ought to know.

Mistinguette, 1875–1956

After a short burst of frenetic activity, the Adventure Bookshop had calmed down. Now it was more like the usual Wednesday morning. Erica could have done with a game of tennis to get her endorphins going, but Brian's mother in Bournemouth had had a funny turn and he said he'd have to stay with her for a few days if that was all right. How could she refuse?

The shop was empty now, with only the soft sounds of a Mozart tape to break the silence. Erica wandered through to the back to make herself a coffee. At least she had a few minutes to herself. Not that she felt very comfortable about it. She didn't much relish being alone on the premises after the events of the previous few days, and aside from her worries about security, she was unsettled in her mind about other things.

Something wasn't right. She could not define it, and Tiger certainly never said anything, but he remained withdrawn. Disconnected from her. She could have a conversation with him and he'd give her his full attention, but then he'd drift off again.

He didn't spend much time in the same room as her, and in bed he seldom came over to her side; spent most of the time facing in the opposite direction. She tried to tell herself it was just a passing phase, and yet sadness gnawed at her. There were moments when she felt she could take it up with him, but they seemed to slip through her fingers before she could properly grasp them, leaving her once more in a vacuum of emotion. She seemed almost marooned by her feelings.

Her train of thought was broken by the sound of the shop bell. She took a deep breath and came out of the back room to find Kate Devon standing in front of the counter.

'Kate!' She put her arms round her and kissed her on both cheeks, and when she stepped back she noticed that Kate's eyes were filled with tears.

'Are you all right? What is it?'

'Oh, I'm sorry. I'm fine. It's just that I haven't seen you for ages.' Her eyes scanned the towering shelves of books. 'Haven't seen this place for ages.'

'We're still here.'

'I'm glad. I wouldn't like to think it had all disappeared. The old world I mean.'

Erica smiled ruefully. 'No. The old world is still here. Limping on.'

Kate regarded her quizzically, as if questioning the fact

that she could be back in her old world and find it just the same as when she left.

'Look, do you want a coffee? I don't mean here. We might be disturbed. I'll close for half an hour.'

'Are you sure? Only I don't want to . . .'

'Of course I'm sure. I want to hear all your news.' Erica pulled down the blind on the shop door, hastily scribbled 'Open again at noon' on a piece of card and placed it in the side window. 'Come on.'

She took Kate to a small cafe further down the alley, and they sat at a table tucked away in the corner where they could talk without being overheard.

'So tell me all about him. Howie, is it?'

Kate replied without much enthusiasm. 'Yes. Howie. In Barcelona this week.'

'And you're not with him? How can you resist Barcelona? All that architecture. Goudi, and the Ramblas . . .' Erica's enthusiasm was in marked contrast to Kate's low-key responses.

'Well, when you've already done it three times it doesn't have quite the original appeal.'

Erica could see that the first bloom of love was beginning to wear off. 'So where are you living?'

'Rome mostly, but I thought I'd come here for a few days. On my own.'

'To Winchester?'

'No. To London. I thought I'd pamper myself in the Ritz for a while.' She gazed wistfully out of the window in the direction of the cathedral. 'Though to be honest I think I'd rather be in a B&B in Winchester.'

'Well stay the night then.'

'Oh, Erica, I couldn't. I've nothing to wear.'

Erica looked at Kate in her well-cut dark brown trouser suit, her brown crocodile boots and her trim bob of blonde hair, then glanced down at her own body encased in nondescript working clothes. For a moment her own sadness resurfaced, then she said drily, 'Well you could make do with the rags you've got on. And we do have clothes shops in Winchester if you need any more.'

Kate smiled apologetically. 'Oh, I couldn't.'

'Yes, you could. And, anyway, Tiger's out tonight and I could do with a bit of company. How do you fancy a girl's night in?'

Kate's face relaxed. 'To tell you the truth, I'd love one.'

'Supper on our laps in front of the fire?'

'Only if it's something ridiculously simple.'

'Well, that's that sorted. All you have to do now is fill the afternoon. You could come and help me in the shop.'

Kate shook her head. 'I think that would be more than I could bear. I'll go and do a bit of shopping. Get myself a toothbrush and things. Maybe another top.' Then she saw Erica grinning at her.

'I know. I haven't changed. Well, not much.'

'You want to do what?' Sarah was looking at Gary as though he'd lost the plot.

'He's the only doctor I know. I'm not going to give anything away. Just sound him out a bit. Anyway, I haven't actually got anything to give away. It's only guesswork.'

'Educated guesswork.'

'Yes, but we're still in the dark really. I've got Ben Atkinson to make some enquiries in Harley Street but I'm not that hopeful. They're a tightly knit bunch.'

Sarah dropped a file on to his desk. 'Well, here you are. Mr Tan's latest movements.'

'Any more visits to Harley Street?'

'Three. One on Monday and two yesterday.'

'In which case he's either very ill or very greedy.'

'He doesn't look especially poorly,' said Sarah briskly.

'But we still don't know for sure that it's transplants he selling, not drugs. And there's still the possibility of the protection racket, even though all the police have come up with so far is a group of layabouts looking for a bit of excitement. We can't go much further until we have a positive lead.'

Sarah sighed. 'I suppose you're right. But just be careful. Don't let anything slip about what you do.'

Gary frowned at her.

'I know. I'm stating the obvious. But I don't want to have to worry any more about you. You're enough of a liability as it is.'

'Am I?'

'More than enough.'

'Enough to make you want to . . .'

Sarah coughed loudly. 'Ahem! Walls have ears . . . even here.' She looked around to check that no one was interested in their conversation. Then she lowered her voice to a whisper. 'To make me want to what?'

'Come home with me tonight,' Gary muttered as he shuffled the papers on his desk.

'Maybe.'

Safe was what Ellie had said it would be. Funny. Christopher felt anything but safe. He had taken ages to choose his tie, checked three times to make sure that he had the tickets, and set off for London in his car allowing two hours for the journey. Maria had said she would already be in London that day. She was meeting her daughter to go around the Wallace Collection. Something to do with her fine arts degree.

She must have detected the apprehension in Christopher's voice. 'It's all right,' she said, 'she'll have gone by the time we meet.'

Christopher stood on the pavement outside the Floral Hall as a cold north wind whipped down Bow Street and away towards the river. The Opera House foyer was crowded already. Had he told her the right time? Maybe she would decide against it. They were irrational thoughts, he knew, but his mind played upon them nevertheless.

Then, out of the melee of pedestrians, came a small figure. At first he was not sure that it really was Maria. She was smartly dressed in a fitted cream coat and her eyes seemed more defined, her whole face more glowing than before.

'Goodness.' The word was out before he could recall it.

'I know,' she said. 'I scrub up well.'

'No, it's just that . . .'

'I don't dress up for work?'

Christopher beamed at her. 'You look lovely.' Then he looked at his watch. 'Time for a glass of champagne?'

'You're in charge,' she said. And then, quite naturally and with no fuss at all, she slipped her arm into his and they walked into the Floral Hall.

Gary had wondered if Sarah's 'maybe' would translate itself into a 'maybe not'. As the end of their working day approached he had carefully, and against all his usual inclinations, avoided mentioning the subject again. They had done more work on Mr Tan. Gary had been out to walk the length of Harley Street and took a look at the particular properties where the Chinese gentleman seemed to have been conducting his business, and then he had set to finding out which of the occupants were his likely hosts.

Sarah had been involved in tying up the loose ends of another case involving a Russian diplomat who had gone missing. It was one of life's anticlimaxes. He had been discovered in Paris under another identity, for no other reason than the job had all become too much for him. What had seemed like a case of espionage had turned out to be nothing more than a rather sad breakdown. Things did not always turn out as you expected.

Gary looked at his watch, then volunteered, 'Right. That's me done.' He pressed the shutdown button on his laptop and got up from his chair.

Sarah watched him from her desk. He glanced over. She shut down her own laptop and got up. 'OK, Mr Flynn. But we'd better not leave together. I'll meet you at Waterloo. Platform nine.'

'Why nine?'

'That's my lucky number.'

Gary was not sure what would happen when they got back to his place. He planned to cook her supper – not the steak and fries a girl might expect from a man of Gary's general demeanour – but sole Veronique. Women generally went for a bit of fish, and he was rather proud of his sole Veronique.

They had hardly got in the door when Sarah turned to kiss him. It was not a gentle kiss. It was hungry and urgent.

He felt her arms around his body, felt them sliding down his back. He cradled her head in his right hand and leaned into her. Slowly he lowered his hand to her breasts and began to caress them. She murmured softly as he slid his hand inside her sweater, but did nothing to resist him.

Eventually she eased away from him gently. 'Come on.' She took his hand and pulled him towards the bathroom.

'What?'

'Got any candles?'

'Er . . . yes . . . I think so. Somewhere.'

'Well you find them. I'll run a bath.'

Gary's feet barely touched the ground. He found the candles. He also found a bottle of chilled white wine. They had their bath, and it was at least two hours before he got round to cooking the sole Veronique.

Simply to sit next to someone who was enjoying watching what you were watching, and who was hopefully enjoying the fact that they were watching it with you, was enough for Christopher. Puccini's music filled the air and saturated their senses. 'Do we have to go?' Maria asked at the end.

Christopher laughed. 'I don't think there's any more.'

Maria looked disappointed. 'No. It's such a sad ending but, oh, that music!'

'Blame your mother,' said Christopher as he walked her out of the Opera House towards his car.

'What?'

'It's probably because you're half Italian that it touches you so much.'

'You're not Italian, and it touches you.'

'Yes, but I'm a romantic.'

'Ah, I see.'

They talked animatedly on the way home, about the opera, about Maria's afternoon with her daughter, about Fragonard's painting of the girl on the swing in the Wallace Collection, which Christopher said he loved, but whose sky Maria found too threatening. 'You wouldn't have got me up on that swing with those thunderclouds.'

When Christopher dropped her off she invited him in for a coffee. He was hesitant. 'If you're sure?'

'Of course I'm sure. Come on.'

She got out of the car before he could walk round to open the door, then led him into the house. They talked easily while she put the kettle on and gathered cups and saucers in the kitchen, then she motioned him through to the small sitting room at the front of the house where they sat and drank their coffee. It was a tiny room, decorated in soft yellows that glowed warmly in the light of table lamps. Christopher sat in a cream armchair, Maria on a small two-seater sofa.

'Perhaps we could do it again?' he asked tentatively.

'Rude not to,' she replied.

'Only next time we'll go out and eat. Then we'll have more time to talk.'

'I might run out of conversation,' she said.

'Do you really think so?'

She paused for a moment, then said, 'No. No, I don't. Not with you.'

Eventually Christopher stood up and made a move to go. Maria stood up, too, and walked towards him. 'Thank you so much,' she said. 'For such a great time.'

'No. Thank *you*. It made such a change.'

It all seemed so desperately polite, thought Christopher. Like two people testing the water. Afraid to overstep the

181

mark. Each wondering what the other was thinking but not daring to ask.

Maria smiled. 'Are you out of practice as much as I am?'

Christopher nodded. 'I guess.' He laid his arms on her shoulders and bent to kiss her gently on the lips. Then he straightened up with his arms still around her and she lay her head on his chest.

'What a day,' she said. 'What a lovely day.'

As Erica had promised, she gave Kate supper on her lap.

'It's nothing special, I'm afraid. Marks and Sparks best.'

Kate, wrapped up in a white towelling robe and sitting in front of a roaring log fire, spooned up the moussaka with a fork and almost purred. 'If you knew how much I longed to do this . . .'

Finally, Erica asked, 'Is it not how you thought it would be?'

Kate was defensive at first. 'I knew what I was doing, Erica. Made up my mind what I really wanted. How could I not be happy? I have everything. A guy who makes a fuss of me, the chance to travel all over the world, and plenty of money. I can indulge myself with whatever I want. That's all a girl needs, isn't it?'

Erica took her time over her mouthful of food. Then she said, 'Is it?'

Kate spoke softly. 'Not really, no.' She put down the plate and picked up her glass of wine, taking a large gulp. 'I don't know why.' She gazed into the roaring fire. 'I remember being so frustrated with Christopher. So annoyed that he never seemed to be able to give me any time. He was always so busy with his patients,' she half laughed, 'or his garden. But the time we did spend together was somehow . . . whole.'

'As in wholesome?'

'No. As in complete.' She turned to Erica. 'Does that make sense?'

'Yes.'

'The trouble was, it just wasn't enough. There wasn't enough of it. I wasn't completely satisfied.'

'Maybe it's not possible to be completely satisfied,' Erica said, softly.

'You don't think I'm someone who thinks the grass is always greener on the other side of the fence?'

'A bit. You did go, Kate. You did have the choice.'

'Yes. I'm just not sure I made the right one.'

'Does Howie know you're not happy?'

'I think he suspects. I've not been the best of company lately. For anyone.'

Erica leaned forward and rested her hand on Kate's. 'We all make mistakes, you know.'

'I've heard that a few times. Not very original. But true in my case.'

'So you think you made a mistake? Looking back, I mean?'

'Yes. Yes, I do. And I wish I could undo it all and start again.'

'Well, there's nothing to stop you is there?' asked Erica. As she said the words she remembered her last meeting with Christopher and the look in his eyes when he had talked about Maria.

Kate looked troubled. 'I don't know.' She picked up the plate of food and spooned a little of it into her mouth. Eventually she asked, 'If I went to see Christopher, do you think he'd take me back?'

'Oh Kate, I don't know. Only Christopher knows the answer to that one. It's been a long time . . .'

Kate pulled her feet up under her body and sat back in the chair. 'What about you and Tiger? You've lasted the course.'

'So far . . .'

'That doesn't sound very hopeful.'

'We're just going through a tricky patch at the moment. Nothing serious. At least I don't think so. We just seem to be in different worlds, Tiger especially. He seems preoccupied. Somewhere else altogether.'

'There's nobody else is there? With Tiger I mean?'

'Good God no! I think I'd know if there was. It's just our age I suppose, and the fact that we've been together so long. It does make you take each other for granted. You do get used to things, perhaps not be as attentive as you used to.'

'Better that than the alternative, believe you me. It's probably just a phase. Probably something to do with work. It usually is.'

'I suppose so. I wouldn't like to think we're going to fall apart. Not after all this time. It'd be such a waste.' Then she realized her lack of tact. 'Sorry. I didn't mean . . .'

'Oh, that's all right. I brought it all on myself and now I'm having to live with it. Anyway, where's Tiger tonight? Off playing dominoes?'

'No. That's Friday nights. He's away on business tonight. Has to stop over in Jersey or Guernsey I think. He's coming back tomorrow.'

'Does he go away a lot?'

'It varies. Sometimes not for a couple of weeks, then he'll have the odd week when he's away all the time. Like last week.'

'And you don't mind?'

'Part of the job. I do worry. About the flying. And I think

about him a lot. But you've just got to get on with it really, haven't you?'

The Jersey hotel where Tiger and Sam were staying over-looked the sea. The little restaurant served excellent seafood, but Tiger was happier with the steak and kidney pudding. They had a bottle of Spanish red with their meal and retired for the night at around half past eleven. Tiger said goodnight to Sam outside the door of her room.

She looked up at him. 'Why don't you come in? Then we can say goodnight properly.'

Chapter 19

And life is given to none freehold, but it is leasehold
for all.

Lucretius, c.94–55BC

Tiger did not appear at breakfast the following morning.
Sam tapped on his door at eight thirty but he didn't answer.
She rang him on the internal telephone. No reply.
Eventually she asked the manager if he could let himself
into Tiger's room to make sure everything was all right. The
manager was reluctant. He suggested that Tiger might have
gone out for a walk. The thought had occurred to Sam as
well, but she had expected to see him at breakfast. At nine
o'clock the manager telephoned Tiger's room. Still no reply.
When, at last, Sam persuaded him to take his pass key and
let himself in, she wished that she had acted sooner.

Sam flew with him in the air ambulance, her face ashen,
her body shaking. A stroke the doctor said. It was a pity

they had not discovered him earlier. A pity that no one had been with him at the time. Sam considered the irony and injustice of it all. If he had agreed to have come to her room she *would* have been with him and been able to act more quickly. But then the very fact that she had been there would have raised other questions.

Would Tiger's unwillingness to be unfaithful cost him his life? How stupid. How surreal. She could not believe it had happened the way it had. Here she was, sitting next to his bed, stroking the back of his hand, waiting for his wife to arrive, and blaming herself for the fact that she had not insisted they break into his room earlier, for taking him out to dinner . . . There seemed to be no end of reasons she could find why it was her fault.

She looked at his prone body, at the wires and the tubes and the drips. How could a man who was flying helicopters in the sky yesterday be so grounded and fettered to a bed just hours later?

The doctor came back into the room. 'Miss Ross?'

She heard her name echoing. She looked up at him with a vacant stare.

'The gentlemen you brought over here – from Southampton – I think they need to be taken back.'

'But what about . . . ?'

'Mr Wilson's wife is on her way. We'll take good care of him until she arrives.'

The reality of the situation bit into her. His wife would be coming. She could get back to her job. She was no longer needed here. 'Yes. Of course.' She got up from her chair and looked down at Tiger, half covered by the crisp white sheet. For a moment she did not see the tubes and the wires; only the naked body of the man, lying there, hardly breathing, his eyes closed against the world. Softly she traced her index finger down the back of his hand, then turned and left the room.

Gary Flynn had two mobile phones. One was a work number, known only to his colleagues, the other was a personal phone. He left the personal one switched off most of the time, milking it for messages at the end of the day, which is why it was not until the evening that he discovered what had happened to Tiger.

Christopher's message was short and to the point: 'Gary, it's Christopher. Bad news, I'm afraid. Tiger's had a stroke and is in hospital in Jersey. Erica's over there with him. Can't tell you much more. He's comfortable but still in intensive care. Give me a ring this evening, will you? I'll be in. Thanks.'

Gary did not ring Christopher. Instead he called in. It was about eight o'clock when he rang the doorbell, Ellie let him in.

'Hello Gary. Rotten news isn't it?'

'The worst,' said Gary, and gave Ellie a light kiss on her cheek. 'Nice to see you again. Are you here for long?'

'No. Going back tomorrow.'

'Your dad will miss you.'

'I think he'll be OK. Got another woman in his life now.' She registered Gary's look of surprise. 'Hasn't he told you?'

Gary shook his head.

'Oh, God! Don't say a word, Gary, or I'm dead.' Then she realized the unfortunate choice of word. 'I'm not doing very well tonight, am I?'

'It's OK.' Gary put his arm round her shoulder. 'Your

secret's safe with me. And don't look so worried. I'm sure Tiger will pull through.'

'I do hope so. Dad's in there,' She gestured towards the sitting room. 'I'll see you next time I'm over. I'm going out in a bit and I expect you'll be gone by the time I get back.'

'Well, you take care of yourself. It's a dangerous place, Africa. Lots of wicked people.'

'Oh Gary, you have such a jaundiced outlook on life. You should get out more. Meet people. Instead of being stuck in that office. The world's not nearly so frightening as you think, you know.'

'So how bad is he?' Gary was crouched over a glass of malt, looking into the fire with Christopher.

'Pretty bad.'

'Bloody ironic isn't it?'

'What do you mean?'

'Well, there he was, saying how we should all put a bit of excitement into our lives and now this.'

'Not the kind of excitement he had in mind.'

'Poor sod. You don't realize how much you take your mates for granted until something happens to one of them, do you?'

'No.' Christopher looked thoughtful, as though he were weighing up Tiger's chances. 'It's a shame they didn't get to him sooner. The next twenty-four hours will be critical. God! I've heard that said a few times in the last couple of days.'

Gary looked quizzical.

'Oh, it's all right. Someone else. Lost a colleague this week and I'm still smarting.'

'It's no easier then, when you're a doctor?'

'I wish it were. I'm sure people think it is. That you can somehow distance yourself. And you can, up to a point. You have to. The old surgeon at college – the one who taught us anatomy – always used to point to one of us and then to the cadaver lying on the slab and say, "That is a person, and that is a body; never confuse the one with the other."'

'That simple?'

'Sometimes. Sometimes not. Especially if you know them.'

Gary took a sip of the whisky, then asked, 'So when will we know about Tiger?'

'We should have a better idea of how he's progressing tomorrow. Find out if everything's working properly.'

Gary looked into the flames again. 'Fragile, isn't it?'

'Sorry?'

'Life. As solid and as strong as a rock one minute, then hanging by a thread the next.'

"Fraid so.'

'Like relationships.'

'That sounds ominous. Has Sarah given up on you? Or you on her?'

'Neither actually.'

'Oh?'

Gary turned from the fire and faced Christopher across his glass. 'How old am I?'

'Younger than I am, you keep telling me.'

'I'm fifty. Been happily bonking everything in sight for a good thirty-odd of those years and now . . .' He sighed heavily and shook his head.

'Oh dear.'

'Yes, oh dear.'

'You poor chap. Is this the one then? You've finally realized the error of your ways?'

'Not the error. It was always fine before. I was very happy to shop around.'

'But not any more?'

'It's taken me a while to work out what it was. It's a weird feeling.'

'Well, you won't be the first person who's taken their time to work it out.'

'It's like . . . well . . . a worry. A kind of fear. And at the same time a thrill. Excitement . . . and sadness . . . all rolled into one. A sort of ache.' Then his mood changed. 'Listen to me. I sound like something out of a woman's magazine. I mean, why can't I get a grip? I'm not like this. I don't do this sort of thing. I don't want any ties, do l? I've been perfectly happy living the way I have. It hasn't hurt anybody. Well, I suppose that's not strictly true, but we were all grown-up. I'd given up expecting anything more permanent.' He took a large gulp from his glass. 'Maybe there's something wrong with me. Maybe I should see a doctor. Bloody stupid! At my time of life.'

Christopher spoke softly and considerately. 'If you want a doctor's opinion I'd say that you're exhibiting the classic symptoms of the most virulent of all afflictions.'

Gary turned to him and asked with a note of sarcastic resignation in his voice, 'Is there any cure?'

'Time, in some cases, will affect a cure. But only in some cases. In others, the effects seem to last a lifetime with varying degrees of severity.'

'And you?' asked Gary.

'Well, I was affected by it once, but it went away. Totally without warning. Quite suddenly and unexpectedly.'

'So you're cured?'

'I thought I was. But I think I might be contracting it

again.' Christopher looked thoughtfully into the embers. 'And there's absolutely nothing I can do about it.'

Gary followed his gaze and murmured, 'It's a bugger, isn't it?'

'Yes,' confirmed Christopher, 'it's a bugger.'

Sarah gazed out over the rooftops from the window of her mansion flat in Wimbledon. They were shining. The rain on the slates was caught in the glimmer of a hundred street lamps. It was not a particularly beautiful view, but tonight it seemed almost like fairyland. She pulled the curtains and slid into bed. Her mind ran over the events of the past few weeks. How different it had been then. How different it all was now. Or how different it could be.

Was it too soon to get into another relationship? Was this another relationship? She knew it could be. Knew that he wanted it to be. But for how long? His record up to now had been six months, and that was ten years ago. His current form predicted a duration around the three-month mark. Three months. That was twelve weeks. Or eighty-four days. Did she want to commit herself – all of herself – for eighty-four days?

She switched off the light and turned over, but she could not ignore the shimmering glow of the street lamps beyond her curtains and the gentle sound of spring rain on her windowpane.

In the soft pool of light cast by the hospital lamp, Erica watched Tiger breathing slowly beneath the oxygen mask. The machines at the side of the bed flickered with lights and neon graphs that mapped the progress of his life from moment to moment. The worries of the past few days were gone now. Light years away. They had been replaced with deeper concerns. With matters of life and death.

There was nothing she could do but wait. Absolutely nothing. Except hold his hand, trying to avoid the tube that was slotted into the back of it, and the plaster that held it in place. She stared hard at his expressionless face. It had been so troubled the last time she had seen it. It didn't matter. Not now. She remembered it, instead, smiling, laughing, expressive and mobile. And asleep. She would watch him sometimes, even after thirty years of marriage, while he slept, and wonder what he was dreaming about. Probably flying, she thought, or thinking up another harebrained scheme for his secret society. Another bit of excitement. And where was his excitement now?

She reached over and stroked the dark hair above his forehead, running her fingers through it and feeling the warmth of his scalp. She thought about the girls who would be coming back from university, to see their father like this. And suddenly she was engulfed by panic at the prospect of losing him. She did not want to be without him. Did not want it to end like this, here in some darkened hospital room, in the middle of an island, in the middle of an ocean, miles away from home.

She felt her eyes stinging, found it difficult to focus on his face, and as the tears welled up and streamed down her cheeks, she whispered softly but with fierce intensity, 'Tiger, Tiger, burning bright . . .'

Chapter 20

A child is owed the greatest respect; if you ever have
something disgraceful in mind, don't ignore your son's
tender years.

Satires, Juvenal, AD c. 60–c.130

Christopher felt like a schoolboy being sent off on a trip by
his mother. It should have been him giving instructions to
Ellie as she packed her bags, but it seemed that a role rever-
sal was in progress.

'You must enjoy yourself. You must let go. Have a bit of
fun,' she urged, pushing more T-shirts and shorts into the
already overstuffed holdall.

'Yes,' he responded meekly.

'And don't let Matt persuade you otherwise.'

'No.' He stood up and walked to the window of her bed-
room, shoving his hands deep into his pockets as he looked
out over the garden. 'What do you think?' he asked without
turning round.

'About Maria?'

'Yes. Do you like her?'

'Does it matter?'

He turned round to face her. 'Yes it does. Very much.'

Ellie's face broke into a sympathetic smile. 'I think she's lovely. We had a chat about you. This week. In the kitchen.'

Christopher looked anxious.

'It's all right. It was very polite. I didn't pry. We just talked about her being here, and how she liked the garden and opera and things. Nothing too personal. But I liked her very much. She's very . . .' Ellie struggled to find the right word, '. . . sensitive. And . . . well . . . nice. And I think it's lovely. And that you should get to know her better.' She looked apologetic. 'Am I being bossy?'

'Just a bit.' Then he smiled. 'But it's kind of you to mind.'

Ellie came up to face him, and lifted her arms until they were round his neck. 'I do mind. Desperately. It's been a rotten time for all of us, but I think we need to move on.'

'That's a very brave thing to say.'

Ellie flopped down onto her bed. 'Probably just fighting talk.'

Christopher flopped down next to her. 'Is this all a front?'

'For what?' she asked.

'For your own sake. To help you cope.'

Ellie looked pensive. 'It was once. But I'm coming through now Dad. It was really awful, you know? Like the worst thing that had ever happened to me in my life. I thought I'd die.'

He felt as though he'd been cut by a knife. 'Don't say that.'

'I'm only saying it now because I feel I can. I'm more on

top of it. It's the reason I went to Africa. To have bigger things to think about. Bigger cares and concerns, if you like. And they helped me put my own problems into perspective.' She put her hand on top of his. 'And you are not to worry about me any more. Or to feel guilty, or anything like that. Just remember Destiny's Child.'

Christopher looked sideways at her. 'What?'

'Destiny's Child – "I'm a Survivor".' She grinned.

Christopher shook his head. 'What will I do without you?'

Ellie got up from the bed and began to zip up her holdall. 'You'll cope, Dad. Even if you do sometimes need a rocket up your bum.'

'That's no way to talk to your father!'

'No, Dad – sometimes it's the *only* way to talk to your father.'

The last week had brought rather too many surprises for Christopher's liking. A bit of honest-to-goodness dullness and predictability would have suited him down to the ground round about now. But he didn't get it. No sooner had he waved Ellie off than a dark figure walked up the garden path of the Manor House. A figure that he had seen only a few days before.

'Hello Dad.'

'Matt? I thought you were only here for a day. You said you were going back to the States after your meeting.'

'Change of plan.' And then, under his breath, 'Change of life.'

Christopher ushered his son through the front door and stood back as he hurried past and climbed the stairs to his room. For a moment Christopher stood there, holding the door open, like a hotel doorman waiting for an invisible guest. Then he came to and closed it.

Maria came out of the kitchen. 'Did somebody just come in?' she asked.

It was evening before they had a chance to talk. Or before Matt was ready to talk. The meeting in London had not been a good one. He had known there were going to be shake-ups; what had not been made clear to him was that he was a part of them. A dispensable part. His job, seemingly quite secure, had disappeared due to a merging of posts. They were sorry, they said, but they could see no way of keeping him on. He had done well for them and they were grateful. They would make sure he had a good reference but they would prefer him to leave now without working his notice.

'Why?' Christopher had asked. 'Why, if you're so good, do they not even want you to work out your notice?'

'Frightened of what I might learn,' said Matt.

'But . . . it's all above board isn't it?'

'Of course.'

'So what are you going to learn that you don't know now?'

'Dad, big business is like that. They want you every waking hour of every day, and then when they've done with you they just want you out from under their feet. In case you make waves, or make life uncomfortable for them.'

'And would you have?'

'No. Of course not. But they may think that my relationship would have made it difficult.'

Christopher did his best to be diplomatic. 'In what way?'

'The guy I live with works there, too.'

'So why would that have made matters difficult?'

'He got my job.'

'Oh. I see.' Christopher offered Matt a drink. He refused, but Christopher poured one for himself. 'And where does that leave you now?'

Matt smiled ruefully. 'Without a job and without a partner.'

'Your decision or his?'

'Mutual.'

'But have you talked it through?'

'Yes. He came over here, too. We've been staying in London. He's gone back to the States. I've stayed here. I'll go back in a couple of days. Tie up loose ends.'

'I am sorry, Matt.'

'Yeah. Me too. Just when I thought I'd got everything sorted. Twenty-two years old with a degree in graphic design and half a flat in New York. And I'll have to sell that now. Not much in the way of assets, eh? Not much of a catch, in business or in . . . well . . . anything else really.'

'Don't do yourself down.'

'I really thought I'd cracked it this time, Dad. The job was good, I had plenty of freedom, you know, artistically, and I had someone who wanted to live with me.'

'And he doesn't any more?'

Matt looked at him questioningly. 'Would you? It's not going to work now, is it?'

'No. I suppose not. What . . . er . . . what was his name?'

'Bill. Bill Symons. We met at work. It just sort of clicked. He's in marketing. More their bag I suppose. Better for business than an arty type, though I did do a bit of business studies as well. Not enough as it turned out.' He sighed heavily. 'Listen to me, trying to justify myself.'

'You don't need to do that. You've had a knock. Well, two knocks. You're bound to feel bruised.'

'S'pose so.'

'God, what a week.' Christopher took a gulp of Scotch.

'Yes. I'm sorry to add to it. And sorry to hear about Tiger.'

Christopher raised an eyebrow.

'Ellie phoned me.'

'Ah, I see.' Christopher started to apologize. 'Sorry. I should have called you, only . . .'

'You probably had enough on.'

'No. It's not that. It's just that . . . well, you get used to being on your own. Silly really. Your world shrinks. Then this week it's suddenly expanded again.'

'Thanks to me and Ellie?'

'A bit.'

'And Maria?'

Christopher looked across at him. 'Yes.' Then he asked, 'Do you mind? I mean, do you really mind?'

'What's it to do with me?'

'A lot. You're my son. I'd like . . .'

'My approval?'

'Well, yes. If possible.'

Matt flopped into a chair. 'I don't know her, so I can't really approve or disapprove.'

'You'll meet her. She's here from Monday to Thursday in the mornings.'

Matt shrugged. 'I'll probably miss her. If I go back, I mean.'

Christopher thought carefully about what to say. He could see his son beginning to withdraw into himself; his usual self-defence mechanism. 'I don't want this to be difficult.'

Matt didn't answer. Christopher carried on. 'It's been eighteen months now. I've hardly seen your mother in that time. I don't know what I can do any more.'

'Have you tried to get in touch?'

'How can I? I don't know where she is most of the time. She has a new mobile phone. She hasn't given me the number. And she's made a life with a new man. What would I look like if I kept ringing her up, even if I knew the number? A pathetic ex-husband who couldn't let go.'

His son did not reply.

'I have to make a new life, Matt. If not I'll just turn into a lonely and grumpy old man and no one will want to be anywhere near me – not even you and Ellie.'

Christopher moved over to the chair where Matt was slumped. 'You two are all I've got now. You'll always have me, but I won't always have you. Ellie will go and get married, if not to that self-possessed doctor then to someone else who'll see what a good catch she is, and you'll do the same.'

Matt made to protest, but Christopher interrupted. 'Oh, I know you probably think that's it; that you'll never bother again. That nobody will ever want you and who cares anyway? That's how I felt. Isolated. Totally alone. And miserable. You can get quite used to it. It becomes an art form. Enjoyable in its own way. Well, undemanding anyway. You don't have to make any effort to stay there, believe me. It's dead easy. But then when someone does come along, when you'd all but given up hope, and you find yourself thinking that they're more than just good company; that there's something else there – a spark of joy, of hope – just remind yourself of this conversation. It doesn't matter one jot whether you're a man with a woman or a man with a man, or a woman with a woman, when you've been battling on your own for over a year and somebody comes along who enjoys being with you you'll find yourself actually wanting to get up in the morning.'

It wasn't until he heard himself speaking; heard himself putting his own thoughts into words that he saw how he had begun to change. That Maria had affected him more than he had realized. He began to smile. 'You notice things – colours, smells. Things you've always taken for granted. It might be a cliché, but it's true. It sharpens your senses. Brings you to life. And it's only then that you understand how dead you were before. You wait and see. And nobody should be denied it, or, worse still, deny themselves the chance to explore it.' He stopped and then wondered if, to his son, this all sounded rather foolish. 'That's all.'

Matt sat quietly for a moment, then stood up. 'I'm going to bed,' he said.

Tiger regained consciousness the following day. Erica was with him when he opened his eyes. He appeared to have difficulty focussing at first, but then he seemed to be able to make her out and smiled weakly.

In a sudden rush of relief Erica lay her head on the bed and sobbed. Then she felt his hand stroking her hair, and she lifted her head to look at him, though she could barely see through the veil of tears.

'Where've you been?' she asked. 'Where've you been?'

Christopher was beginning to wonder if he would ever practice again. The locum work at Romsey had dried up – the missing partner had returned from holiday just in time to deal with the onset of a flu epidemic – and nothing else had materialized. He tried not to think about it too much. Tried not to get down. Convinced himself, in Micawber fashion, that something would turn up. Soon with any luck.

In the meantime he found solace in the fact that his garden had never looked better at this time of year, even if a nagging voice reminded him that he had hardly enough money behind him to retire and take up full-time estate management just yet.

He was forking over a flowerbed by the wall when the voice assailed him. 'So this is how you spend your time off. Digging up the daisies.' It was Gary.

Christopher was surprised to see him. He could not recall when Gary had ever been to the Manor House during the day. Come to think of it, he didn't think he'd ever seen Gary during the hours of daylight, except on the rare occasions when he had visited the surgery, and even then it would most likely have been in the evening.

'I thought you only came out at night!' he exclaimed. 'What are you doing here now? You must be really love-sick!'

Gary grinned apologetically. 'No. It's not that. It's something else. Can I come in?'

The day was mild, the daffodils were in full bloom, rippling like a yellow sea, and Gary and Christopher sat on the white bench underneath the yew tree.

'This is a bit disappointing,' said Christopher.

'Why?'

'I normally only sit on this bench with a woman.'

'Difficult times,' said Gary. 'Be grateful for small mercies.'

'I've thought of you as many things but never as a small mercy,' confided Christopher. 'So what are you doing around here, during the day?'

'Oh, I've got the day off,' Gary lied. 'Thought I'd come round and take you out for a pub lunch.'

'Very thoughtful. But I'm not sure I could stomach lunch at the Hare and Hounds – all that cholesterol. And with Tiger . . . well, you know.'

'Any news?'

'Out of danger. Still in hospital on Jersey. They don't want to move him yet, but Erica called to say he's regained consciousness.'

'Thank God! That's worth a celebration on its own. Anyway, there are other pubs around here, aren't there? The Seahorse, that's a good one.'

'Oh, well, if you're going upmarket then I'll join you.'

'I tell you what, though,' said Gary, doing his best to sound offhand. 'I was reading something in the paper that you might know about, but it staggered me . . .'

'What's that?'

'Well, I was reading about all this illegal trading in body parts. For transplants and stuff.'

Christopher looked startled for a moment. 'Oh, yes?'

'I mean, I know it goes on in the States. But does it go on here as well?' He hoped he sounded casual, but something in Christopher's demeanour led him to believe that he might not have succeeded.

Christopher cleared his throat. 'I have heard rumours.'

'Rumours? Is that all?'

'I was trying to be diplomatic. No. Rather more than rumours. It does go on here. Shamefully. There was at least one member of a large hospital's staff who was convicted of supplying material. Bones it was, in that case. But it goes on with organs as well. Strictly illegal of course.'

'So what happens?'

Christopher relaxed a little. 'We have around ten thousand bone transplants a year, so there is a demand for good bones, strange as it may seem. Seven thousand people are waiting for kidneys but there are only three thousand kidney transplants a year. It's actually harder to get a kidney than it used to be.'

'Why's that?' Gary asked.

'Road safety. Our records have improved. Fatal accidents are one of the main sources of organs. Safer roads mean fewer deaths, fewer deaths mean fewer kidneys.'

'So where do we get them from?'

'Abroad in the main.'

'Right. Now I was reading about that.'

'Yes. Most of them come from India. Well, they did until new laws were passed. There was a time, not so long ago, when India was known as the Great Organs Bazaar.'

'That easy?'

'Not any more.'

'I was reading about other countries that do it, though. Moldova, for instance.'

'Yes. It makes my blood boil.'

Gary nodded in agreement, then asked, 'Do you have much involvement with transplants?'

Christopher looked uneasy again. 'A little. I've had patients who've needed them. But I don't have any involvement in locating them. That's down to the hospitals.'

'So everyone stands an equal chance of getting one, then?'

'They should do.'

'But they don't?'

Christopher sighed. 'Money talks, I'm afraid. Even in medicine, it saddens me to say.'

Gary noticed that Christopher had become tight-lipped. His jaw clenched, as though some memory had been reawakened. Then he asked his sixty-four-thousand-dollar question: 'You don't know people who trade in body parts do you?'

'Good God no! Not illegally.'

'Is there a legal way?'

'I do know people who have helped others to jump the queue. Because they can pay. It's not illegal as such but I really can't condone that sort of thing.'

'Unethical?'

'Totally.'

Gary moved the conversation along. 'Of course, you know where the majority of illegal organs come from nowadays?'

'Nigeria?' offered Christopher.

'No,' said Gary, pausing before playing his trump card. 'China.'

Chapter 21

The truth is rarely pure, and never simple.
The Importance of Being Earnest, Oscar Wilde, 1854–1900

'So did you learn much?' asked Sarah.

'Well, I learned that there's enough illegal trading going on over here to make it a very profitable business,' confirmed Gary.

'Did Christopher know anybody involved?'

'No. Not that he would have told me if he had. But I know Christopher won't have any personal experience of it. Far too upright to get himself entangled in that sort of thing.'

'You make him sound dull.'

'Do I? I didn't mean to.'

They were walking along the Thames Embankment, taking a lunchtime stroll. Like previous days in this unusually mild March, the weather was set fair, with little wind and spells of sunshine that were strong enough to warm the back of your neck. Sarah stopped and leaned over the granite wall of the riverbank, looking down at the muddy water.

'I think he's rather lonely. Such a waste.'

Gary leaned on the wall next to her. 'I reckon you've got rather a soft spot for the good doctor.'

'Oh, I wouldn't say that. I just thought he was too good to be on his own, that's all.'

'Like me.'

She glanced at him. 'Was that a question or a statement?'

'Not sure.'

'Are you fishing, Mr Flynn?' She looked down at the river. 'Because you won't catch much in this water.'

'Just because it looks a bit murky doesn't mean it's not full of hidden treasure, you know. You can't always go on appearances; you should know that in our job.'

Sarah turned to look at him and leaned back on the wall. 'What, exactly, are you trying to say?'

Gary remained staring at the water. 'Just that sometimes things change almost without you noticing them. This river used to be one of the dirtiest in Europe. It couldn't support a single fish. Now it's one of the cleanest, but you wouldn't necessarily know that just by looking at it. Appearances can be deceptive.'

'I see. So you think a leopard can change its spots?'

'I wouldn't go that far. But spots can fade, can't they?'

'I'd like to believe that, but I'm not sure I can.'

He turned to her. 'Come home with me tonight.'

'No. Not tonight.'

'Why not?'

'Because I can't come home with you every night.'

'Why not?'

'Because . . . because it's all so sudden. All so quick. I need time.'

'But I thought . . .'

'Gary, I'm not saying "no" full stop. I'm just saying . . . don't rush me. That's all.'

Christopher had thought that he would take Maria to the Hotel du Vin in Winchester. It was smart in that shabby-chic sort of way, with a warm atmosphere. There was always a good buzz of conversation, plenty of people to watch and enough tables in corners to allow them to be tucked away.

Instead, he found himself being taken out by Maria. 'You took me to the opera, so it's only fair that I should take you out to supper.'

'Only if I can pay,' had been his response.

'Certainly not,' had been hers.

Which is how they came to be sitting in the Red Dragon.

'You do like Chinese food don't you?' asked Maria after the waitress had seated them at their table. There was a worried note in her voice. Christopher seemed to be uneasy.

'Yes. Love it. It's just that . . .'

'You don't like it here.'

Christopher snapped out of his reverie and smiled at her. 'Of course I do. I was just thinking about something somebody said to me, that's all. It's not important.'

'Only Charlie was never fond of Chinese food. I suddenly wondered if . . .'

Christopher laid his hand on hers. 'It's fine. Don't worry. I've heard a lot about the place and it'll be good to try it out.'

After a glass of wine Maria began to relax. 'I don't remember the last time I came out to dinner. It's not something we ever did. I suppose that's why I got interested in cooking.'

'Elizabeth David?' He recalled the books on her shelf.

'Yes. And others.'

'I've always thought she must have been a bit scary. A bit of a man-eater by all accounts.'

Maria tried to suppress a smile. 'It's only the culinary techniques that are in the books, not tips on how to treat a man.'

Christopher laughed. 'Tell me about Charlie.'

Maria's smile faded.

'Unless you don't want to?'

'No, it's all right. Not much to tell, really. We married quite young. He was very attractive, very persuasive. In the end I gave in and we got married. Had two children. He was away a lot. Driving lorries on the continent. I suppose I realized something was wrong when his trips got longer and longer. When he came back he was with me in body but not really in mind. It's funny, isn't it?'

'What?'

'Men. How they think you won't notice things.'

'What sort of things?'

'Oh, the fact that their mind is somewhere else. I mean, we're not clairvoyant, but we can tell when something's not right. By all those little things – telephone calls that you interrupt; when they say good-bye very quickly then put the phone down; when they go out for a paper at a strange time of day. That sort of thing.'

'Yes.'

Then she said lightly, 'I'm sorry. You shouldn't have reminded me. I'm not really the suspicious type. Quite happy really. Quite straightforward. On an even keel. Most of the time.'

'Do you miss the company?' he asked.

'Yes. Yes, I do. Not that I had very much of it.' Then she stopped herself. 'Listen to me. We came out to be together, not to talk about the past. But what about you?'

'Oh, married to the job for thirty-odd years, married to a wife for twenty-odd. Job stayed, wife went, then job went. All a bit of a disaster really.'

'How did the children take it?'

'Badly at first. They were older – I mean, at least they weren't in their teens. But I don't think it's easy when your parents split up, whatever your age. It still comes as a shock. Ellie coped with it better than Matt. He always got on better with his mother than with me. Not that we got on badly. It's just that they seemed to have an easier relationship.'

'Father and son rivalry?' asked Maria.

'A bit I suppose. But it wasn't just that. He's gay. I think he thinks that he's been a disappointment to me.'

'And has he?' Maria asked gently.

'No. Not at all. It was a bit of a shock, if I'm honest. But I'm a doctor. I've seen enough of it over the years to know it happens. It doesn't embarrass me or anything like that. But I'd be lying if I said it hadn't made it more difficult; hadn't made the break-up harder, simply because they both continued to share the house with me – when they were at home. I always felt that Matt would rather have been with his mum.'

'You must feel very bitter.'

Christopher sighed. 'No. Not bitter. Sad. Guilty. But not bitter.'

'And now?' she asked.

The look of intense concentration departed. His face

relaxed and broke into a smile. 'Right now I'm happier than I can remember.'

Maria looked self-conscious; as though she had been caught searching for a compliment. Her discomfort was relieved by the arrival of the food, which they spooned out and began to eat.

'How about you?' asked Christopher. 'Are you happy?'

'Yes. More than happy. Content.'

'Perhaps that's the secret.'

'Contentment?'

'Yes. Instead of asking, "Are you happy?", perhaps what people should really ask is, "Are you content?"'

'Isn't that like resignation? Like giving in?'

'I don't think so. I think it's about getting in touch with reality. About balancing aspirations and actuality.'

'That sounds very deep.'

Christopher brightened. 'And very boring.'

'Not boring at all. Thoughtful. Accurate. Considerate. Just what a doctor should be.'

'And a bit safe?'

'Is that what you want to be? Safe?'

'Not really. I think there are times when you have to take risks. Calculated risks.'

'Even in relationships?' she asked.

Christopher was silent for a moment, then he said, 'I think it's a mistake always to rely on your head. I think sometimes you need to let your heart have a bit of a free reign.'

She smiled at him. 'I do so like being with you,' she said.

'And you,' he murmured. 'And you.'

Maria took a deep breath. 'Don't you wonder sometimes, how different it could have been?'

'Mmm?'

'If we'd been born in a different time. Jane Austen's time. I think that sometimes when I look at her name engraved on the floor of the cathedral. How different it all was then.'

'The medical treatment wasn't nearly so good,' said Christopher teasingly.

'No. But the manners were there. Men would bow on meeting a lady, and the lady would curtsey to the man.'

'You'd like to go back to that?'

'No. It's ridiculous. But it was just . . . well . . . the observation of niceties. You know . . .'

'Like letter writing?'

'Yes. Do you write letters?'

'Yes, I do. I think the kids think its silly. They think that I should fire off e-mails like they do. But I like writing letters. I like the paper, and the pen and the ink. I can think about what I'm writing, then fold it all up and put it in an envelope. It seems to me to be special. It seems much more personal than an e-mail.'

'Yes. You're right. It's special. Not ordinary.'

At that moment the waitress came and asked them if everything was all right. Christopher looked up to assure her that it was, and as he did so he noticed a movement in the far corner of the restaurant. A Chinese gentleman in a suit had stood up to greet another man who had just come in. The greeting was quite muted, not ostentatious in any way, but Christopher gazed at them transfixed. The Chinese gentleman was smartly dressed and smoking a fat cigar. He motioned to the other gentleman to sit opposite him, and a waitress poured them both glasses of Scotch whisky. Now that they had sat down they were obscured by the other diners, but Christopher had seen enough.

Maria noticed the change in his mood. 'Are you all right?

'Sorry?' he responded absently.

'Are you sure you like this food?'

'Yes. Yes. It's fine.'

She laid down her chopsticks. 'You know what I was saying about men not thinking that you notice things?'

'Mmm?'

'Christopher!'

He came back to earth. 'Sorry. Yes.'

'What is it? What's wrong?'

He took a deep breath. 'Do you ever do those puzzles in newspapers?'

She looked at him with a bewildered expression. 'What sort of puzzles?'

'Connections, I think they're called. You have to decide how one person who has apparently nothing to do with two or three other people is actually connected to them.'

'Related you mean?'

'Yes. In a way. But not always by blood. They may all have been in a film that was directed by a particular person, or they may all wear wigs or something like that.'

Maria looked genuinely worried. 'Are you sure you're feeling well?'

'Yes. Yes I am. I'm very well, but I've just had what I believe they call an epiphany.'

'I thought that came after Christmas.'

'Usually it does. But in my case I think Christmas has come early this year.'

Maria was still insistent about paying and Christopher overcame his natural inclination to overrule her. He walked her back home through the lamp-lit streets as light rain began

213

to fall. Their conversation seemed more dislocated than normal. Maria knew that for some unaccountable reason his mind was elsewhere.

He kissed her politely at her front door and declined to come in for a coffee. She smiled bravely, but could not ignore the rising feeling of disappointment within her. Whatever it was that had happened in the Red Dragon, it had changed his attitude towards her. She could not imagine what it was, and Christopher, it seemed, had no urge to tell her.

The warm spell of weather went as quickly as it had come, and within twenty-four hours March had turned into a lion rather than a lamb. Squally gusts of wind bent double the stems of the newly opened daffodils and rain lashed against windowpanes. The sky turned from azure blue to threatening pewter grey, the moisture-laden clouds bowling by impatiently and shedding their chilling rain with uncalled for generosity.

Having worked late the previous night, to occupy his mind and avoid dwelling on the fact that Sarah had declined his offer of hospitality, Gary was in no rush to turn up at the office. He had a lie-in, and at eleven o'clock he was walking across Lambeth Bridge, bending forward to slice through the wind. The dull brown Thames below was being whipped into frenzied wavelets, and a lumbering barge slowly butted its way upstream. It was the sort of day that made him grateful he worked in an office.

She would be there already. Sitting at her desk. He could see her in his mind's eye, and his heart leapt. Strange how, having lusted after her for so long, he had now become close to her. Well, closer. There was a difference in the way she affected him now. Before she had been a distraction. Now

she was so much more. Sometimes he had to fight to concentrate. But when they worked together there was a new
dimension to things. A new dimension to his life.

As he walked through the door she looked up and smiled
at him. 'Good morning!'

'I wish,' he replied.

Sarah got up and looked out of the window. 'Not good, is
it? Not to be out there.'

'I knew it. Don't tell me I've got to go out in it.'

'Not till tomorrow.'

'Why?'

'Mr Tan's on the move. Went to Winchester last night
apparently. To the Red Dragon.'

'Damn!'

'Yes. We picked the wrong night.'

'And . . . ?'

'The boss thinks it's time we moved in.'

'I thought I was in charge of this op?' Gary sounded irritated.

Sarah picked up a file and handed it to Gary. 'You would
have been if you'd turned up early enough. We were just
about to send out a search party. Read that . . .'

Gary opened the file and read the first page in silence.
'So we've got him?'

'Yup.'

'And it is transplants?'

'Yup. We managed to get some intelligence on one of the
firms he's been dealing with – after a long process of elimi-
nation.'

'So it's not a protection racket?'

'Nope.'

'Yes!' He punched the air. 'So we're setting the trap?'

'As we speak. And you're a Harley Street specialist.'

'I am? I thought we were sending Ben Atkinson in when we got this far?'

'Ben called in sick this morning. He's gone down with the flu and we don't want to cancel the appointment.'

'Which is when?'

'Mr Tan's expecting you at three o'clock tomorrow afternoon at the lounge in the Savoy '

'Bloody hell! Couldn't we have made it any later? I've not done any prep.'

'Well, we could have made it next week, so that you had time to thoroughly acquaint yourself with the manner of a Harley Street specialist,' said Sarah with a hint of sarcasm, 'but we thought that Mr T. might have got bored waiting and pushed off back to Beijing.'

'Bugger!' muttered Gary under his breath.

Sarah handed him a passport and a wallet. 'Documentation.'

Gary opened the passport and read out loud, 'Dr Andrew Wilson. Ha!'

'What's the matter?'

'They could have chosen a better name.'

'What's wrong with Andrew Wilson?'

'Oh, it's just that it's Tiger's real name. Perhaps that's an omen.'

'A good one?'

'I hope so.' He closed the passport and looked through the wallet, muttering as he did so. 'What am I meant to do, then? Go up to Mr Tan and say, "Got any organs for sale guv?"'

Sarah frowned. 'Don't be ridiculous. You know the form. Proof of identity and a case full of cash. It's all been arranged.'

'But I know bugger all about surgery.'

Sarah gave him a withering look. 'Mr Tan's not going to ask you to demonstrate your skills with a scalpel, is he? Not in the lounge of the Savoy. All he's interested in is your credentials and your money.'

'But do I look like a surgeon?'

'No. I'd put you down more as an ear, nose and throat man.' Sarah nodded in the direction of the hat rack. 'There you are.'

Gary walked over and took down the suit carrier. He laid it on his desk and unzipped it, then looked at the label above the inside pocket. 'Henry Poole. Bloody hell. Savile Row. How do you know it'll fit?'

'Luckily you and Ben are the same build.'

'Are we?'

'Yes. Almost identical,' said Sarah, archly.

'I won't ask you how you know that,' grumbled Gary.

'It's not what you think. Women just notice these things. Anyway, as Mr Tan knows a good suit when he sees one he wouldn't be too keen to deal with a Harley Street specialist who was dressed by Top Man.'

'I can't believe that all Harley Street specialists have their suits made in Savile Row. What about the shoes? Lobb, I hope?'

Sarah bent down and picked up a box. She removed the lid and took out a highly polished black brogue. 'Church's, I'm afraid. And before you ask, no they are not new. They need to look as though you've worn them before.'

'OK. I know the ropes.' He sighed and sat on the edge of his desk. 'I just wish that I'd had a bit more notice that's all.'

*

Christopher was sitting at his study desk. Maria was cleaning the bathrooms. He'd greeted her with a kiss on the cheek, but she had seemed distant. Not her usual bright-eyed self. Perhaps she had had some family upset. He would ask her as soon as he had a moment. Maybe when they had coffee. He'd been trying to sort out in his mind his precise plan of action when the phone rang. It was Monty Loveday, the coroner.

'About our conversation the other day,' said Monty.

'Oh, don't worry, Monty. I decided not to proceed. I didn't do anything about it.'

'No. I know you didn't. But I did.'

'Oh?'

'Yes. I thought that if you had your suspicions, maybe I should, too.'

'But Reggie's body had been left to science. It had already gone when I spoke to Dr Armstrong.'

'Yes. But I tracked it down. Some of the organs had already been removed, but the pathologist examined what was left; ran some blood tests and suchlike.'

'And?' Christopher waited anxiously for Monty's reply.

'Clean as a whistle, I'm afraid. No traces of anything untoward. No marks – other than the bruising you'd expect from a car accident. I thought you'd like to know. Just to put your mind at rest.'

'Right. Thank you, Monty.' Christopher put down the phone, thought for a few minutes, then picked it up again and dialled a number.

'Hello, surgery.'

'Could I speak to Stella Walters please?'

'Just a minute.' The line went silent, then, after a few

seconds, a woman's voice answered 'Dr Silverwood's practice.'

'Hello Stella, it's Christopher Devon.'

'Dr Devon! How are you? How nice to hear from you.'

'Thank you. Stella, I'm so sorry about the news. About Reggie.'

'Yes. Terrible shock. It's so difficult having to answer the phone with his name, but then not every patient knows yet, so I have to.'

Stella had been Reggie Silverwood's secretary for ten years or more. She was a stalwart of the health centre; an older woman who combined secretarial efficiency with a kindly disposition toward the patients. Christopher listened as she explained how sad they all were, then he asked, 'Reggie wasn't a diabetic, was he?'

'No, certainly not. Why do you ask?'

'Oh, it's just that he'd donated his organs and I knew that if he were a diabetic that wouldn't be the case. Then I thought that the condition might have developed more recently. I was just wondering if it could have caused him to have had a blackout while he was driving.'

'No. Dr Silverwood was very healthy, for his age. A bit worried about the flu epidemic that's going round at the moment.'

'Yes, aren't we all.'

'But he took precautions. He had the flu injection the day he died.'

'Did he?'

'Yes,' said Stella. 'He said he thought he'd better. So that he could stay well enough to keep treating his patients.' Her voice tailed off, overwhelmed by emotion. Then she recovered herself and continued, 'I'm so sorry, Dr Devon, only, as I said, it's been a bit of a shock.'

'Yes. Of course. I'm sorry to ask questions, Stella. There's just one more. Can you tell me who gave him the flu injection?'

'I saw him just before he went in. It was Dr Cummings.'

Chapter 22

Men's souls are naturally inclined to covetousness; but
if ye be kind towards women and fear to wrong them,
God is well acquainted with what ye do.

Koran

So there it was. All neatly laid out in front of him. The
things he had not wanted to believe. The things he could
hardly believe. But there was now no doubt in his mind.
Christopher picked up the telephone to make his final
call.

'Dr Silverwood's surgery. Can I help you?'

'Stella, it's Christopher Devon. I'm sorry to bother you
again, but I wonder if you could put me through to Dr
Cummings.'

'Oh, I'm sorry, Dr Devon, but he's finished surgery and
gone.'

'Is he out on his rounds?' Christopher asked, hoping he
could intercept him.

'No, he's not. He's gone off for a couple of days. Said that he would not be contactable. Can I give him a message when he gets back?'

'No. Don't worry, Stella. I'm obviously too late.'

And then the front doorbell rang. He got up from his desk and went downstairs. In a week of unexpected callers, this one was the most surprising. Standing in front of him on the doorstep, her hands plunged into the pockets of her long red coat, was Kate.

She was more friendly than he would have expected. Excitable almost. He put it down to nerves. Kate had always been highly strung, and this would be her chosen way of peace making, though it had been long enough coming. She looked thinner. Somehow more grown-up, which struck him as being an odd thought to have in your head about a fifty-year-old woman.

'So how have you been?' she asked, while he busied himself making coffee.

Where did he begin? How could you explain 'how you had been' eighteen months after someone had left you? He thought it best to regard it as a rhetorical question and shrugged.

'I meant to call more. To check on how things were but . . . well . . . it never seemed to be the right time.' Kate sat down at the kitchen table and undid the gold buttons on her coat to reveal a smart black polo-neck dress and a single strand of pearls.

'No,' said Christopher softly. And then, 'How is . . . er . . . Howie?' He tried not to fall over the words; to ask the question in as level a tone as he could manage.

'Fine. In Barcelona at the moment. Clinching some deal or other.'

Kate looked around the kitchen, at the familiar furniture, the plates on the wall, the vase of daffodils by the sink. It was hard to bear. She seemed to be looking at an album of her life, from inside the pictures. 'Gosh!' was all she could manage for a few moments.

Christopher did his best to keep the conversation going. To make it easier for her. 'So how long are you here for?'

'Oh, just a few days. Not long. I go back the day after tomorrow.'

'I see.'

'But I don't have to.'

Christopher was not quite sure what she meant. 'I'm sorry?'

'I don't have to go back tomorrow. I could stay.'

He still did not grasp her meaning. Thought that she must mean she could extend her stay to see friends or something.

He put a cup of coffee in front of her and sat down opposite. 'You know about Tiger?' he asked.

'Yes. Dreadful. But at least he's pulling through. I've been speaking to Erica. The girls are with him now as well.'

It surprised him that she had been in touch with their friends. Hurt him a little that she had wanted to talk to them, but not to him. He continued, 'They should be able to bring him home soon. Well, back to Hampshire anyway. Start getting him back to normal. I think they're hopeful of a complete recovery.'

'Yes.'

He sipped his coffee.

'I meant . . . I mean . . .' Kate hesitated. 'I could come back here. Come back to you.'

At first he was not sure he had heard correctly. The

223

words reverberated in his head, then he lowered his cup and set it carefully on the saucer. 'I see.'

Kate's words tumbled out in a jumble. 'I think I made a mistake. I shouldn't have gone. We should have talked more. I didn't really think it through.'

'No.'

'What do you think?'

'What do *I* think?'

Kate nodded.

Christopher took a deep breath. 'I don't know what to think.'

'Could we try again?' she asked. 'Give it another go?'

Of all the things he thought might happen when he saw Kate standing on his doorstep, this one had never even crossed his mind. He tried to formulate words to respond, but could only say, 'I don't know, Kate. I don't know.'

'But it was me who left. You were happy weren't you? With the way things were? It was me who made the mistake. Not you.'

'I *was* happy with the way things were. At least I think I was.' He looked reflective, as if weighing up the past situation. 'Yes, I was. But that was almost two years ago. I've had to adjust. Get used to things being different. I don't know whether I can pick up where we left off. Not just like that.'

'But you would have me back; if it could be like it was?'

'But how can it be like it was? I can't just discount what has happened.'

'You could if you forgave me.'

The words bit into him. They were designed to. And the truth of what she said sank home. Wasn't she right? He had longed for her to come back; to be able to make a fresh start. Now she was offering the one thing he'd almost given up hoping for. A chance to avoid all those years together being wasted. Was it only his lack of forgiveness standing in the way?

'Yes. If I could forgive you. But that would mean I thought it was all your fault. And it wasn't. It was mine.'

Kate reached out for his hand, but he picked up his cup before she could reach it. 'It doesn't matter whose fault it was. The important thing is that we can carry on. Not as if nothing has happened, I know, but to make sure it doesn't happen again.'

'Do you think we could be certain?'

Kate sighed. 'Nothing's certain. But I really would like to give it a go. Wouldn't you?'

Christopher got up from the table. 'I don't know. I need time to think. Time to get my head round this. It's so completely unexpected . . .'

Kate rose to her feet and began buttoning up her coat. 'Think about it. Please. I'm staying in the Hotel du Vin. I'll call you.'

'No. No, let me call you. I just need time . . .'

He walked Kate down the path from the front door to the garden gate. She kissed him lightly on the cheek and squeezed his hand, then got into her taxi and was driven away.

From the bathroom window, Maria watched her go.

Christopher walked slowly back up the path to the front door, oblivious to the figure in the upstairs window. He climbed the stairs to his study and quietly closed the door. What to do now?

*

225

'So let's get this straight shall we?' Gary was pacing the office. 'We know Mr Tan is going back to China the day after tomorrow, yes?'

Sarah ran her finger down a sheet of paper that lay in front of her on her desk. 'Yes, he's booked on the British Airways sixteen-forty flight from Heathrow, Terminal Four. Flight number zero three nine.'

Gary cocked his head on one side and spoke almost in parenthesis, 'Isn't intelligence wonderful?' He hoped she would notice the double meaning. Then he continued, 'Except that he won't get on it.'

'Not if everything goes according to plan,' confirmed Sarah.

'So he's expecting me at three p.m. in the Savoy?'

'He's agreed to meet Dr Wilson, a Harley Street special-ist, to discuss a regular supply of organs for his clinic.'

'But he wants money there and then?'

'It's his way of making sure that the doctor is serious. Otherwise he could end up supplying organs and not getting his money. Except that if he didn't get his money, I'm sure he has a few heavies who could be relied on to apply pressure.'

'You know, considering that we had so little information a week ago, it's amazing what we've got now.'

'Why do you think Ben Atkinson's gone down with flu?' asked Sarah.

'Overwork?'

'Exactly.'

'So what does Mr Tan know about me – I mean about Dr Wilson?'

'He knows that Dr Wilson is a respected practitioner who's forty-nine, accomplished in his job and runs a thriving clinic.'

'Does he know what he looks like?'

'No. He hasn't met him. He's met one of his colleagues.'

'When was this?' asked Gary.

'Yesterday. Ben managed to get a guy into one of the clinics. They'd had an approach from organ vendors before and declined any involvement, but we managed to persuade them to call Mr Tan and arrange an appointment.'

'He's good, Ben, isn't he? Shame about his health.'

'Don't be unkind.'

Gary looked suitably chastened. 'So I just go in and meet Mr Tan and strike up a conversation? Ask him what he can supply?'

Sarah pushed a piece of paper forward on the desk. 'There are some notes here. The sorts of things you can ask. You'll be wired for sound, of course, and we have the numbers of all the bank notes. Not that we should need them. Mr Tan will be intercepted as he leaves the hotel and we'll then have all we need.'

'OK. Well, I suppose I'd better do my swotting. Make sure that I sound as though I know what I'm doing, though I can't see myself getting through *Gray's Anatomy* in an evening.' He paused, then asked, 'I don't suppose there's any point in asking you . . .'

'Not tonight,' said Sarah. 'Maybe tomorrow. When we've got something to celebrate. *If* we've got something to celebrate.'

The time seemed to fly by. Christopher had been sitting at his desk for more than an hour. He had not done anything except think. He was not sure he was any further forward. The two dilemmas shimmied around in his head but he seemed unable to resolve either of them. He jolted himself into full consciousness and looked at his watch. One o'clock. Lunchtime. He would go downstairs and find Maria. He would not burden her with either problem, but at least her presence would improve his frame of mind. They had hardly spoken earlier in the morning. She had seemed preoccupied and he himself was hardly at his most communicative. He would make it up to her over lunch, however unwilling his mind would be to deal with other things.

The kitchen table was laid out with cheeses and fresh bread, jars of pickle and some freshly cut ham. Propped against the jar of mango chutney was a letter, addressed simply to 'C'. He pushed his finger underneath the flap and opened the envelope, sliding out the folded piece of paper inside.

Dear Christopher,

I'm sorry not to see you before I go, but I just wanted to say thank you for your company over the past couple of weeks. It has been such fun being with you and I shall treasure my visit to the opera always. My mother will be back with you next week and I will explain that you prefer a light lunch to pasta. I do hope we can meet again sometime.

With love and thanks,
Maria.

P.S. I have made sure there is plenty in the fridge.

He sat down at the table and lay the letter gently in front of him. He had forgotten that Luisa would be back on Monday. And then the reality of the situation dawned on him. He had been so tied up with his own mental agonies, so bound up in his own little world that it never occurred to him that she must have seen Kate come into the house. And leave. What must she have thought?

He reached out for the portable phone and rang her number. But there was no answer.

Tiger was sitting up in the hospital bed. He was feeling sorry for himself and was not in the sunniest frame of mind. Erica sat beside him on the uncomfortable chair and did her best to cheer him up.

'They say you can come home in a few days. It won't be long now.'

Tiger spoke with care, enunciating the words as clearly as he could, 'Bloody pain. Just want to fly.'

Erica squeezed his hand. 'Hey! You've been lucky. So lucky. It could have been much worse. Let's just be grateful for that, shall we? You'll fly again one day, you know that. You'll fly.'

Tiger shook his head. 'I don't think so. Not now. Sorry. Not very good company.'

'That doesn't matter. You're here. Still here. That's what matters.'

'And what about the shop? And the man in black?'

'Oh, that seems to have died down. Nobody's seen him since. I don't think he can have had much success. They reckon he was a one-man band, and not a very good one at that. And there have been no more bricks through windows. It looks as though it was those yobs after all.'

'So much for my secret society. Didn't really do much good, did I?'

Erica stroked his cheek. 'You did your best.'

Tiger inclined his head to one side and gazed into her

eyes. 'Do you still love me?' he murmured. 'Even after all this?'

'Of course I still love you. I'm not going away, you know. I'm afraid you're stuck with me.' Then she frowned with mock seriousness. 'As long as you want to be stuck with me?'

Tiger forced his unwilling mouth into a smile. 'Yes, please,' he said. Then his eyes closed and he drifted off to sleep.

Christopher tried Maria's number again that evening. But there was still no reply. Matt was out for the evening, Ellie was back in Africa and here he was sitting at his study desk in the glow of the desk lamp. He had not eaten. He didn't feel like it. His appetite had deserted him. He couldn't even face a drink. He didn't know what he felt about anything any more. But he did know one thing: by tomorrow he would have to have both problems sorted out. One of them to allow him to be able to live with himself, and the other to allow him to be able to live with somebody else.

Maria wished she did not have to sleep at her mother's. But then her mother didn't have much of a life. Two weeks away with her brother in Italy weren't much of an annual holiday, and at least her mind would be at rest if Maria could spend a few nights there, she said, to keep the cat company. Company for a cat, maybe that was her lot now. She lay awake on the narrow bed in the spare room feeling lower than she could remember.

It was her own fault. She should have been more assertive. Like her mother. Should have made her feelings better known. But that was not her style. He must have guessed mustn't he? That it wasn't just a friendship?

But if she were honest with herself, that's all it was. So far. How could she claim it was more? There seemed to be a bond between them but it remained, as yet, largely unexplored. The rest was in her mind. Her imagination. Her dreams. She realized that she simply did not know. And now his wife had come back. She had left soon afterwards, but probably only to go and get her things. If that were not the case he would have explained it to her wouldn't he? Especially on her last day. Maybe he had forgotten. Been distracted.

And then she had left the note. Saying good-bye as though she thought the whole arrangement was temporary anyway. So there you are. That was probably that. She had had her chance and missed it. What a fool she was. What a slow, oversensitive fool.

Chapter 23

Tender-handed stroke a nettle,
And it stings you for your pains;
Grasp it like a man of mettle,
And it soft as silk remains.
'Verses Written on a Window in Scotland',
Aaron Hill, 1685–1750

Gary did not sleep much that night. He lay awake thinking about the proposed meeting with Mr Tan the following day, and about Sarah. Was she cooling towards him? Why had he let her get to him? What if she told him it was all getting too much? Too intense? That he'd caught her on the rebound and it would be better if they kept to a working relationship, nothing more.

At half past six in the morning he was up and sitting at the desk in his flat, running over the likely events of the day in front of him. He felt unusually nervous. He always felt apprehensive about an operation like this, but not as jumpy as he felt today. He made himself a cup of strong coffee with the intention of calming his nerves. It was only partially effective.

He had a shower, a long one, then towelled himself down and sat in his robe watching as dawn broke over the cathedral city. The morning light was watery and palest pink, gradually turning to icy white. He looked at the suit hanging on the wardrobe door, at the shoes on the floor beneath it and at the shirt and tie on the back of the chair. It occurred to him at that moment, for the first time in his life, that he was getting too old for dressing-up.

Christopher had arranged to meet Monty Loveday in the cathedral close at Winchester. The day was cold and the sky the colour of parchment, with dove-grey clouds rolling in from the west. He'd hoped they might have been able to sit outdoors at a table in front of one of the little cafés that were dotted around the side streets. It would be easy to talk there, more difficult to be overheard. But as they met the weather broke and a heavy shower forced them to seek shelter in the cathedral.

'Not the best place to talk is it?' muttered Monty as they strolled quietly down the north aisle.

'Well, we can walk in the rain if you'd rather,' said Christopher.

'No thanks. I don't want to order my own post-mortem.' Monty chuckled. 'What is it then? Why the cloak and dagger?' His hands were pushed deep into the pockets of his trousers, his suit jacket and raincoat unbuttoned so that he looked rather like a gangly version of Columbo.

'Can I level with you?' asked Christopher.

'S'why I'm here,' replied Monty.

Christopher spoke softly. 'It's about Reggie Silverwood.'

Monty Loveday looked impassive. 'I gathered as much. Go on.'

'I don't want this to sound like the ravings of an embittered doctor who is out for retribution.'

'So it's something to do with Randall Cummings?'

'Yes.'

Monty stopped walking. 'Has he been up to something?'

'I think it's almost certain.'

'So what's your theory?'

'Well, it *is* only a theory, but I just have a feeling that it's an accurate one.'

Monty walked on slowly and Christopher moved with him. 'I've known for some time that Randall has been preferential in his dealings with patients. Encouraging some of them to go private. Telling them that he could offer them better care that way.'

'Disagreeable but not illegal.'

'Not as such, no. But I know for a fact that in the case of at least one kidney transplant patient the organ was withheld and given to someone who could afford to pay for it.'

Monty stopped walking again. 'Are you certain?'

'Perfectly certain. I'd checked that a kidney was available and had the patient lined up for it. At the last minute Cummings diverted the kidney to another patient, known only to him, and as a result my patient was unable to receive the transplant and died before another kidney became available.'

'Did you challenge him about this?'

'Did I? I raised merry hell at the time, and within a week I'd been given the push.'

'And Reggie Silverwood? Did he know about it?'

'Not at the time. Nobody did. They must have thought it

234

odd that I went so quietly, but that's all I could do – pack my bags and go. I knew that if I said anything it would undermine the confidence in the practice and the reputations of all the other doctors.'

'So you put your head in the sand?'

'Yes. But only because I was trying to put my patients first.'

Monty looked at him questioningly.

'Yes. I know it was wrong, but on balance it seemed to me to be the right course of action at the time. I see now that it wasn't.'

'And what's brought about the change of mind?' asked Monty evenly.

'Reggie rang me the night he died. He was on his way to meet me when he had the accident. He sounded particularly low on the phone. Said that he'd discovered something that he was unhappy about. Something to do with Cummings. I suggested he come round for a talk.'

'And you think he'd discovered Cummings's . . .' he searched for a suitable phrase, '. . . lack of fairness?'

'I'm pretty certain so, yes.'

Monty leaned against a pillar, his hands still in his pockets. 'But he never got a chance to tell you?'

'No.'

'And you think his accident was suspicious?'

'Yes, I do.'

'Why so?'

'Because Reggie might have looked frail but he was as strong as an ox. Always had regular health checks – blood pressure, cholesterol levels, that sort of thing. I wondered if he'd developed diabetes lately. That might have resulted in a blackout, but apparently he was as sound as a bell.'

Christopher lowered his voice to a whisper, 'Then I discovered that just before he left to see me he'd had a flu injection.'

'Wise man, they're going down like flies around me.'

'He'd been given the flu injection by Randall Cummings.'

'So?'

'If Randall Cummings hadn't injected him with flu vaccine, but had given him an overdose of insulin instead, the symptoms would be just like those of a heart attack. And there would be no trace of anything untoward at a post-mortem because by then the insulin would have been broken down by the body's metabolism.'

Monty Loveday whistled under his breath. Then his expression changed to one of incredulity. 'But it's a bit fanciful, isn't it? Do you really think Cummings would have resorted to murder just to stop Reggie blowing the whistle on a bit of unethical medicine?'

'Not just unethical. Illegal.' Christopher explained about his sighting of Randall Cummings at the Red Dragon, sitting down with the Chinese gentleman. He confided, also, that it had not been the first time that Cummings had been seen there in such company. 'And do you know where the vast majority of organs for transplant come from nowadays?' he asked Monty.

'India?'

'China.'

'So you think Reggie had rumbled Cummings and was about to blow the gaff?'

'Yes. And in doing so he would not only have ruined Cummings's career, but also stopped him from earning hundreds of thousands a year in backhanders.'

'That much?'

'Oh, yes. The illegal organs market runs into millions. There was a case in nineteen ninety-nine when bids for a kidney from a live donor reached five point seven million dollars on an auction website before the company realized what was going on and pulled the plug. If you're rich, and dying, you'll pay anything to stay alive.'

'You can't prove that Cummings injected Reggie with insulin though.'

'No. I can't. And I wouldn't voice this to anyone but you. But if these other developments amount to more than a coincidence then there's no way I can ignore them any more.'

'So where's Cummings now?'

'He's gone away for two days and we don't know where. He simply told the surgery he wouldn't be back until tomorrow and they have no way of contacting him.'

'And if he's a doctor in general practice and nobody knows where he is you reckon there's something not altogether above board going on?'

'Exactly.'

Monty thought for a moment and looked at his feet. Then he said, 'Sounds like something from a novel. Only much more squalid than hers.'

Christopher looked down. They were standing alongside the grave of Jane Austen. 'Yes. I just hope it's not my overactive imagination that's brought me here.'

'Come on,' said Monty.

'Where to?' asked Christopher.

'We're going to the police station.'

They brought Tiger home that afternoon. He was not the easiest of patients. 'More of an *impatient* if you want the truth,' Erica told her daughters. They had offered to come home, to help look after him, but Erica had said she could manage. She wanted some time with him to herself. Time to get through to him without distractions. She worried about the shop, about whether Brian would be able to cope, but decided that he would have to rise to the challenge. It was more important that she was here.

Mercifully, Tiger's stroke had not been as severe as they first thought. His recovery was steady, and if no great strides were made each day then he was still moving forward slowly. He could walk quite well now thanks to the ongoing physiotherapy. His face was still a little numb and his speech still not clear. But the feeling was coming back into his arm.

Erica put an armchair by the window so that he could sit and watch what was going on in the cathedral close.

'I'm not a bloody invalid,' he insisted.

'No. Just a pain in the neck,' Erica had remarked. 'Here you are. A cup of coffee. And try not to dribble.'

He gave her a withering glance and muttered, 'I don't know why they couldn't send me home with one of those nice nurses. Could you send out for one? Or an au pair?'

Erica shot him a glance. 'You're improving.'

Tiger took a sip of coffee and grinned. 'Daren't do otherwise. Not with you on my back.'

She came and crouched by his chair. 'Are you going to be nice to me or just plain horrible?'

He lifted his hand up and stroked her cheek. 'Sorry, love. Just a bit knocked, that's all. Want to get back to normal. Hate being like this.'

'You will. But you'll need rest as well as exercise.' She stood up and walked across the room. 'By the way,' she asked, 'what happened to the girl who was with you? Sam, wasn't it? She didn't come to visit you in hospital, did she? Only I wanted to say thank you.'

Gary was standing by the office window dressed in his suit. His nervousness manifested itself in its usual way – he was drumming his fingers on the windowsill.

'I wonder if you ought to take a mac?'

'What?'

Sarah examined the sky. 'It looks a bit grey. I wonder if you should take a mac?'

Gary sighed heavily. 'I'm on my way to meet a man who'd probably bump me off as soon as look at me and all you can worry about is whether I should take a raincoat?'

'Well, we don't want you going down with flu like Ben Atkinson. If we lose two of you then we really are up shit creek.'

Gary smiled sarcastically. 'Don't worry. I'll take my paddle. Talking of which, has the money come?'

'It's on its way.'

'How much?'

'Fifty grand.'

'Oh, that'll do nicely.'

Sarah went and sat down at her desk. 'That's about a month's salary for you isn't it?'

'I wish. Mind you, it would be worth running away with you now, wouldn't it? Come on. Never mind the operation, let's just sneak off to the Caribbean and lie on some sun-soaked beach.'

'No,' she said. 'I can't really do that.'

'Why not?'

'Got to have my hair cut tomorrow. Can't miss my appointment.'

'Oh. Shame. Perhaps I could take somebody else.'

'You do and I'll break your legs,' she murmured.

'What?' he spun round to face her. At that moment the door opened and a man came in with a suitcase.

'Is there someone who can sign for this?'

Gary walked forward. 'That'll be me.'

'Check it first please, sir.'

Gary laid the case on the desk and pressed the catches to release the locks. He lifted the lid and gazed on the money, neatly bundled with elastic bands.

'There's five hundred in each bundle, sir, and there should be a hundred bundles. Will you count them, please?'

Gary went through the laborious process of counting the money, then signed the form on the clipboard. 'There you are. You'll never see me again.'

The man ignored the comment. 'Thank you, sir.' He took his clipboard and left the room.

'Well, there it is then. It's make your mind up time. Either you elope with me now or your chance has gone forever.'

Sarah pushed her chair back and lifted her legs up on to her desk.

Gary watched the long limbs unfurl. 'I do wish you wouldn't do that at work,' he said.

'Does it unnerve you?' she asked.

'Hugely.'

'Good. I like "hugely".' And then she added, 'You will be careful, won't you? You won't do anything stupid.'

''Fraid I can't promise that,' he replied. 'I've been doing stupid things all my life. Too late to stop now.'

Chapter 24

Rule 1, on page 1 of the book of war is: 'Do not march
    on Moscow . . .'
Rule 2 is: 'Do not go fighting with your land armies in
    China.'

Lord Montgomery of Alamein, 1887–1976

Monty Loveday had been quite impressive at the police
station. He was not a man to throw his weight about, but he
had known the Chief Inspector – another old-car enthusi-
ast – and that had, to use an appropriate metaphor, oiled
the wheels. The Chief Inspector accepted that Christopher's
theory involved a good deal of conjecture, but felt that at least
they had enough reason to bring in Randall Cummings for
questioning. He made it clear, though, that at the moment
there was little concrete evidence of malpractice, apart from
Christopher's own knowledge of Cummings's willingness to
provide organs to those who could pay for them. Whether
they could get Cummings to admit to any other misdeeds he
thought doubtful.

Coming out of the police station the two were in less than high spirits. 'The trouble is that you and I know from experience that there's something untoward going on, but in law we probably haven't got a leg to stand on. Not without some sort of definite proof,' complained Monty.

'He didn't look totally convinced, did he?' mused Christopher.

'Oh, I know Tom well enough for him to know that I wouldn't bother him without good reason. I wouldn't worry on that score. But they can't do anything until Cummings bowls up again, and that's not likely to be until tomorrow if what you say is correct. Where he is now is anybody's guess.'

Monty said good-bye outside the police station and Christopher headed for home.

The unmarked car took Gary from the basement garages of MI5 into the centre of London. It dropped him off in Regent's Park Crescent, just a short walk from Harley Street where he hailed a taxi. It was force of habit. A superstition in a way, but he liked to start his journey from the right place. Asked where he had picked him up, the taxi driver would have said, 'Harley Street'. It mattered somehow. Tennis players had their little rituals before they played a big match. Gary had his. The attaché case sat underneath his elbow on the back seat. He travelled down Harley Street and Regent Street, across Piccadilly Circus and down Haymarket, turning left at Charing Cross into the Strand. The cabby dropped him off opposite Savoy Court and he crossed the road and walked down the short cul-de-sac that led to the entrance of the hotel.

The lobby was reasonably busy, which made him feel better. Staff behind the polished wooden desk to the right

242

were dealing with enquiries and allocating rooms. There was a steady trickle of visitors to and from the bar on the left. He looked at his watch. Three quarters of an hour early. He crossed the floor and went down the steps into the lounge. He would sit in a corner. Out of harm's way but where he could watch any comings and goings. It also meant that if Mr Tan were meeting anybody else before him the situation could be used to advantage and any such visitors intercepted as they left. It would be a shame to miss the opportunity.

He took in the four members of MI5 who were scattered about the lounge. One was sitting on his own reading a newspaper. Two others, a man and a woman, were having tea. A fourth was tucking into a large plate of pastries at a low table.

Gary felt nervously to check that the microphone was in the right position, and that the equipment was switched on. He looked around again, and this time located Mr Tan. He was seated halfway down the lounge on the far side, and with him were two men. They were all three crouched forward over the low tea table which was set with cups and saucers. Mr Tan was talking quietly and the other two were listening intently.

After a few minutes Mr Tan sat back and the other two men talked to each other. One of them, Gary could see, was quite fat with grey hair. The other a sparely built man. Both wore grey suits. Doctors? Or dealers?

Gary leaned on his right hand and spoke softly to his wrist. 'Hope you've clocked the two guys.'

After another twenty minutes of intense conversation the two men nodded to each other as if they were in agreement, at which point Mr Tan reached into his briefcase and pulled out an envelope which he handed to the fatter of the two men who slipped it into his inside pocket.

After a few more pleasantries the two men got up to leave. They shook Mr Tan by the hand and walked across the lounge, up the stairs and out into the lobby.

Gary looked at his watch. Fifteen minutes to go. He got up and walked across the lounge to the gentlemen's cloak-room where he went into a cubicle, locked the door and once more checked the contents of the case. He sat down on the closed lid of the lavatory and thought through his approach once more. He checked his watch again. One minute to go. He stood up, flushed the lavatory, waited a moment, then unlocked the door and walked out. The attendant who brushed the shoulders of his jacket for him gave him a knowing wink. He was one of Ben Atkinson's sidekicks.

Gary straightened his tie in the mirror, picked up the case, took a deep breath and walked out of the cloakroom and into the lounge. It was exactly three o'clock.

Christopher needed air. And space. He pushed the wheel-barrow across the garden and through the sea of daffodils down to the bottom of the orchard. There, on the banks of the stream, he sat on the wooden bench and watched the water trickling by. It had been a dry winter. The stream was shallow and playful in its notes, not the deep and tumbling torrent that it could be. He tossed a twig into the water and watched it slowly pirouetting out of sight. How different it used to be, when they played here with the children. Where was she now? he wondered. She was still not answering her phone. He had called her twice at lunchtime. He would call again this evening. And if she were not there? What then? Supposing she had changed her mind? What if she decided that there was clearly no point in pursuing this relationship any more? Could he still turn back the clock?

The questions came thick and fast, but the answers did not. What must she have assumed from his attitude? Damn! Why had he been so negative?

His mind was a miasma of disorganized thoughts. But at least he had done what he could about Randall Cummings. Now he would have to await developments. And repercussions. Would it affect his own employment prospects? More than likely. He looked around at the garden. The fruit trees were on the verge of bursting their buds and the first glossy tufts of bluebell leaves sprang from the banks of the stream.

Maybe he would pack it all in and just be a gardener. He didn't need much. As long as he had enough to keep the house going, he could do the rest himself. He looked at the old mellow bricks and the white-framed windows, the old tiles on the roof encrusted with dull green moss. It was the house he was married to now. The house and the garden. It would be nice, though, if that did not have to be the beginning and the end of it.

Mr Tan stood up with an outstretched hand as Gary approached. He was taller than he had appeared in the photographs, and more heavily built. He gave a curt bow as he shook Gary's hand and said, 'Dr Wilson, how good to see you.' His smile was broad and Gary saw that among the even row of teeth there was one large, gold crown. He hadn't noticed that in the photographs either.

'Mr Tan.' Gary inclined his head in a gentle nod, in the

way that he assumed Dr Wilson would incline his head if he found himself in this situation.

Mr Tan motioned Gary to sit and then said to a passing waitress, 'May we have some tea please. China.'

Gary smiled. 'Lapsang?' He could not resist the remark.

'Of course. It is very difficult to find in Shanghai. Most people do not like it. They consider it to be inferior. I, on the other hand, am very fond of it.' He turned again to the waitress. 'And some scones please. With jam and clotted cream.'

His English was impeccable, if a little old fashioned, and Gary found himself suppressing a smile. He thought that he had better get down to business. 'So you think you can help me, Mr Tan?'

'That rather depends, Dr Wilson, on what it was you had in mind.'

Gary slipped into what he hoped would sound like surgeon mode. 'We have a busy clinic, Mr Tan. We perform, on average, three kidney transplants a month and we could perform many more if we could get hold of the organs.' He hoped that 'get hold of the organs' sounded all right. Mr Tan remained impassive and so he continued. 'We also carry out bone transplants and liver and heart transplants, though these are not so frequent as the operations for kidney replacement.'

Mr Tan nodded. 'So what exactly would you be requiring from me?' he asked.

'We could use another three kidneys a month, certainly, if the current situation is anything to go by but, naturally, we would like a flexible arrangement which would allow us to use more or less than this according to patient demand.'

'That could be arranged.'

'What I do need, Mr Tan, is assurance that the kidneys are in perfect health and that they will arrive in good condition. We have important clients and for the continued success of our practice we cannot afford to use substandard material.' He hoped that did not sound too industrial.

'You need have no worries on that account, Dr Wilson. Our kidneys are all from healthy people.' He hesitated. 'Well, people who were healthy before they were . . . before they gave their kidneys up for transplantation.'

Gary was warming to his role. 'We do try to keep up our standards of surgery, Mr Tan, and I cannot state too strongly the need for reliable tissue.'

'Of course.'

'Which just leaves us with the subject of cost.'

At this point the waitress came with the tea tray. Gary wished she had not. He was just getting into his stride.

'Ah, tea. A great British institution is it not, Dr Wilson?'

Gary muttered to the affirmative.

'And a great Chinese institution, too,' confirmed Mr Tan.

The waitress took what seemed to be an inordinate length of time setting out the cups and saucers, the milk jug and sugar basin, the plate of scones and the jam and the cream. By the time she was laying their butter knives neatly on the side of the plates Gary had almost reached breaking point. But he took a deep breath and said nothing. The waitress departed and Mr Tan rubbed his hands together. 'Shall I be mother?' he said, smiling broadly. The gold crown glinted in the light from the chandelier as he began re-arranging the cups.

Gary tried again. 'So, as I was saying, Mr Tan, we just have to sort out the financial arrangements.'

'Yes. Yes, of course. But first the tea.'

Mr Tan bowed gently, then silently set to work. First he poured a little of the tea into a cup. The he emptied the contents of that cup into a small bowl the waitress had provided. The he poured the tea into two more cups, bowed again at Gary and pushed one of the cups towards him. His next question was not one normally associated with the Chinese tea ceremony.

'Would you like a scone?'

'No. No thank you.'

'They really are very good, Dr Wilson. The Savoy Hotel makes a very good scone.'

For the sake of appeasing Mr Tan, Gary took a scone, wondering when, if ever, this elaborate ceremony would end.

'Help yourself to cream and jam.'

'Thank you.' Gary tried to look interested in the scone, and spooned on the strawberry jam and then the cream.

Mr Tan did the same. All outside influences faded into insignificance as he concentrated intently on the matter in hand. The construction work completed, he raised the embellished scone to his mouth, opened wide and took a large bite. As he chewed the mixture of scone, jam and cream the expression on his face was one of rapt delight.

Gary sipped his tea.

When Mr Tan's scone had disappeared, he wiped his hands on his napkin and leaned forward. 'Have you brought the first instalment with you?'

Gary tapped the case. 'Fifty thousand. That was what we agreed, wasn't it?'

Mr Tan bowed his head. 'To seal the agreement.'

'Would you like to check it?'

'There is, I am sure, no need.'

Bloody hell! thought Gary. All that bother and he's not even going to open the bloody case. He contained his irritation. 'And in future?' he asked.

'In future you will let us know your needs through the agreed channels and we will supply exactly what you want, when you need it.'

'As simple as that?'

'As simple as that, Dr Wilson.'

'And what sort of notice do you need? I mean, how quickly can you get the organs to us?'

'Generally within a week. Ten days at most, but that would be in unusual circumstances.' Mr Tan drained his cup. 'Would you like a refill Dr Wilson?'

'No, I'm fine thank you.'

'But you have not eaten your scone.'

Gary smiled knowingly. 'I'm afraid I have to watch my cholesterol, Mr Tan. I can't rely on statins to do all the work for me.'

'Ah, of course. The doctor must take care of his health.'

'Just so.'

Mr Tan shook his head. 'And so must I, regrettably. One scone will have to do. But then, as you say, Dr Wilson, you can have too much of a good thing, can't you? And that would never do.'

Gary was anxious to move the meeting to a close. He had all he needed now. The recording would be sufficient to incriminate Mr Tan. He just had to be seen leaving the hotel with the money.

'So, there is just the question of contacts then,' confirmed Gary. 'The "agreed channels" you mentioned.'

Mr Tan reached into the inside pocket of his jacket. Gary

tried not to make the involuntary movement he would normally feel subject to on such an occasion and sat quite still. Mr Tan pulled out a large black leather wallet, opened it and took from one of the compartments a visiting card. He leaned forward and slipped it into the top pocket of Gary's suit jacket.

'If you just ring that number with the details of what you need, Dr Wilson, you will find that everything will fall neatly into place.'

'Thank you. I'm very grateful.' Gary made to get up.

Mr Tan rose with him. 'I look forward to a long and continued association, Dr Wilson. I am sure you will not be disappointed.'

'I am sure I will not, Mr Tan,' replied Gary, making the greatest effort not to look too pleased.

The two men shook hands, and bowed to each other, and Gary walked across the lounge and up the stairs into the lobby. As he did so, he breathed a deep sigh of relief, and noticed that the palms of his hands were dripping with sweat.

He looked over his shoulder and saw, in the distance, Mr Tan slipping a bank note underneath the plate of scones and picking up the attaché case and his own briefcase.

Smartly Gary walked through the swing doors at the front of the hotel and turned immediately left into the corner of the taxi rank, pressing himself hard against the wall.

Mr Tan came through the door twenty seconds later and hailed a taxi. But he did not reach the door of the cab. As he approached it, two burly men – one dressed as a businessman, the other as a hall porter – converged on him from either side. One of them took the briefcase and pushed his left arm up behind his back, the other eased the attaché case from his right hand, but before he could pin back Mr Tan's other arm, the Chinaman struck out at his assailant and knocked him off balance, then slammed his elbow into the face of the other man. In that split second he broke free and ran faster than a man of his size could ever have been expected to, past the row of taxis in the courtyard and on towards the Strand, his arms flailing.

But as he rounded the corner a third agent, who had supposedly been selling newspapers, performed a neat flying tackle and brought Mr Tan to the ground with a heavy thud. Winded himself, he stood up and leaned over his captive, ready to prevent any further attempts at escape. At that moment, before anyone could reach out and stop him, Mr Tan slipped his hand into his pocket and then into his mouth. Gary ran to give assistance, but by the time he had covered the twenty yards that lay between them, he could see Mr Tan's body being convulsed with heaving spasms.

He knew that it was too late. Mr Tan's lips were purple and his mouth contorted in agony. Gary could see the gold crown glistening in the sunlight. He could also see a speck of clotted cream on Mr Tan's chin.

Chapter 25

In her first passion woman loves her lover,
In all the others all she loves is love.

Don Juan, Lord Byron, 1788–1824

There was something therapeutic about tedious manual labour, thought Christopher as he ran the mower over the lawn. The blades were set high, but the fact that there were now stripes on the grass lifted the whole garden. He emptied the final load from the grass box into the wheelbarrow and put the mower away in the shed. His body felt more at one with life now. Instead of being weary and tired, he was invigorated. He smiled to himself. Why it should surprise him after all these years he did not know, but a little work in his garden went a long way towards making him feel whole.

He glanced up as he walked across the lawns that flanked the house, and saw Matt walking towards him. Matt, who always looked so ill at ease in a garden, as though he found it a threatening and alien environment. He walked across grass as if, at any moment, it could leap up and devour him. He didn't seem to trust it.

'Hi!' His greeting was brief.

'Hi! Are you off or just back?'

'I'm out for a couple of hours then back, if that's OK?'

'Sure. Whatever.' Christopher tried to sound easy going.

Matt looked hesitant. Then he said, 'I gather mum came round?'

'Yes. Who told you?'

'She did. She rang me.'

'I see.'

'She said she offered to come back.'

Christopher knew where the conversation was going. 'Yes, she did,' he confirmed.

'What did you say?' Matt asked calmly.

'I said I didn't know. That I wasn't sure.'

Christopher saw the look of incredulity on Matt's face.

'But I thought you always wanted her back. You said that you still loved her.'

'I did still love her. I do still love her, but I don't know that it would work out. And please don't use that phrase "wanting her back". It makes it sound as though she's some kind of possession. Lost and found.'

'Well she is, isn't she? In a way? You were married. You belong to each other. You agreed that when you signed the marriage certificate.'

Christopher was irritated now. 'Look, Matt, if you're going to talk to me as though I'm someone who isn't fulfilling the words on the contract I'll be forced to remind you that it wasn't me who broke the agreement in the first place . . . but I really don't want to have this conversation with my son about his mother.'

Matt kicked at a lump of grass. 'I just don't understand. You go on for ages about wanting her back, then when she offers to come back you turn her down.'

'I haven't turned her down. I just said that after almost two years without her it isn't an easy decision, that's all.'

'So you will have her back?'

Christopher seldom raised his voice. He did so now. 'I don't know, Matt. I don't know. I can't just sweep all that time, and everything that's happened, under the carpet. I need to work out what I think. To consider whether it really would work out again. Can you see that?'

His son shook his head as though the person he were trying to communicate with was being deliberately obtuse.

Christopher opened his mouth to speak, but Matt beat him to it.

'I'll be back in a while, then. I'm going into town. I need a couple of shirts.'

He turned on his heels and walked back across the lawn and down the garden path. Christopher opened his mouth to shout after him, but he thought the better of it and just watched his son go.

Gary did not enjoy the debriefing. He did not enjoy being involved in an operation which resulted in anybody's death. In cases like this one there was always a risk of attempted suicide, and he was angry that one of his colleagues had been too slow to prevent Mr Tan from slipping a cyanide capsule into his mouth. It was unjust anger, he knew. His colleague was pretty devastated, too.

He pulled off his tie and slipped off his jacket then sat down at his desk and leaned forward with his head in his hands. The operation had been successful in terms of stopping Mr Tan, but it would have been more fruitful had he still been alive.

Sarah came back into the office with two mugs of coffee. 'Do you want anything in this?'

Gary looked up. 'No thanks, it'll be fine as it is. Want to keep a clear head.'

'Don't blame yourself,' she said. 'You know it's counter productive.'

'That sounds very matter of fact. Very calculating.'

'Hey!'

He looked at her apologetically. 'Sorry. Just a bit pissed off. Thought we'd got it all sorted and then . . .'

'Well, you've got the two guys downstairs.'

Gary took a sip of his coffee and said, 'Yes, there is that. Do you want to come and have a look?'

'Yes. Yes, I do.'

The two men were being interrogated in a dimly lit room. Gary and Sarah walked into the room next door which was on a higher level. They looked down on the scene through one-way glass. They could see the men, but were themselves invisible to the room. They could hear the conversation through speakers.

Two MI5 agents were questioning them and didn't seem to be getting very far.

One of them was leaning on the far wall and saying, 'We saw Mr Tan give you the envelope full of money. We know that you took it willingly. What was it for?'

Neither of the two men spoke.

Sarah whispered, 'That fat one . . . wasn't he in the Red Dragon that night?'

Gary looked at the large man in the grey suit who was

now perspiring heavily. 'I don't know. I can't say that I remember him, though I did have other things to concentrate on that night.'

Sarah smiled at him.

Gary turned and spoke to a woman who was taking notes on the seat behind him. 'Have we got their names?' he asked.

'Yes,' she said, and flipped back the pages on her pad. 'The fat one's name is Randall Cummings and the thin one . . . hang on . . . here we are . . . Montagu Loveday.'

Christopher showered and changed. His mind was clearer now. He would not rush things. He would take his time and do it properly. Matt was right in one respect at least. He did still love Kate. You could not be married to someone for almost thirty years without loving them. Well, you could, but you'd be a fool to yourself if you stayed, and he flattered himself that he was no fool. Foolish, maybe, but that was different.

He poured a large Scotch for himself and took it into the sitting room. Then he ran his finger along the shelf of CDs behind the sofa. *La Boheme*? No. Too tragic. *Tosca*? Too many recent memories. He settled on *The Barber of Seville*. Rossini would lift his spirits. Keep him forward thinking. He took a slug of Scotch and heard the opening bars of the overture. Then he heard the doorbell. It would be Matt. He must have forgotten his key. He got up and walked across the hall to the front door. It was not Matt. It was Kate.

'Hello,' she said.

He had not expected her to come back so soon. She looked radiant, her hair and make-up fresh, as though she were about to go out.

'Oh! Hello!' Then, by way of breaking the ice, 'You look smart. You must be going somewhere.'

Kate shrugged. 'Only here.'

Christopher was taken aback. 'Oh, I see. Well, come in.'

He took her coat, then gestured towards the sitting room. It seemed odd, doing that to your own wife in her own home. Well, what *was* her own home.

'Drink?' he asked.

'Thanks.'

Christopher did not have to ask what she wanted. He left her for a moment and went to the fridge in the kitchen to get her a glass of chilled white wine. When he came back she was sitting at one end of the sofa, with the music playing behind her.

'I'm sorry. I'll turn it down . . .'

'No, really. It's fine.'

'No. I know you don't like it.' He adjusted the volume so that the music was barely audible.

'I didn't expect you back so soon.' He sat down opposite her in an armchair.

'No. Only I didn't want to wait any longer. To see what you thought.'

He looked at her sitting on the sofa. Her blonde hair was immaculate, her face seemed to be shining and she wore a little black dress and black tights, her legs crossed at an angle. She looked almost like a model, and astonishing for her age. He had been lucky to catch her all those years ago. The envy of all his friends.

'Yes,' he said quietly.

'What do you think?'

'I still love you, Kate.'

'I still love you, too,' she said eagerly.

257

'I don't know how I've managed without you.'

'Nor you.'

'But I just don't think . . . I can't see how we can pick up where we left off.'

'No?' She looked crestfallen.

'Please don't think I haven't thought hard about this. So hard. I've remembered all the good times we had, and I do know that I still love you . . .'

'But not enough?'

He paused, marshalling his thoughts. He wanted to explain clearly and fairly what he thought. To convince her that he was not just turning his back on what they had had. 'When you left . . . I didn't know whether I could carry on. I was so . . . well . . . bereft is the only word I can think of. I don't remember life ever looking so bleak. We'd been together for so long. We were such a part of each others' lives. Life without you was not something I'd ever contemplated. We'd been through such a lot together – all those years without money, then the children, and bringing them up. Going through all those traumas with Ellie and her boyfriends. And with Matt. You were so good with Matt and I was so . . . clueless.'

'No,' she protested.

'Oh, I was. You were much more sorted. Took it all much more evenly. I got there in the end, but it was harder for me than it should have been. I didn't do as much for him as I could have or should have, really. I'll always regret that.'

'But it's all right now.'

'It's better. But I don't think he really understands me, even though I try to understand him. I love him very much, but I do find it hard to tell him.'

'So isn't it worth it carrying on for them?'

'Kate, you can't build a marriage solely on a love of children. Especially not when they've left home.'

'But you've said you still love me.' She was leaning forward on the sofa now, willing him to agree.

'I do. But I can't go through it all again.'

'Because I'm not worth it?'

'Don't say that. It's just not true. I can't go through it all again because I can't feel the same as I did.' Christopher put down his glass and clasped his hands together, almost as if he were trying to contain and channel his emotions. 'When you went my world fell apart. I wanted to call you. I was desperate to get in touch, but you didn't leave an address, or a phone number. You even changed your mobile number. How could I find you?'

Kate looked down, embarrassed. 'I'm sorry. I shouldn't have done that.'

'Then one day I bumped into a couple in the street – patients – and they asked me if I had enjoyed my stay in the Dorchester the night before. Said they'd seen you there and so assumed that I'd been there, too. They obviously didn't know. So I went there. I was walking up to the hotel when I saw you come out. You had your arm in his. You were laughing. You looked so happy. Then he kissed you on the cheek and helped you into the back of the car. I just stood there, looking. Feeling so foolish. Foolish for having lost you.'

'I'm so sorry,' Kate whispered. 'I had no idea.'

'I saw clearly then that it was my own fault; for not having let you know how much I loved you. How much I needed you. I don't know how I got through those next few months. It sounds dramatic, but I do know what living hell is now, and I wouldn't wish it on my worst enemy. I did come close to giving up. I had the means. I even ordered the tablets. But then I got so angry with myself. Angry that I could think of going and leaving my children. What would they think of a father who took the easy way out?'

Christopher took a sip of his whisky. 'And then, to crown it all, I got the push. Not that that was anything to do with us. Not really. Though I suppose there were some who thought it was. No wife, no job, no prospects. Not much of a catch really.'

Kate sat quite still, the tears welling up in her eyes.

'But the anger helped. It made me bloody-minded enough to get through. If you'd have come back at any time then, though, I'd have found a way. I'd have had you back, in an instant. But you didn't. There was no call. No message. Nothing. So I had to carry on. The guys were kind – Tiger and Gary – tried to take me out of myself. I just got my head down and kept buggering on. There was no joy in it. Not for over a year. And then I just got so worn down by it all. Thought that if I didn't do something soon it would just be a waste of a life. And so I've tried. And nothing has really happened yet. But something might. And I'll try and be up for it if it does.'

'I see,' said Kate, softly.

'I'm so very sorry. I don't want to do this. God knows I never wanted it to happen. But I can't go back there, Kate. I can't risk it again. I'd love to say yes, let's give it another go, but I really don't have the appetite for it. I'm so very sorry.'

The room was silent, apart from the faintest strains of an operatic aria that seemed miles away. Kate sat quite still for a few moments, gazing into the middle distance. Then she got up and moved to the door. 'I'd better be going.'

'Where? Where will you go?' he asked.

'Oh, back to my hotel. Then on to . . . wherever it is this week.'

He looked at her standing there. The woman with whom he had shared more than half of his life, knowing that if he said the word she would stay. But he could not bring himself to say it, and she slipped on her coat and walked out of the front door, closing it quietly behind her.

Christopher stood there for a few moments, listening to the echoes of moments past, then turned, and saw Matt standing in front of him.

His son stared at him without speaking and then, very softly, murmured, 'Oh, Dad!' He walked forward and put his arms around his father's shoulders, burying his head in his neck. Christopher could not speak, but he could feel the tears of his son running down his skin.

Matt took a large gulp of the malt whisky. He had almost stopped shaking now. 'I had no idea you were there,' Christopher said. 'I'm sorry you had to hear.'

Matt shook his head. 'I didn't mean to be. I came in and heard voices. I just couldn't go.'

'They weren't really for your ears, you know. The things I said. They were between your mother and me.'

'I know.'

'I wouldn't want Ellie to know.'

'Of course not.'

After a few moments Matt said, 'Those things I said. I had no right to. I had no idea. I mean . . .'

'Well, there we are,' Christopher said with finality.

'Dad?'

'Yes?'

261

'I'm sorry I was a complete bastard.'

Christopher half laughed. 'Oh, I don't know. Not a complete one. Just a bit of one. And you have got a few things on your mind.'

'I guess.'

Christopher perched on the arm of a chair. 'Funny, isn't it?'

'What?' asked Matt. 'How we all seem to just miss sometimes? I try to understand you and don't quite get there, and you try to understand me . . .'

'And don't get there either. Yes.'

'At least we try, Dad. At least we try.'

Christopher nodded, then drained his glass and got up.

'Another one?' Matt asked.

'No. I can drive on one, but not on two. And I have to go out for a while.' He turned in the doorway. 'We'll get there, Matt. In the end. Both of us.'

Chapter 26

A woman's friendship ever ends in love.
Dione, John Gay, 1685–1732

'Bloody hell!' At that particular moment Gary could think of nothing else to say.

'How come you didn't know what Randall Cummings looks like?' asked Sarah. 'He's from your neck of the woods.'

'Because I have my own doctor – Christopher – and although I knew *of* Randall Cummings I'd never met him. Tiger knows him because he used to be Erica's GP, until he gave Christopher the push, then she took her business elsewhere.'

'What about the other one?' she asked. 'Montagu Loveday.'

'Not met him either. Apparently he's our local coroner.'

'And they were in it together?' Sarah was scrutinizing the two men through the glass.

'It looks like it, though neither of them is giving anything away.'

'But they look so ordinary.'

'Always the way, isn't it? Never be fooled by appearances,' he muttered meaningfully.

The two of them listened to the one-sided conversation being conducted in the room next door. The agents were getting little satisfaction. Cummings had taken off his jacket now. It was on the back of his chair. He was mopping his brow with a white handkerchief. Monty Loveday on the other hand was coolness personified. He sat upright and looked straight ahead.

'We have the envelope, gentlemen. We know you were dealing with Mr Tan, and we know what Mr Tan deals in. It is illegal in this country to profit from the sale of body parts.'

Cummings cleared his throat. 'We don't know anything about that. We were just being paid for some medical advice we had offered him. Consultancy work. Nothing more. That's what consultants do – provide advice.'

'Advice and clients. You were lining up clients for Mr Tan and taking a cut of the proceeds. You were working on commission. How much did he give you for each kidney he managed to sell? There was five thousand pounds in the envelope. That must have been very expensive consultancy work.'

Monty Loveday spoke without looking at his interrogator, 'We really have nothing more to say. We admit we met Mr Tan and we've told you why – he wasn't a well man and we were offering him medical advice. We can't know the business of everyone we deal with. Lots of people from the world of big business require confidentiality, and that's what we give them. Admittedly we should have been more careful about the way in which we were paid, but I really can't believe that you put us through all this just because we were avoiding VAT.'

Gary looked at Sarah. 'Cool customers aren't they? Bloody cool.'

'Is he right?' asked Sarah. 'Have they really got no more to go on?'

'No. We didn't tape the conversation so we can't get them on that. We couldn't get anyone in close enough.'

'So are we stuffed?'

'Looks like it,' said Gary. 'We might have put the wind up them because we're on to them, but they're not going to crack.' Then his mood changed. 'Hang on a minute.' He left the room. Sarah wondered where he had gone. She half expected him to appear in the interview-room to see if he could do any better. Instead, a few minutes later, another figure came through the interview-room door. It was a woman with a tray containing the possessions of the two men. She whispered to one of the agents who then put it down on the table.

'You can have these back now,' he said.

The relief on the faces of Cummings and Loveday was plain to see. There was nothing to incriminate them. They were about to be released. Each leaned forward and scooped up their respective belongings, putting them into their jacket pockets and standing up in readiness to leave.

Sarah heard the door open behind her. Gary came in, carrying his mobile phone and a visiting card.

'What are you doing? Gary this is hardly the time to be making personal calls. And they seem to be letting them go. What can we do?'

Gary held up the visiting card. 'Mr Tan gave me this. This was to be my – Dr Wilson's – contact whenever he needed body parts.'

The card had nothing on it except a mobile telephone number. Gary punched in the numbers. Through the loud-speaker they could hear the ringing of another mobile phone, and through the glass they saw Randall Cummings put his hand into his jacket pocket.

Tiger was sitting in his chair by the window, and Gary was looking out over the cathedral close.

'Have you told Christopher yet?' asked Tiger.

'No. I thought I'd nip over there after I'd called on you.'

'He'll be a bit shocked. I think Monty Loveday was a friend of his.'

'I have a feeling that he won't be surprised about Randall Cummings.'

Tiger looked up. 'You think he knew?'

'I think he had an inkling. Don't know why I say that. Just a feeling.'

'Do you think they'll give Christopher his job back?'

'Can't see how they could refuse. Not after all this. He is a great doctor and Randall Cummings isn't nearly as popu-lar.'

'How did you come to hear about it, then?' asked Tiger. 'I didn't see it in any of the papers?'

'Oh . . . er . . . I heard it from Sarah. She has a friend who was involved in nabbing them.'

'God, I bet that was a bit of a case. Think how much undercover work they must have had to do. Must have taken them ages.'

'Yes, it did . . . er . . . apparently . . .'

The sparkle had come back into Tiger's eye. 'So this Sarah . . .'

'Mmm?'

'Is she involved in police work then? Investigations?'

Gary feigned ignorance. 'Oh, I don't think so. She's a civil servant like me. Leads a very sedentary life. You know me, anything to avoid expending effort. Unless it's horizontal.'

'Yes.' Tiger looked at him sideways. 'You know, the thing I've always thought about you, Gary?'

Gary ,was still looking out of the window. 'Mmm? What?'

'I mean, I'm probably way off the mark, and giving you credit for far more than I should, but I've always thought you were a bit of a dark horse.'

Gary turned to face him 'Me? Nah. Straight as a die. What you see is what you get.'

'Oh. Really?'

'Yup.' Gary spread his arms wide. 'An open book, that's me.'

Tiger looked unconvinced. 'And Sarah. She's still on the scene then?'

'At the moment.'

Tiger grinned. 'At the moment! Ha! If you're an open book, Gary Flynn, then there's one thing that anybody can see.'

'What's that?'

'That you've never been so besotted with a girl in all your life.'

'You reckon?'

'I reckon.'

'Well,' said Gary, 'you might just have something there. Perhaps leopards can change their spots.' He knelt down by Tiger's chair and looked up at him. 'And what about Tigers? Can they change their stripes?'

Tiger looked serious. 'I might have to. Not sure if they'll let me fly again. Bloody determined to try though. Nothing else like it.'

'Haven't you had enough excitement for a bit?'

A look of something that even Gary could not quite identify flickered across Tiger's face. 'For the time being, yes. I thought it would be a bit of fun. But in the end it turned out that it wasn't worth the candle.'

Gary could not quite understand. 'So if you can't fly, what will you do instead?'

'Well, there's a lot to be said for running a bookshop.'

At that moment Erica walked into the room with two mugs of tea. Tiger turned to acknowledge her, then looked back at Gary. 'Especially if you're in love with the owner,' he said.

'Soft bugger,' said Gary.

'Yeah. Suppose I am really.'

'It won't last, you know.'

'I wouldn't bet on it,' said Tiger. 'No more than I'd bet on you and Sarah not lasting. But time will tell. It's learning to be content with what you've got really, rather than chasing dreams. That's the trouble with dreams. When you're living them they feel like reality. And everyone underrates reality.'

'Sometimes,' said Gary, 'I haven't a bloody clue what you're talking about.'

The surgery was as busy as ever. Christopher managed to find a parking space round the back and walked in the side door, hoping to have a word with Stella Walters about Randall Cummings. He did not manage it. Instead Stella's office was occupied by the Chief Inspector that he had visited that morning with Monty Loveday.

'Hello Dr Devon. Have you got a minute?'

*

The tea had sugar in it, but Christopher still couldn't taste it. 'Monty Loveday?'

'I'm afraid so,' confirmed the Chief Inspector. 'It was as big a shock to me as it is to you. We built cars together. Or took them apart . . .'

'But we were with him only this morning.'

'After which he shot off to London to meet Cummings.'

'So they were in it together?'

'Apparently so. As a coroner I suppose Monty was a handy accomplice.'

'But why? I thought he couldn't stand Randall Cummings.'

'It was all a front, clearly.'

Christopher was finding it difficult to take in. 'But why did he come with me to see you?'

'Because he thought that if he didn't you'd become suspicious.'

'Risky though?'

'A calculated risk. He'd know that the evidence you had was circumstantial, nothing more. He'd know that we wouldn't have enough to go on.'

'And then he went off to London. To meet Cummings.'

'Another risk. But the meeting must already have been planned by then, and they wouldn't want to risk losing their money.'

'All for the money . . .'

'No other reason. They've admitted it now. They'll both be convicted.'

'My God!' said Christopher. 'And to think I worked with him all those years.'

'Yes, sir. We never really know people as well as we think we do, do we? The ones that are close to us.'

'Apparently not.'

'But I have to say I'm a great believer in instinct. Gut reaction. It let me down this time, but it doesn't often,' mused the policeman. 'But then, being a doctor, I suppose you've no time for that sort of thing?'

Christopher pushed away the cup of tea and stood up. 'Oh, I have. I don't think that the occasional mistake like this one should get in the way of your true inner feelings. They don't let you down very often, and sometimes, officer, you just have to take risks, don't you? What sort of life would it be if we played safe the whole time?'

Christopher tapped on the door. There was no reply. Then he heard a lot of muttering and the bolts were slid back on the inside. The door opened to reveal Luisa Bassani.

'Doctor Devon! What you doing here? I back on Monday.'

'Hello, Mrs Bassani. Yes. Yes, I know. I was just wondering if Maria was in?'

'No. She not in. She out. She go to cathedral to do flowers.'

'She . . . ? Oh! I had no idea she did the flowers.'

Luisa looked at her watch. 'She always good at – how you say – arranging? If you go you maybe catch her.'

'Fine. Yes. Yes, I'll do that.' He backed down the narrow gravel path and walked quickly down the street, lest Mrs Bassani should detain him further.

He was crossing the cathedral close when he saw the familiar figure walking towards him.

Maria did not notice him at first. She seemed to be in a world of her own. She almost walked right into him when he said, 'Hello!'

She looked up, squinting in the late shafts of spring sunshine and shielding her eyes in order to see. 'Oh! Christopher. Hello!' She hesitated. 'What are you doing here?'

'I came looking for you.'

'But my mother is back. She'll be cleaning for you from next week. I thought I left a note?'

'Yes, you did. But I wanted to give you this, anyway.' He pulled an envelope from his pocket and handed it to her.

'What is it?'

'Open it and see.'

Maria looked confused, but she tore at the flap and pulled out the letter inside. She opened it and read the words:

Dear Maria,

It is with great regret that I have to terminate your employment as of today. However, I was wondering if there would be the faintest possibility that our relationship might continue on a less businesslike footing. Should you be able to see your way to carrying on being in my company even more frequently than you have been to date, with a view to a more permanent relationship, I would be most grateful. This is not something I ask without a great deal of forethought. Neither is it something that I take lightly. Unless, of course, you would prefer that I did so.

I hope this letter finds you well, and I have to say that an early reply would be appreciated.

I remain, madam, your humble and obedient servant,
    Christopher Devon

Maria folded up the letter and slipped it back in the envelope.

'How early would you like your reply?' she asked.
Christopher thought for a moment. 'Now?' he said.
'As soon as that?'
He nodded silently.
'Well, then, Doctor Devon, you'd better come home and meet my mother.'